I0765534

THE Home Studio
AUDIOBOOK HANDBOOK

In loving memory of Nodge and Ada
without whom none of this would have happened

THE Home Studio AUDIOBOOK HANDBOOK

Written and illustrated by
Martin Hussingtree

THE Home Studio
AUDIOBOOK HANDBOOK
© Martin Hussingtree

This first edition 2024
Published by SHORTLIST SELECTED

ISBN: 978-1-3999-4405-2

Martin Hussingtree has asserted his rights under the Copyright, Design and Patents Act, 1988 to be identified as the author of this work.

www.audiobookhandbook.com

Cover design & illustrations by Martin Hussingtree
Printed & distributed globally by IngramSpark
Formatted & Typeset by Fakenham Prepress Solutions

Contents

Foreword

I feel very honoured that Martin asked me to write a Foreword for this book. **There is nothing like this Manual anywhere.**

My passion is writing – but when I was looking for a narrator to turn some of my novels into audiobooks, I found the process on ACX confusing to say the least! I therefore looked for an instruction manual but did not find anything.

I am a hybrid author, which means that some of my work is with conventional publishers and some is independently published. Most of my career as a writer has involved carving out my own pathway – and doing my own research. I quickly discovered that some books explain things more clearly than others!

THE Home Studio AUDIOBOOK HANDBOOK explains everything clearly and concisely. The author knows what information needs to be supplied – and what is reasonable to expect from a narrator. It was useful to find out how the process works from the narrator's viewpoint – even though I wasn't intending to do it myself.

I communicated with a number of prospective narrators before accepting Martin's offer to work with me. I have found him consistently professional in his attitude, clear as to what his requirements are and great fun to work with. I would have no hesitation in recommending him as a narrator.

Sue Johnson
www.writers-toolkit.co.uk

Sue Johnson is a poet, novelist and playwright. Her work is inspired by the Worcestershire countryside near her home, eavesdropping in local cafes and reading a wide range of novels and fairy-tales. When she's not writing she enjoys cooking, walking, yoga and visiting National Trust houses.

Sue's short stories have been published in many UK women's magazines as well as *Allas* in Sweden and *That's Life* in Australia. She also writes books aimed at helping other writers.

She published two novels with Indigo Dreams Publishing – *Fable's Fortune* and *The Yellow Silk Dress*. Her third and fourth novels – *Fortune's Promise* and *Apple Orchard, Lemon Grove* were originally published by Endeavour Media and are now republished by Toadstone Press. Her fifth novel *The Girl With Amber Eyes* began life as a My Weekly Pocket Novel.

Apple Orchard, Lemon Grove, Fortune's Promise and *The Girl With Amber Eyes* are also available in audiobook format. They are narrated by Martin Hussingtree (narratorsuk@gmail.com).

Sue has published three joint poetry collections with poet and environmentalist Bob Woodroofe (www.greenwoodpress.co.uk).

Sue is very fortunate to have lexical-gustatory synaesthesia – which means she interprets some words and names as a specific taste. Synaesthesia in some form affects 4% of the population and is a gift, not a problem. Sue has created a short guide to the condition entitled *Synaesthesia: tasting words in a rainbow of sound* which she hopes will help others.

Sue is a *Writing Magazine* Creative Writing Tutor and also runs her own brand of writing classes.

Further details of her work can be found at www.writers-toolkit.co.uk

Follow Sue on Twitter – @SueJohnson9

Sue lives in Evesham, Worcestershire, UK.

Preface

My life has seen the highest of highs and the lowest of lows. I've mixed with all sorts, from Royalty to rogues, characters (lots of them), craftsmen, Directors of multi-national companies to down-and-outs, all the time, over many years, enriching my latent love of words and laughter.

My father and grandfather were both classically trained architects, so it was natural that I was born with a pencil in my hand, constantly creative and wondering how things went together. I would have been an architect too if the professional body the RIBA hadn't changed their entry requirements when I was 16.

Instead I went in for a new idea called professional construction management, which many years later, in between building everything from hospitals to houses and bridges to high street banks, led to me writing articles for the national trade press and reference works for the Chartered Institute of Building. I was even elected their youngest Fellow and was presented to HM The Queen and HRH Prince Philip at St. James Palace in London.

Prince Philip was taller than me, like a steely eyed hawk sighting a mouse. Surprisingly, maybe because he was bored or hungry, in the sarcastic manner for which he was well known, he asked me "...and what are *YOU* supposed to be good at?" Without thinking my mouth blurted out "...knowing what can go wrong, sir."

Looking back on things, I suppose that probably has been what I am good at. As Einstein said "A clever person solves a problem. A wise person avoids it." So, many years later, after my world collapsed in the severe Recession of the 1990s, a very dark period in my life, I eventually found myself in the supposedly wonderful world of audiobooks. Except there were so many things that didn't seem right, not thought out, confusing and one or two chancers taking unsuspecting folk for a ride.

So, in a nutshell, I suppose it was a case of learning things on the job, as what information there was, was and still is, confusing and incomplete, and poorly presented. That led me into creating *THE Home Studio AUDIOBOOK HANDBOOK* over the last three years, which will hopefully provide both authors and narrators with more confidence and a constructive and mutually beneficial way of going about things.

Even as I have been writing and illustrating this, the commercial world in which this subject finds itself is evolving. I intend to update the contents every year or so, in order that it never loses its relevance.

I hope you find this helpful.

I would like to dedicate my work to my children: Emma, Sally & Toby and their partners: Martin & Katy and my grandchildren Molly, Kitty and Charlotte, not forgetting Judy who has spent many years putting up with and looking after me and trying to work out what I'm doing.

I would also like to acknowledge the kindness, support and assistance from Sue Johnson; James Neal of Pendas Computer Services Ltd; The friendly folk of Findaway Voices; the support staff at Audacity; Steve & Nigel at Zimprint; Kim Storry and Terry Money at Fakenham Prepress Solutions; Ian Roberts for proof reading; and Emma Spiers for all her help with websites and podcasts

Martin Hussingtree
(narratorsuk@gmail.com)
Warwickshire, England

Disclaimer

I have intentionally written this manual as a conversation, a companion guide to have beside them, to help folk who might otherwise be put off considering converting their stories into audiobook form and those who might wish to record and produce audiobooks themselves.

Currently on relevant websites there is much unnecessarily daunting specialist technical jargon, and an unnecessary over-emphasis on legalistic contractual complexities. They have the potential for draining disputes in what is, after all, a straightforward, creative, hopefully amicable and rewardingly satisfying collaboration between the two kindred spirits of an author (assuming he is the Rights Holder) and his chosen narrator.

With this manual by your side, it should be a joyous if not sometimes a challenging but rewarding experience and achievement.

I taught myself, as best I could, and in the process I developed my own opinions and ways of looking at this relatively new and forever growing world. I made mistakes, oversights, as you and I will both continue to do. Hopefully we will both learn from them.

If I have inadvertently made genuine mistakes or errors of judgement on technical matters, then I apologise, but can only offer the thought that they were never adequately and patiently explained by others in the first place.

For simplicity I have written this in the first person, as a male. That in no way should be interpreted as demeaning, to what I hope will be, many female readers, authors and narrators who open these pages and find them useful.

I have done my best to avoid infringing anyone's copyright and if I have, I apologise, and claim Fair Use Under Section 107 of the 1967 Copyright Act where allowance is made for criticism, comment, news reporting, teaching, scholarship and research, which is all this manual attempts to do.

My objective, amongst others, is not to challenge or criticise the status quo but to raise issues for others to consider, and which, as the subject has evolved and continues to do so, topics and valid points of view which might have been inadvertently overlooked.

Part One

THE Home Studio
AUDIOBOOK HANDBOOK

Introduction

How wonderful the versatile English language has become, in all its forms. To be able to unite all of those across the world who speak it as a first or a second language and who are able to listen to audiobook recordings of stories and adventures, both real and fictional for pleasure, inspiration or simply information to improve their communication and understanding.

I am fortunate to live in a part of the world which, over centuries, has been instrumental in shaping the English language and its culture. I live but a few minutes from where writer and playwright William Shakespeare was born and lived. In more recent times, the notorious publisher and poet philanthropist Felix Dennis who set about restoring Shakespeare's beloved magical Forest of Arden. Within an hour's drive eminent composers Elgar and Holst gained inspiration from the countryside around, as did country boy Laurie Lee who wrote his famous lyrical work *Cider with Rosie* and similar stories. Just a little further on was where the almost forgotten and persecuted martyr William Tyndall, following in the tradition of Geoffrey Chaucer, the father of English Literature, is commemorated.

Seven hundred years ago, Tyndall was in exile in Belgium, in those days the home of mass printing, in a bid to simplify Catholic religious texts, making readings understandable to less educated, mostly peasant congregations.

Tyndall painstakingly translated the scriptures from ancient Latin and even earlier Greek and smuggled them across the North Sea into Catholic England. They were the first Bibles printed in everyday English so that the humblest ordinary man, a ploughboy, could read for himself and understand what was denied him by the convoluted Latin of the controlling Catholic Church and the intransigence of Henry VIII. Much of every day English speech contains words given to us by Tyndall.

Hopefully, this "How-To" manual, might, in its own small way, make it simpler for non-technical folk to better understand, use and enjoy what some modern day websites, by their very nature, have made questionably complex, unintentionally difficult to navigate and tedious to use, often achieving the exact opposite effect – a lack of straightforward simplicity, like the turning of a printed page.

THE Home Studio
AUDIOBOOK HANDBOOK

This year, 2024, sees this manual, the inaugural edition of what is the first publication of its kind. It covers numerous neglected and important aspects of commissioning and producing a quality audiobook for sale to the general public.

Since I began writing this first edition of *THE Home Studio AUDIOBOOK HANDBOOK* in the Summer/Autumn (Fall) of 2021, I became aware of certain changes taking place within the established global audiobook publishing and distribution market. Together with the Covid pandemic affecting almost everyone including me, this has disrupted the publication until now.

My concern has been to produce a work which is currently accurate and as far as is possible, beyond factual criticism. It has not been easy, because information which has traditionally been available in published book form is now only available in (forever updated without warning) website form. To the non-technical middle aged mind it is far more difficult to cross reference.

So, please take pity on me if you're otherwise disposed, but I assure you I'm doing my best to make it easier to understand for the many other non-technical folk who might be involved in this process … and I believe there are many.

As a picture is supposedly worth a thousand words, I have created a fully illustrated, comprehensive, all-in-one-place, self-help companion. A "How-To" manual for my fellow non-technical participants and anyone else who might like to find their feet and be part of this rapidly expanding exciting revolution.

THE Home Studio AUDIOBOOK HANDBOOK is both a reference work and an instruction book, written by someone who has learned the hard way, in the absence of anything like this to guide him. It is intended to issue revised (print-on-demand) versions each year or so in response to constructive criticism, evolving software and website development, the commercial world and the practices and procedures of others which affect the current situation. It will save hours of being mesmerised and discouraged, aimlessly wading through voluminous (mostly unhelpful and confusing) website pages which might lead you into being swamped by diversions into things which are both irrelevant and technically bewildering.

This manual will enable anyone who has determination, patience, a reasonable voice and who speaks clearly, and can fund the relatively modest expense of creating their own recording environment like mine, to audition for and produce professional standard audiobooks for sale across the world wherever English or any other language is spoken.

It is NOT necessary to be a trained actor or a qualified sound engineer. This manual will tell you all you need to know in a straightforward manner. DO NOT be apprehensive.

It is NOT easy, nor is it a get-rich-quick venture, but with perseverance and practice it is possible to develop it from an absorbing, otherwise entertaining hobby into a full-time occupation with a worthwhile return or a supplementary income. This manual is designed to help you do that.

There is also a busy niche market for voice-over work for a myriad of opportunities in advertising, information, broadcasting and many more, but that is not the main purpose of this work. For those who are interested in trying that it might be worthwhile to have a look at fiverr.com

It is hoped that this manual might also inspire those who are retired, disabled, housebound, disadvantaged, down-on-their luck or unemployed or those who might feel they've been thrown on life's scrap heap to consider this as a worthwhile option.

For simplicity, this manual concentrates on the two audiobook industry dominant players, both American, they are Amazon's Audible.com and their operating arm ACX (Audiobook Creation Exchange) and Spotify's Findaway Voices.

Technically and administratively they are similar. Should that change, subsequent editions of this *AUDIOBOOK HANDBOOK*, will take that into account. Those two organisations seem to have different cultures. As with most things, much depends on which you find to be most user-friendly and who you are most comfortable with. The differences seem to lie with their approaches to contractual and commercial matters, and the number, spread, and variety of those outlets to which they distribute your quality controlled audiobooks. In other words YOUR AUDIENCE.

What is an audiobook?

If you are in the process of writing fiction, or you've already written a book, you should have a pretty good idea of what you are doing, so I won't dwell on that. But if you want to expand your market exposure and opportunities, by converting it into an audiobook, that is a sound idea (no pun intended!).

Comparatively, for an author, it requires very little effort from you. First and fundamentally printed books and audiobooks are DIFFERENT, although the words are the same. They are consumed differently. Their readership is probably different.

Reading is different to listening. One is in the form of a traditional printed-on-paper book, the other is hidden inside an electronic "gadget" of one sort or another. The selling front cover of a traditional book and that of an audiobook need not be the same, even if the title is. For one thing they are of a different shape or size.

There are good arguments for them being different, especially as an audiobook is a collaborative venture where, to my mind, both the author and the narrator should be seen as equals.

In what is known as market testing, commercial publishers, in common with many other product manufacturers with specialised resources, "A/B market test" by using different branding, colours, messages, slogans, brand names, typefaces, images, etc. to see which sell more than the other. It is relatively simple and inexpensive for authors, with time and determination, to do the same.

The way ACX, for example, set things up by default, seemingly, is that the author alone is left to decide on the audiobook cover. Wrongly, in my view, the cover used is usually the same as that of the paperback version, without mentioning the narrator's name, which is both lazy and discourteous at least.

Without the narrator's name, it is tantamount to saying that the audiobook is not worth listening to. Because that is what a buyer is going to do – LISTEN TO IT! The first law of sales is to make the product available, obvious what it is, and why it is worth buying. What's in it for the buyer or the person that they are going to give it to? Enjoyment, excitement, escapism or knowledge, etc.? Study packets, boxes and bottles on supermarket shelves – ALL designed by clever people to satisfy a need, a desire, solve a problem, compel you to buy theirs rather than those of a competitor. You wouldn't buy them if you hadn't a reason, would you? The buyer does not want to have to guess. Solve their problem or dilemma – instantly! Companies have spent a lot of time and money deciding that.

Commercial publishers promote audiobooks on the basis of the (paid a lot) "celebrity" narrator's name. Not everyone, by a long way, will recognise who that person is, but at least they sound as if they ought to know of him or her, and they should be worth listening to.

Before any audition, the narrator should be given the chance to see what the audiobook selling cover might look like with their name as prominently displayed as that of the author. If that can't be done, in view of the amount of the narrator's time and effort involved, in my opinion, the narrator would be wise to decline an invitation to partake in a royalty-share option, because if nothing else, it will indicate the author's lack of interest in actively promoting it which would not work to the narrator's advantage.

How audiobooks evolved

In 1877 Thomas Edison invented the phonograph making it possible to record the human voice speaking. His test piece was reciting "Mary had a little lamb".

Over the next 40 years, either side of World War I, pioneers such as English gentleman Cecil Sharp eventually embraced the new technology by "collecting" traditional folk songs in the UK and USA so that they wouldn't be lost to future generations.

In due course, anthropologist J.P. Harrington, drove the length of North America to record oral histories of Native American tribes for the same reason.

Fifty years later, the American Foundation for the Blind and the Library of Congress set up a "talking books" initiative to make books available to the partially sighted. The first talking books were recorded on LPs for playing on a gramophone. They included the Bible and some Shakespeare.

After World War II, in 1954, a New York publisher produced the first commercial audiobook of poetry readings by famous Welsh writer Dylan Thomas who had been invited to tour the USA when parts of his famous radio play for Welsh Voices *Under Milk Wood* was adapted for an American audience and performed by five local American actors. Spoken word records were almost unheard of at the time.

Three years later the Listening Library was set up in the USA to provide schools and libraries with the earliest commercial audiobooks.

In 1963 a compact audio-cassette tape player for listening to music was invented by Dutch company Philips which was to go on to revolutionise audiobook creation.

Gradually, some public libraries started stocking audiobooks (or talking books as they were still known back then). Traditional book publishers began releasing spoken versions of hardback novels.

In 1979 Sony launched their "must have" ubiquitous low-cost mass market portable audio-cassette tape player "Walkman" which over the next 30 years in production and with continuous refinement sold over 200 million units world-wide.

In 1982 the CD-Rom (digital compact disk player read-only memory) jointly developed by Philips and Sony was launched, progressively taking over the ever-growing audiobook market from cassettes. The format was developed, as computer design evolved, because they could store far more data than the integrated computer hard drives of the day.

Over the next 25 years or so, talking books were being sold in 75% of regional and independent booksellers across the USA. It had grown to a $200 million industry.

By 1997 the term "audiobook" had become well established. Sales had eclipsed CDs which were in rapid decline.

The following year, 1998, a company called Audible pioneered the world's first mass-market digital media player named "The Audible Player" specifically designed to play audiobooks. They sold for $200 each and were advertised as being "smaller and lighter than a Walkman". They held 2 hours worth of audio to be downloaded from audible.com, the first to establish an online library website on the emerging internet.

In 2003, Audible supplied the earliest audiobooks to the 30-year-old Apple Computers for their iTunes Music Store. Two years later, Audible released "Audible Air" which allowed audiobooks for sale to be downloaded by the general public to their hand-held electronic devices.

In 2008, after ten years of rapid growth, the ever-acquisitive far-sighted Amazon, itself a phenomenal success story, seeing the audiobook industry's potential, bought Audible to develop their own sci-fi and fantasy audiobook range to complement its already thriving innovative paperback book publishing business.

In 2011, Audible launched Audiobook Creation Exchange (ACX). Since then it has gone on to publish over 150,000 audiobook titles, becoming the incredibly successful online Rights marketplace and production platform which operates in the USA, Canada, the UK and Irish Republic.

Meanwhile, in Ohio, another US state, Findaway had been into audiobooks since 2002. Four years later they had started with their manufacturing

Playaway audio player business servicing US libraries and schools in widespread communities across the vast North American continent and many US military communities all over the world. Playaway's compact durable devices gradually replaced compact disk players.

Findaway's business grew with their subsidiary "Audio Engine", which has evolved into the audiobook industry's largest business-to-business audiobook delivery platform, powering Findaway's huge catalogue of audiobooks and those of most distributors around the world.

With the object of making every book in the world available as an audiobook, they launched their subsidiary Findaway Voices in 2017/18. It is an audiobook production and distribution service for independent authors, narrators and publishers throughout the world including those serviced by ACX. Currently it has more than 325,000 titles, twice as many as ACX.

In 2019, *Forbes*, an authoritative, influential American business magazine, noted for its research and performance league-tables, reported that US audiobook sales neared $1 billion, growing at 25% year-on-year. The audiobook publishing industry passed that mark a year later.

In 2022 the 15-year-old ever-acquisitive Spotify with 433 million global listeners to their music and podcast platform bought market leader Findaway. Their recently announced (September 2022) intention is to distribute audiobooks directly to listeners, initially in the ACX backyard of North America. Audiobook sales globally are set to continue growing exponentially.

Originally a Swedish, predominantly music, audio streaming and media services provider, Spotify has become the world's most popular audio streaming subscription service with more than 381 million monthly active users and 172 million premium subscribers. They have a presence in 178 markets and more than 70 million tracks including 3.2 million podcast titles.

Spotify has transformed the way people access and enjoy music and podcasts. It intends to do the same with audiobooks. Gustav Soderstrom, Spotify's Chief Research & Development Officer stated:

"Together, Spotify and Findaway will accelerate Spotify's entry into the rapidly growing audiobooks industry, enabling faster innovation and bringing audio-books to Spotify's hundreds of millions of existing listeners.

Findaway's technology infrastructure will enable Spotify to quickly scale its audiobook catalog and innovate on the experience for customers, simultaneously providing new avenues for publishers, authors and independent creators to reach new audiences around the globe.

The acquisition positions Spotify to revolutionise the space in the same way as music and podcasts, powering content to reach a wide audience on its global platform.

It is Spotify's ambition to be the destination for all things audio both for listeners and creators. The acquisition of Findaway will accelerate Spotify's presence in the audiobook space and will help us more quickly to meet that ambition".

Findaway Founder & CEO Mitch Kroll adds:

"We're excited to combine Findaway's team, best in class technology platform, and robust audiobook catalog, with Spotify's expertise to revolutionise the audiobook space as we did with music and podcasts. Together with Spotify we have the opportunity to innovate and democratise the audiobook ecosystem".

Kroll who went on to say:

"We founded Findaway with the recognition of the power of the spoken word through audiobooks and the unique opportunity to empower storytellers and connect them with listeners. Findaway supports more than 80 different localised languages from various countries of the Earth.

We look forward to combining our leading technology tools and world-class team with the reach of Spotify's platform to provide an enhanced audio experience for creators, publishers and listeners around the world."

According to Spotify, the audiobook industry is currently valued at $3.3 billion but is expected to grow to $15 billion by 2027.

The statements above were taken from Press Releases and other public pronouncements and are included here for general information. I look at it like this:

In my view, ACX, Audible and Amazon are as one. They manufacture and retail audiobooks direct to the consumer though the internet. They wholesale audiobooks to their competitor Apple who then sell them through Apple Books/iTunes in 4 specific countries – USA, Canada, UK and Ireland.

Findaway with a different technology history have been predominantly distributors to 40+ retailers (including ACX and Apple) and hirers (libraries) across the world, in many countries, as well as selling direct to consumers. Now under the control of Spotify, effectively a huge hirer of musical output, Findaway have effectively broken Amazon's seemingly virtual monopoly.

It is an on-going evolution, still in motion as I write, which is one of the reasons why this manual is a print-on-demand book so that it can easily be revised to reflect whatever changes take place in the future.

Part Two

Authors

An audiobook? From an Author's point of view

One way for authors to earn more money from their printed novel is to create an audiobook version. This *AUDIOBOOK HANDBOOK* was mainly written for those wanting to transform their printed novel, which is read and imagined personally, usually quietly by one individual, into an audiobook to be listened to by any number of people through headphones, speakers or on the radio.

An audiobook is a performance to an audience, even if it is just one person. The first recorded example of characterisation of multiple diverse voices as opposed to simply reading text was *Under Milk Wood* by Dylan Thomas in the USA in 1954, 70 years ago. Now regarded as a classic, the voices were the conversations and thoughts of the residents of a small sleepy Welsh coastal village (modelled on New Quay) "as time passes" during a 24-hour period. It was "the beginning of the beginning", as the story began.

As such, an audiobook is a totally different commodity to a printed book. It adds another dimension. It brings an author's words to life through someone else's voice, which may or may not be the author's choice.

Listening to an audiobook performed well and sympathetically might be seen by some as preferable to, and in many cases, more convenient and enjoyable than reading the printed book.

Authors are traditionally solitary souls totally in control of what they do. An audiobook, if it is to be commercially successful, and which satisfies the author's imagination, must be seen as a collaborative venture. The author delegates some of that control to another person, probably personally unknown, on the basis of a very brief connection, through an agent, a friend or acquaintance or through a somewhat limited third-party audition.

From an author's point of view, the potential for disappointment can be overwhelming. Rather than take the perceived risk, an author might decide against it.

The whole purpose of this book is to eliminate, or at least minimise, that perceived risk. To be successful, any arrangement has to be of mutual benefit and of a common understanding.

Both parties, authors and narrators MUST have that common understanding, a meeting of their minds and a desire to create something "special".

In time honoured traditional industries and processes, "the rules" are documented. Training is undertaken, tested and accredited by a recognised and respected external body.

Commercial audiobooks, on the other hand, are relatively new, and other than the somewhat sketchy technical requirements of certain websites, the relationship between author and prospective narrator is left very much to chance and open to interpretation.

My background is in a traditional industry, construction, notable for its disputes and a framework which evolved to minimise and resolve them. You might say that I became an expert in "misunderstandings".

Forty years ago, I got fed up with being in the midst of incessant arguments. My researches took me back to 1870 when construction contracts began to be standardised. In due course, other conventions took the same path. In spite of that, disputes continued. Seemingly no-one had looked into it before. Disagreement was accepted as inevitable or an occupational hazard.

I came to understand why this situation prevailed. The Chartered Institute of Building published my book *The Standard Form of Contract in Times of Change* in 1983. It exposed an inconvenient truth. The supposedly independent professional arbiter in any dispute, corrupted by commercial considerations, could no longer be relied upon to be as impartial as the contract required him to be. The time-honoured concept had been debased.

So, my concern for the inadequacies of our modern audiobook regime are well founded and potential failings all too obvious.

My motive for writing this book is to enable commissioning author/ Rights holders and/or their agents, if they have one and they wish to, to use *THE Home Studio AUDIOBOOK HANDBOOK* as a specification governing the work and the relationship between author and narrator, to which both parties should formally agree before auditioning or starting recording.

If you have written a novel, the biggest mistake an author can make with an audiobook is choosing an inappropriate narrator to be your voice actor. He has to be able to carry 80+% of your words, potentially over maybe several hours. So, your audience must be content to listen, preferably eagerly, to that voice for that length of time. Would it bore YOU?

If you don't fancy anyone from an audition, try the same exercise again with others in a few weeks' time. There are lots to choose from on registers alone. Maybe find one of your own. You are under no obligation or pressure to choose anyone. Follow your own selfish interest and instinct. The "fit" must be right. Something you can look forward to.

A voice actor/narrator must be capable of CONSISTENTLY and CREDIBLY performing voices of as many differing characters, of both sexes that you have created, in such a way as to hold your listener's attention throughout.

An author should think deeply, without rushing a decision, maybe taking advice from other writers, before even considering an audition. Can a man do female voices? Different ones? Can a woman do men's deeper voices? Tenor, baritone and bass? Convincingly?

In Part Three – Narrators, I give the example of my recording *Fortune's Promise – A Regency Romance* a 208-page novel written by Sue Johnson. There were 83 different voices of both sexes (including a parrot).

I make the point that your Audition Script MUST have a selection of carefully chosen speeches by leading characters as well as the narrator's voice. Get that wrong and your listener or prospective buyer will give up!

If you elect to have an audition, your Audition Script should be a selected random collection of deliberately testing "snippets" rather than one or more pages. An audition is an author's only way of avoiding the mistake that he might regret when it is too late.

You are NOT obliged to have an audition as such. Alternatively, you might consider a "Schedule of Voices" whereby you might provide a carefully chosen passage of, say, 100 words for each of a number of the main characters so you can judge how they complement each other.

As an author commissioning a narrator/producer you will have a parental interest in the likely end product with your name on it. To give you some idea, ACX, for example, offers many samples of audiobook recordings for you to listen to depending on keywords, genre, gender, language, accent, compensation (royalties), vocal style, voice age, location, Audible approved.

Be aware that some established North American/Canadian voices, predominantly professional actors, may belong to an actors union with set PFH (price per finished hour) hourly rates which some authors may regard as expensive.

Authors can of course invite someone they know or who has been recommended to audition, or you can just post the audition on the ACX website and see who turns up. Whatever you choose to do, you must follow ACX steps.

Choosing a Narrator

The way the audiobook making process has evolved over the last 25 years has seen Rights-holders in the form of large scale commercial publishers engaging well-paid established "names" and commercial, predominantly music-making, studios with expensive equipment and specialist sound engineers to narrate stories and documentaries as a means of securing sales to cover and recover hefty overhead costs to capitalise on the emergence of the new technologies and the public's increasing desire to consume them.

Evolution doesn't stop. It continues. The emergence of Amazon and Kindle amongst others completely changed the balance of influence of God-like publishers who no longer control writer's options.

Nowadays there are many more authors in print than ever before. Increasingly they turn their thoughts to the possibilities of readers becoming listeners.

My experience is that most authors are not particularly well off financially. Cashflow is often a problem. So, matching the financial clout of long established commercial publishers is beyond their budget. This manual was designed to address that problem, at least to some degree.

The process begins with a published book. The author, or whoever they have sold the Rights to, has to find or engage a narrator who needs to see a benefit for what might well be many hours of hard work, especially if he or she is also to act as sound engineer, editor and liaison with the audiobook publisher and distributor.

So, there are cost implications. How much? When or how is payment made? How and when, if at all, does the author see a return on investment?

Both ACX and Findaway Voices (both in the USA) have many narrators on their books, all anxious to promote themselves. Their websites enable you to find them.

Understandably, many of them are in the USA and Canada, and of those, many are professional narrators, actors and voice-over specialists. Some are famous. Many belong to the SAG-AFTA performing arts trade union (Screen Actors Guild-American Federation of Television and Radio Artists) representing 160,000 individuals formed from the merger in 2012 of SAG (founded 1933) and AFTRA (1937). As I revise this text prior to publication (July 2023), they have come out on strike, downed tools, for more money.

It would be wrong to call it a closed-shop, but it will be true to say that it influences a narrator's "going-rate" as perceived by those in North America.

Findaway for example, for a fee, offer to suggest reliable narrators known to them who have experience of your sort of novel and the voices that it contains. Maybe a case of "the devil you know …"

On the other hand, there is nothing to prevent you from sourcing your own narrator or doing it yourself. This manual shows you how and gives you in-depth knowledge of what you should be looking for. It was designed effectively as a specification of what your expected narrator should do and sound like.

Part Five – The **AUDIOBOOK HANDBOOK AGREEMENT** provides a far simpler procedure for governing such a relationship than others do.

Auditions

Both ACX and Findaway maintain a comprehensive register of narrators for authors to choose from, as well as giving authors freedom to find their own, and for narrators to approach authors.

ACX display a list of auditions, requested by published authors for which both new and established narrators can apply. That is because their parent company, Amazon, only takes audiobooks from their previously published traditional paper books and ebooks sold by them, mail order over the internet.

Unlike ACX, Findaway has an inexpensive paid-for option to suggest suitable experienced narrators from their list and also to project manage the whole process and relationship between the author and the chosen narrator. Being American, their register operates like that of ACX.

In all cases, it is for the author, typically, but not necessarily, the Rights holder, to choose who will perform their written/published story/content in audiobook form.

If the potential narrator is a stranger, even if they have a proven track record, the author needs to satisfy themselves in the present circumstances that he has the wherewithal to sustain the effort of narrating and producing the author's particular publication, often over several weeks and months to the standard expected, both technically and artistically.

As such it is in an author's interest to question the proposed narrator/producer's motive in committing his time to what can be both time consuming and an arduous task.

Recognise that it is a collaboration, a partnership, hopefully a long-lasting friendship in which you need to be confident in the narrator that you choose. This brief list is given in Appendix Part Two for you to copy.

✓ What's in it for him? It is important you know that.

✓ Is it just for money? For recognition? For experience? The challenge? Has he done it before? Does he intend doing more?

✓ Can you sense that he will enjoy creating your audiobook? If you can't persuade yourself on that, best find someone who will.

✓ Has he got other interests which may take precedence over your work?

✓ Does he have a steady income from another activity or source, or a pension or social benefit? Because if not he might be obliged to abandon your project to earn some money elsewhere.

✓ Has he other commitments or deadlines which will get in the way of finishing your audiobook?

✓ Is he in good health or expecting to go into hospital? Has he any problems with ailing dependents?

✓ Has he got a track record of similar work? Are there any reviews or any relationships with any other authors?

✓ Is his offer too good to be true? Is he over optimistic? Are you running a risk that he might give up part way through, or take a prolonged sabbatical?

All or any of those considerations, or other factors unknown can have an impact on your plans or aspirations.

I cannot stress this strongly enough, and I make no apology for repeating myself. *THE Home Studio AUDIOBOOK HANDBOOK* is designed to be used as a specification to avoid getting off on the wrong foot. Both author and narrator need to have a copy.

You now have to consider what commercial arrangement can be made with the narrator/producer that you choose or can afford.

If you have not done this before, and you feel vulnerable in this strange situation, the following might give you a sense of proportion:

The audiobook I created of the novel *Fortune's Promise – a Regency Romance* by Sue Johnson (my third for her) was about 75,000 words long. In Per Finished Hour (PFH) LISTENING terms (automatically measured by the project screen) the 75,000 words took 7½ hours of listening, at a rate of hearing of 10,000 words per hour.

That covers the main text in 36 chapters of differing lengths, plus a Prologue and an Epilogue, Opening and Closing Statements and a Retail Audio Sample. I had to voice act the voices of 83 different people of all ages, sexes and types, from the well-to-do to peasants (see Part Eight). It turned out to be a highly complex undertaking.

Listening time is easily and automatically measurable and therefore comparable. Recording and editing time is not and is infinitely variable.

To produce that particular audiobook of 7½ hours listening time took 25 calendar weeks of recording and editing. That equates to a rough rule of thumb of 3,000 words (75,000/3,000 = calendar 25 weeks) of written text converted to ACX publishable standard completed each calendar week of work.

This is fact NOT supposition! It is an experienced narrator diligently processing a complicated novel to the highest standard.

Findaway, by comparison, work on the suggestion of 9,000 PFH words of listening per hour.

Nowhere do either ACX or Findaway offer guidance as to how long, and what effort goes into recording and editing. Do they even care? How long is a piece of string you might ask? A fair question.

The answer I would give, is that it all depends on the number of speaking characters and the incessant start-stop of their exchanges. It makes the painstaking editing process very time-consuming.

The simplicity of just reading a straightforward script bears little comparison with the audible creation of a large and disparate cast-list with the complexity of many intricate situations and relationships requiring further research before and during recording.

To emphasise my point, I reiterate. I work on my own in my home studio as you will see in Part Six. The finished 75,000 written word audiobook listening time (PFH) was 7½ hours. It took me 25 calendar weeks, each of 5½ working days (140 days in total) of 5 hours net of intense concentration each day recording, but mostly editing and arranging to meet ACX requirements.

Narrators charge their hourly rate at PFH. So, in the above Findaway example they might charge 8.33 hours (75,000/9,000 = 8.33) at their PFH rate.

So, you can see that to be paid for 8.33 hours to cover 25 calendar weeks (six months) of arduous complex work is unrealistic. A full-time professional narrator could not make a living on that basis. To rely on what ACX or Findaway voices or others might tell you, can be totally misleading when dealing with anything beyond straightforward reading, which is why it is necessary for you to be totally confident that your narrator will get to the end without giving up part way through.

Others might disagree, they might suggest something better, quicker. If it comes down to a matter of opinion, it is only worth listening to if the other person has real first-hand experience. But always remember, it is NOT the recording that governs the time, it is always the EDITING.

Try getting a friend or two to act (with feeling) as narrator speaking out loud for a couple of chapters so you can time them. It might afford you a better approximation to give you greater confidence before you ask a stranger to do it.

It is your risk, as author, to evaluate, which is why it is so important to get the audition right. Your sales, reputation and peace of mind depend on it.

With an outline knowledge of the narrator's circumstances, the author should consider what their PFH hourly/daily/weekly/annual remuneration might be in the short and long term, bearing in mind that the non-negotiable PFH rate is determined by the listening time, as it is progressively logged up on the project screen. That is what the author is obliged to pay. You need to ensure that the narrator realises that.

The author should be sensitive to that reality and provide fully detailed notes to enable the narrator to do his best, particularly at audition. An example pro-forma is given as an Appendix. It should not come as a surprise to the narrator, many chapters later, that some detail was not provided earlier which causes a whole unravelling of recorded chapters up to that point.

A narrator wants to enjoy what he is doing and take pride in what he has done. It is in the author's interest to encourage, and when appropriate, to compliment the narrator. It's sure to pay dividends in the long run.

Audition Scripts

As far as audiobooks are concerned, the first place where things can and will go wrong is failing to choose the best or most appropriate narrator for the job.

The degree to which it might go wrong depends on the amount of thought that goes into the Audition Script or Schedule of Voices which is entirely the responsibility of the author. Computer folk talk about "garbage IN = garbage OUT" and so it is with an Audition Script.

The care taken by the author at this point will pay dividends in sales of the published audiobook and the listener's enjoyment.

The chosen narrator as voice actor has to give the gift of life to the author's characters who have been fermenting inside the author's head, arguing with one another, or loving each other for many months.

So, for me, a more informative, reassuring suggestion is to create a bespoke Audition Script from a series of passages, or paragraphs of the main characters memorable speeches, split between the sexes, and if that requires more than the "2–3 pages or 3–5 minutes" suggested by ACX, then so be it.

At that point neither ACX nor Findaway are in the picture. They have nothing to do with it. They are not checking. So, they can't complain. Their suggestions of what to do are unhelpful, lack understanding and are ill-informed, especially in works of fiction, which sets the seeds for problems later on.

The author also knows which and where are the most dramatic scenes which will make or break the listener's experience. It doesn't matter whereabouts that action takes place in the order of things. It doesn't have to be the first few pages, but it does have to be amongst the most memorable.

Authors shouldn't be scared to follow their inclination, if getting the right narrator to re-enact that conflict at audition stage will give him the most confidence and reduce his constant anxiety so much the better.

A novel for example has 80+% of one voice, that of the narrator as scene setter and lynchpin. It has to be a warm, soothing voice that is expressive and easy to listen to, not harsh or shrill, with words deliberately spoken and clear, not mumbled. The remainder is made up of a cast of maybe many varied characters who carry the main action, reaction, emotions and crises whilst telling the story between them.

The listener's over-riding interest is in following the voices of one prime and a few other main characters and the interplay between them. So, it is logical for an Audition Script to be mainly about them.

The Audition Script is of far greater importance to an author than the casual reference by ACX. It is almost like delivering a baby. The midwife can make all the difference to that traumatic experience, the memory of which will last a lifetime.

So that potential narrators, as voice actors, can give the most credible performance, the author should append a potted biography of each of the characters, and their voices/accents. For without it, the whole process is meaningless and can lead to avoidable disagreements. It is for the author alone to decide who, male or female, is best suited.

It is totally unreasonable for a lazy author to expect a narrator to spend hours reading a book from which he may gain no benefit.

It is perfectly reasonable for the narrator to be assured that he will be paid and not penalised. It is also commercially reasonable for the author to have a "hold" over the narrator's reimbursement, a "retention". That can be achieved by the narrator's reimbursement NOT starting until the author has approved two uploaded, technically acceptable chapters (including any Prologue).

The outstanding retention monies can be paid in a timely manner once the final chapter (including any Epilogue), Retail Sample, Opening and Closing Statements are acceptable.

Whilst there is nothing wrong with ACX or Findaway dispensing monies received from sales to both the author and the narrator, it is not essential that they do so. The author can pay the narrator direct once he gets paid. It's a question of transparency and mutual trust.

Just like the current unexpected actors and writers strike in the USA (July 2023) anything can happen in life – even to a narrator, his family, his equipment and so on. Any ESTIMATE of how long the audiobook might take should be given and taken in good faith. Guidance is given elsewhere in this manual as to what might be regarded as reasonable. There should be no threat of penalty, which is counter productive.

Pressurised deadlines are inappropriate in audiobook work, where tolerance, give and take is essential. So long as there is appropriate dialogue between the parties it should be possible to avoid dispute.

There should be no reason for either ACX or Findaway Voices, who have to co-ordinate their workload across numerous other projects, to get anxious about progress as they too have access to the project workflow screen and messages and can see how things are going.

Should any sort of misfortune, which would disrupt the orderly progress of chapter submission, befall the narrator, or he feels the parties have irreconcilable differences, he must advise the author immediately.

Depending on the difficulty and its known or unknown duration and when it occurs in the sequence of uploading chapters, the author must decide what is prudent, given that to go back and start again with another narrator is going to be both time consuming, tedious and probably more costly in the long run. It all comes down to how well and wisely the author chose the narrator in the first place hence my preoccupation with the Audition Script and the first 15 minutes recording.

In that situation the author is expected to be tolerant and patient. But if they feel that with no foreseeable solution to the matter it is necessary to terminate the Agreement at that point, then they must advise the narrator in writing through the workflow messaging system and ask for all payments made to be returned.

The author should NOT be entitled to cancel, or claim a refund, once 25% of the text has been recorded, submitted and technically approved.

However, if the author's actions in that case are perceived as petulant, or acting on a whim, with no previous adverse comment recorded on a chapter-by-chapter basis, or based on a third party's intrusion, then the narrator would have strong grounds for not returning any money.

In the event that the Agreement is based on a split payment whereby the narrator has a reasonable expectation of several year's worth of regular royalties (or compensation) and the author revokes that Agreement, he should pay the narrator the remainder of the 100% of his recording fee of

PFH x workflow measured listening hours x 5 times by way of compensation for the unearned income.

Life is a succession of risks. Mostly, nothing ever goes wrong, and little thought is given to what might have happened *IF* … .

But occasionally things don't go according to plan for one reason or another. In the case of an audiobook, progressing by repeated approval and payment on a chapter-by-chapter basis gives both parties the best chance of minimising any (should they have one) perceived risk. That will also depend on how far they have got, and if they did reach an impasse who will sort it out?

Neither ACX nor Findaway Voices contracts offer independent mediation facilities. Both deliberately excuse themselves from any involvement. That's not what they're in business for.

Instead, they both direct aggrieved parties to the civil Courts of their respective States in the USA, New York or Ohio, or commercially minded rubbing-their-hands with glee anonymous mediators.

Anyone who has ever been involved with civil actions, anywhere, will shudder. They are unpleasant and stressful, especially those like me in the UK who have seen the antics of the USA legal system on TV. The sums of money involved are unlikely to be worth arguing about to that degree. As I said, life is a risk.

My suggestion is to ONLY deal directly with "the chosen voice" that you feel has empathy with your words, who cares, and can consistently and competently represent all of the different characters in your story (and enjoy doing so) in a way which will hold the listeners' attention for hours. Trust your instincts.

Control and Communication

IMPORTANT! After choosing a narrator, the author's next control point comes with approving the first 15-minute recording. There is no compulsion or logic that that MUST be the first chapter or Prologue. What it should be is all or much of the most testing chapter, the pivotal point of the story, the one the author might be most anxious about, which has a fundamental effect on the whole story. This is the enactment of the Audition Script for real. Failure to do that can ruin everything.

In that case, the mechanics of uploading a recorded chapter to ACX or Findaway Voices (Spotify) in the wrong numerical order are easily overcome. The project screen system facilitates that.

The methodology which I have described in this manual enables necessary corrections and adjustments to be made as every chapter is uploaded.

Both the ACX and Findaway systems provide the narrator with the opportunity to advise the author whenever a new chapter, or a corrected one, has been uploaded. Equally, there is nothing to stop the author sending messages to the narrator. It enables both parties to have a constant dialogue, frankness and appreciation, to avoid festering misunderstandings. It also commits the author to confirming, chapter-by-chapter, that he is satisfied by the quality and progress, denying him the opportunity to complain at a later date.

Consequently, disputes over content and performance are avoided.

Narrating an audiobook is NOT a repetitive manufacturing process, any more than writing a novel might be, or an artist painting a portrait or even a sculptor. There are so many things which can influence the length of time it takes to complete an audiobook that no narrator should commit himself to, or be held to, a guaranteed timescale, nor should it be expected.

An honest estimate can be given in good faith, and the author updated, but until he gets into the rhythm and feel of the first few chapters, the narrator will not know, particularly if he is inexperienced in that sort of work.

Under no circumstances should a narrator agree to work under the fear of a deadline penalty clause. Nor should any author, caring for his own work, expect it. The author must not be impatient.

Being paid on an uploaded, technically checked, author approved, chapter-by-chapter basis, ideally with an initial goodwill and final payment basis incentivises the narrator's efforts and removes his financial risk.

The other thing for the author to give thought to early on is the Retail Sample which prospective purchasers will listen to before deciding to buy or borrow his audiobook. There should be a synergy between the Retail Sample and the Audition Script. Effectively they do the same job.

His narrator won't need to know what excerpts the author wishes to use in the Retail Sample until they have uploaded the last chapter, Opening and Closing Credits. What is important is that YOU, the author KNOWS in advance so you can select a few minutes worth of intrigue, mystery, excitement, or cliff-hanger in the same way that cinema trailers entice people to turn up when the movie is coming to town in a week or so.

Apart from its title, the audiobook specific visual front cover, the 5-minute-long retail sample recording is the "MUST BUY ME" factor offering an emotional experience of some kind. Suspense! What's next?

All of those things will be dealt with in Part Nine – **Audiobook Marketing**.

But before you do anything, the same with Findaway Voices, go to the ACX.com website, first page, top line, *SEARCH*. The drop down menu offers you *TITLES ACCEPTING AUDITIONS*. There you can browse published audiobooks in your target market, so you can see how they display themselves, how they are selling, and imagine how yours might fit in.

You'll soon realise that the ACX.com website is very extensive, compre-hensive and saturated with volumes of information which can be difficult to take in and navigate. It can overwhelm you. It is easy to get lost and forget how you got there. It's not as easy as turning pages in a traditional "how-to" printed reference manual such as this, which you can have open at the side of your screen.

Hopefully this manual might make things simpler. To find anything out, identify your topic on the extensive ACX main menu, which is like the trunk of a tree with many branches, and appears on every screen page and work from there. For example, you can click on Authors; Authors as

Narrators; or Narrators on their own before you branch out into greater and greater detail.

A good idea is to constantly print out things to remember on good old-fashioned paper and make an indexed physical folder of relevant topics which you'll find far easier to work with than having to constantly remember which navigational path to follow.

Part Three

Narrators

An Audiobook? From a Narrators point of view

Both American ACX and Findaway have registers of narrators/producers and welcome new applicants through their respective websites. Many of those registered are professional actors and voice-over artists operating in a predominantly American unionised environment of "the going rate" but there is no obligation on outsiders or newcomers to conform.

Traditionally after an auditioning process at the author's invitation, and an agreeable timescale, the successful narrator will work on payment upon completion and approval by the author.

Both ACX and Findaway are scrupulously correct in making royalty payments on time when they are due.

Payment is made on the universally understood basis of a narrator quoted PFH – *NOT* how long it takes to make and agree the work which takes much longer than it does to listen to the finished result.

Under those arrangements, the narrator derives no income, which might be for several months until the audiobook is finally approved and available. Factors beyond a narrator's control.

In all of that time, of potential uncertainty, whilst the author has written agreements with either ACX or Findaway Voices, **the narrator has no such Agreement or safeguard with anyone**.

Without a formal agreement such as that offered by Part Five – the **AUDIOBOOK HANDBOOK AGREEMENT**, the narrator is exposed to questionable risks leading to expensive time-consuming debilitating legal arguments in far-off jurisdictions described in legalistic gobbledygook in both the ACX and Findaway Agreements.

One of the reasons why unionised narrators' rates are so high, as in any business, they have to factor in contingency sums in case the relationship with the author breaks down for want of simple certainty, or any other uninsurable misadventure covered in normal commercial practice.

Neither ACX nor Findaway insist on the use of narrators from their respective registers. Nor, so it would seem, are they against any formal or informal Agreement between the author and his chosen narrator who could be a personal acquaintance or of mutual recommendation.

Audiobook publishers, such as ACX serving Amazon Group interests and Findaway Voices serving a global network of independent distributors are the means by which you reach your listeners wherever they are in the world and from whom you potentially derive an income.

Traditionally those organisations rely on authors alone to decide where an audiobook is promoted. The narrator whose voice the audiobook buyer listens to, and likes, largely through a sample excerpt, is influential in effecting the sale. In my view, wrongly, the narrator doesn't get a say.

So a narrator, persuaded to enter a royalty sharing arrangement in an Exclusive deal, tied into ACX for seven years or so, for example, finds himself in a weak position where he has no control over the audiobook cover design which supposedly attracts buyers, but might not, the purchase price governing the commission paid, which ACX can cut, or the global market placement into which he has no input. It could be seen as a costly mistake which might not be realised until many months later.

On the other hand, an unknown narrator may consider that such a situation is a price worth paying for getting a foot on the ladder. Portfolio building is a long-term strategy. That is how I got started, so I know the pitfalls.

Be wary of anyone acting as a well-meaning intermediary, introducer or "literary" agent so-called who claims to be the Rights holder. Their motives may not be as straightforward or honourable as you might hope. I speak from bitter experience.

Recently (July 2023) I received the following email from ACX regarding an audiobook that I had narrated and recorded on a split royalty basis for a so-called literary agent three years earlier:

"We are reaching out to you regarding the ACX productions listed below.

We have conducted an extensive review, and during that review, these productions raised a significant number of flags across multiple data points:

xxxxxxxxxxxxxxxxxxxxxxxxxxxxxxxxxxxxxxxxxxxxxxxxxxxxxxxxxx

Our investigation identified suspicious activity related to the ACX Rights Holder associated with this title, and as a result, we have terminated the Rights Holder's account. Accordingly, we have removed the title listed above from sale on Audible,

Amazon and iTunes. We apologize for any frustration or difficulty this may cause you. Please know that your ACX account as a producer remains in good standing with ACX/Audible. We are constantly working to improve the creator experience, and have introduced a number of on-site features and internal processes to ensure the legitimacy of ACX projects. If you have any questions about future auditions please let us know.

Thank you for using ACX. We wish you the best with your future productions.

Regards, ACX Team, The ACX Team"

What that means is that I receive no future royalties from that Agreement, nor is it worthwhile the time, effort and cost of pursuing that individual. If nothing more, it justifies my writing this manual to warn other vulnerable narrators to only get involved on the basis of the advice given here.

Evaluating opportunities and challenges

If you feel that you have, or friends have told you that you have a "nice" voice and you have studied this manual, and feel that you have the confidence to make it work, the following section will tell you what you need to know, and to have, to become a narrator working from home.

To my mind, providing you have a basic income or pension, savings or a charitable family to support you for a year or so, and a small space, with minimal external noise for your exclusive use, then it is an ideal occupation for established authors who wish to self-narrate their own books or those of other authors, or for the actively retired, redundant, housebound, disabled or anyone else who would like to do it for an interesting, rewarding pastime or anyone who might, for whatever reason, feel lonely or depressed.

Is narrating worth doing? That will depend on your objectives. Whatever they are, it is essential that you evaluate the opportunities and/or challenges that are presented to you. It is enjoyable work and will introduce you to many nice folk that you might otherwise never have met, some of whom will become good friends.

If nothing else, it is a worthwhile achievement of which anyone can be justly proud, and which relatively few others will achieve. You don't need to be clever, or sporty, nimble or quick, or a member of a team. You don't need to be big and strong, good looking, the life and soul of the party, extroverted or sociable or creative like an author or a painter is. You just need to be persistent and believe in yourself.

You WILL gain confidence and respect and along the way you will earn yourself a modest income and with your name on the cover you'll gain the recognition you deserve.

If you are a beginner, your prime objective is likely to be getting a foothold in building up a track record of reliability and credibility. In that case, beggars can't be choosers. Commissioning authors evaluate their risk in terms of cost, commitment and reputation. Are you worth the risk to them?

Even if you are a beginner, and you don't have any connections with friendly authors, you can always join a local writers group and build up a portfolio of sample random recordings of (internet search) "Out of copyright {Public Domain} book titles" and register with ACX on their established register, or the recently reorganised Findaway Voices as a producer for authors to choose from. You need to demonstrate your ability and reliability, so they choose you on merit with no risk to them.

Nothing will annoy an author more – and get your relationship off on the wrong footing if you stupidly agree, or are bullied into agreeing, a tight production schedule which is beyond your experience or capabilities. It is far better to pass up on that opportunity than have a dissatisfied customer.

Start off by targeting books that are no more than 50,000 words long with few characters. Children's books are ideal to start with. You will be under less pressure. Ask for the least remuneration you can afford, as many authors are not well off financially.

This manual will give you guidance on how long things take for an experienced narrator. Every book is different in length and numbers and complexities of characters.

By now you will have a good understanding of the amount of work involved in narrating and producing an audiobook to professional standards. It is important NOT to waste your time and effort on an audiobook that is unlikely to become popular enough to reward your contribution. Research! Choose the genre wisely, Romance for example. Ideally try to follow an author who has had a book(s) published, and subject matter which has a good following, but maybe is yet to have an audiobook.

You can do that by studying Amazon categories and sales statistics and ranking which will cost you nothing except your time or the impressive K-lytics.com for comprehensive data on their subscription service which you can easily cancel at any time.

Today (November 11th 2021) on ACX, as I write this there are:

✓ 1,234 titles open for audition across many categories/genres.

✓ 672,902 narrator/producers doing more or less what I do, in their own way, but don't let that put you off. They're not all likely to be active and looking, and may not want to do what you do, and if they did, the author may not be able to afford them. Besides which they probably won't have a voice or accent like yours is, or what you offer is not what the author wants.

✓ 267,531 titles for sale across Amazon, Audible.com and Apple Books (formerly iTunes)

How successful your audiobook might be is dealt with in Part Nine – **Audiobook Marketing**.

The importance of the Narrator's Script

As its name implies, a Narrator's Script is produced by and for the narrator alone. It is his control panel. It is NOT to be confused with the Audition Script which is produced by the author for a different purpose. They are not the same thing.

An audiobook is an intimate performance to an audience, usually of one, an individual listening through headphones on a plane or train, speakers or on the radio by himself.

The chosen narrator of the audiobook, or the author as the narrator IS in fact one of the characters with a voice or sound of their own. The narrator has by far (80+%) more words to process than any fictitious character. It is they, individually and as a group and the interplay between them which tells the story. The narrator makes it happen. He sets the changing scenes, settings, lighting, locations, date and time and influences the mood or atmosphere.

As a narrator I work from my annotated script laid out in a specific way to enable me to highlight, mark or underline the text (I use the easy-to-read Palatino Linotype font), spaced out and sized to effortlessly read the authors words at a comfortable distance, saying and interpreting them in the way that they were written. Work with what best suits YOUR eyesight, to feel comfortable and avoid mistakes. Do not have it imposed upon you.

The author holds the complete text on his computer which, when asked, he should transmit digitally by email for downloading so that the narrator can rearrange the spacing, margins, typeface and sizing so that he can print it out to suit his way of working. The narrator may then mark up and annotate what will then become the Narrator's Script.

On no account should the narrator be asked to, or expected to, read direct from the author's published book. To do so is contemptible. If that were to happen the narrator should decline to go further, as it deprives the narrator of his ability to control the quality of the sound. It's just asking for trouble.

A narrator's home recording studio, in this context, only needs to be adequate enough to satisfy Findaway and ACX.com's stated audio quality requirements. Two of those are technical issues concerning the performed sound quality provided by the equipment available. The third concerns the interfering sound of the background environment which detracts from that performance. All of that will become clear in Parts Six, Seven and Eight.

The capital and running costs of a purpose-built professional sound studio are NOT necessary for our purpose, nor is that of a trained sound engineer. We are NOT going to record music which has far more sophisticated requirements.

All that is required is a comparatively small, enclosed space big enough for one person, the narrator, to be comfortable for a few hours, standing up or sitting down without feeling cramped, ideally but not essentially with some natural light and ventilation.

Artificial light, mechanical heaters, anything with a fan such as a ventilator risks introducing unwanted noise which will be picked up by a sensitive condenser microphone, even if you, a human being, can't hear it and often you can't, the microphone will.

A comfy, preferably swivelling, chair, with a bench or table needed for drinks, papers and anything else the narrator needs to have to hand as I will show you in Part Six – **The Home Studio.**

The key to a good, recorded sound, apart from the condenser microphone and audio interface, is soft wall and floor surfaces. They absorb and deflect the invisible bouncing sound waves and prevent echoes and reverberation.

Think of sound like a snooker, billiards or pool ball which bounces from one "cushion" to another on a soft baize covered surface until it gradually slows down and eventually stops.

Horizontal, hard ceiling surfaces deflect sound waves down on to hard, vertical surfaces from which they bounce around unless you stop them. External noise transmitted through an occupied floor above or from activity below the recording floor can be problematical, but with patience and planning they can be overcome.

In reality, recording is relatively quick compared with what comes next. It is the editing, correcting and compiling which takes the majority of time.

Wait for any interruption/disruption to stop or adjust the times when you need to record until things calm down. Outside noise from thunder and traffic to thoughtless neighbours does NOT affect listen-through or playback editing because you will be using quality headphones, so you always have something else you can be getting on with.

As you will see from the following pages, this writer uses a spare guest bedroom in a modern house overlooking a garden and fields beyond, on the edge of a quiet village in middle England. A bathroom is adjacent and a kitchen below, both of which can create annoying domestic sounds and clatter from time to time, as do the birds nesting in the climbing roses on the external walls surrounding the window and the occasional noisy agricultural machinery in the field beyond the fence. From time to time helicopters and light aircraft can be a nuisance, as can migrating swans and geese.

Yes, it may sound idyllic, but noise and nuisance are an occupational hazard for everyone.

The narrator must decide on how they wish to split up recording into manageable units of work. As he annotates his working script and becomes familiar with the characters and their situations, he will get a feel for how much time, how long, a "chunk" should be, depending on the number and interaction of voices over a variable time span depending on concentration, tedium and complexity.

I've found that round about 20 minutes finished listening time, registering on the project screen, give or take, is comfortable. Another criteria is that an essential Audacity ACX-Check (see later) tends to have a processing time limit of about 25 minutes or so, necessitating longer chapters to be split up and processed into two or maybe more.

It is important for the narrator/editor/producer to feel that he is making progress in the often lengthy, time-consuming process of constructing an audiobook. There is nothing more demoralising for a runner in a marathon than to have nothing to gauge his progress by. No landmarks to aim for, no scenery to pass, no spectators to smile, wave and shout encouragement, no target to achieve.

Long chapters can be tedious, as can those with extensive conversations. Because of that they tend to take longer to record.

Analysing the task

The term "Voice Actor" is probably more appropriate when it comes to audiobook work, because in a range, or cast, of characters, differing voices need to be used to identify and distinguish who is speaking and how they are saying it.

The term "Narrator" is appropriate for the bits in between when the characters are brought to life or when simply reading or looking at something. A bit like a knowledgeable tour guide or sports commentator might. The essential characteristic is that a narrator is himself alone. It is however one word instead of two and more convenient to use.

For the purposes of this manual, a narrator/voice actor in an audiobook is unlike a stage or film actor (although they can be one and the same). An actor has to convincingly become just the one character that they are portraying in situations interacting with other actors in a time limited performance before a live audience in a theatre or auditorium or in a film.

A voice actor, in bringing to life a previously written script or work by a third person, an author, such as in a novel, has to convincingly and consistently, over several hours of listening time, often spanning days or even weeks of recording time, portray to individual listeners, any number of fictional characters, their situations and locations, at all times transporting the listener into an author's otherwise unbelievable world of plausible make-believe.

What the voice actor can never know is when and where the listener will switch off his delivery device, and when and where they will resume, and to what degree that listener will recall the story thus far, and what their level of concentration will be.

Some might have the misconception that all of this is merely reading aloud, like they might have done at school. That is far off the mark.

A trained actor is very talented, as are some good amateurs. They have to have many skills because they are performing predominantly visually with actions, sometimes subtle, almost imperceptible expressions and mannerisms. Research is necessary to communicate the life and times of the characters. The need for an audience to "imagine" the action is minimised.

In audiobook work much of that trained expertise is superfluous. It is NOT necessary to have the years of training at drama school or an on-the-job apprenticeship in a repertory company, although it will help. The contents of this manual will go a long way towards preparing a beginner to being able to successfully audition for audiobook work, providing a creditable outcome and basis for future commissions.

The voice actor's role is to make the author's words "imaginable" in the listener's mind. There are no artificial theatrical sound effects to help him. The voice actor is truly the storyteller. Emotion and sensitivity are needed to be transmitted to, and to be felt by, the listener whose mind, the inner eye, is the stage upon which the action is taking place.

Before you begin recording you should have annotated your Narrator's Script to identify when OTHER VOICES are speaking, i.e. the characters, because that is when the narrator, as narrator is NOT.

The narrator must judge how long other voices are speaking, and whilst the moving cursor continues across the screen as recording takes place, the narrator must remain quiet. This will create gaps in the Timeline waveform, which will become obvious in due course.

The lengths of gaps will, for now, be a guess, especially in a conversation where characters are talking to each other. The duration of each gap will be adjusted in the EDITING process and again when those speeches are patched in later. All of this will come with experience and is nothing to worry about.

ALWAYS REMEMBER in EDITING, it is easier and quicker to DELETE gaps and parts of gaps than it is to add them in afterwards.

The following is a real-life example of what happens next. Part Two of this manual dealt with the ACX audition process upon which this presentation is based. This segment is relevant to that, but is dealt with here, logically, for simplicity.

In this example, the published novel is *Fortune's Promise – a Regency Romance* by well-known author Sue Johnson, for whom I have recorded two of her other novels previously. The action takes place in rural middle England around the early 1800s. It is an A5 paperback of 208 pages covering 70,000+ words in 38 short chapters.

Now for the important bit. Please refer to spreadsheet screenshots A–E on the following pages. They illustrate all of the characters and the chapters and pages on which they will appear.

There are 82 "voices" plus a parrot (talking mynah bird), of which, 37 are female and 45 are male. The sex of the parrot is unknown.

Of the female voices, four of them are LEADING characters with frequent involvement. The others, the SUPPORTING female characters are infrequent and crop up all over the place. Of all of the women, 16 are classed as YOUNG (Y), 15 are variously MIDDLE AGED (M), whilst the other six are OLD (O).

Apart from one elderly lady with a superior social affectation, all are from varying social levels of English rural society, predominantly the county of Worcestershire in middle England with accents to match.

Fortune's Promise by Sue Johnson - Leading Characters - Prologue to Chapter 12

Y = up to 30
M = 31 -60
O = 60 plus

Chapters with page numbers below

Ages	Leading Characters	Sex	Prologue	1	2	3	4	5	6	7	8	9	10	11	12
Y	Lucinda Beckford	F	4,5	8,10,11			27,28,		36,38,39,	42,43,44,46,47,48,49,			59,	61,64,65,	
Y	Hannah	F		8,			27,28,			43,44,46,				61,62,64, 67,	
Y	Georgiana Milburn	F				18,19,22,24		32,33,34			51,52, 54,				
O	Lady Sophia Beeching	F						32,							
Y	Adam Lennox	M						30,34,				53,54,55,	58,59,60,		
Y	Giles Milburn	M				15,19,	25,26,					56,	58,59,60,		67,
Y	Oliver Gray	M				19,23,24,									
Y	John Beckford	M							37,38,	45,47,48,				63,64,65,	
M	Josiah Beckford	M	3,5,6	10,					37,40,	42,43,44,45,48,					
M	William Milburn	M				17,18,		33,34,			51,				

Fortune's Promise by Sue Johnson – Leading Characters – Chapters 13 to 25

Y = up to 30
M = 31 –60
O = 60 plus

Chapters with page numbers below

Leading Characters

Ages		Sex	13	14	15	16	17	18	19	20	21	22	23	24	25
Y	Lucinda Beckford	F	69,70,71,	74,75,76,77,78,79,80,81,82,		85,86,87,88,	90,91,93,96,	99,100,105,106,107,	112,113,114,115,116,117,118,121,	126,127,128,131,132,	136,137,139,141,142,			150,151,152,	153,155,
Y	Hannah	F	69,	74,75,77,78,79,80,81,82,				105,106,107,	112,114,115,116,117,118,119,121,122,	124,127,128,129,130,131,132,	136,137,139,140,141.			152,	153,154,155,
Y	Georgiana Milburn	F			84,	86,									
D	Lady Sophia Beeching	F					94,95,	108,109,							
Y	Adam Lennon	M	69,70	78,79.				102,110,111,	120,121,122,123.	128,129,132,			147,148,		
Y	Giles Milburn	M			84,		90,92,93,94,9	108,			139,142,143,	145,146,	147,148,		
Y	Oliver Gray	M													
Y	John Beckford	M		81.				104,							
M	Josiah Beckford	M				86,	91,93.	103,104.							
M	William Milburn	M								126,					

B

Of the male voices, six are LEADING characters with frequent involvement. The others, the SUPPORTING characters, are infrequent and crop up all over the place. Of all of the men, 19 are classed as YOUNG(Y), 19 are variously MIDDLE AGED (M), while the other seven are OLD (O).

Apart from one, the villain, an aggressive scoundrel with a false "posh" affectation, all are from varying social levels of English rural society, predominantly Worcestershire with accents to match.

As an aside, you might like to know that the world-famous BBC radio soap *The Archers* (broadcast globally) – with multiple professional actors in a professional studio in Birmingham, with all of the necessary rural sound effects, plus technical support – is based on fictitious village life in that part of the world (reputed to be Inkberrow), just a few miles from where I live.

Importantly, the narrator with a non-acting part has to differentiate voices sufficiently to create that illusion. That is best achieved by analysing where similarities might occur on the same page and chapter and adopting voice tones to ensure that listeners are not confused as to whose voice it is that they are hearing.

That is best done by ascribing different characters with different voices – normal; high; low; soft; harsh; loud; aggressive; lyrical, etc. – slow speaking; drawling; staccato; rapid speaking; accent and so on. Then to record, for each character in the narrator's Schedule of Voices, a "palette" (as in an artist mixing his paints) of his or her voice for a reference of consistency as a waveform file. It does not need to be more than any paragraph or a few sentences. It does not even have to make sense, but it MUST be distinctly different.

Then on a chapter-by-chapter basis, copy and paste from the waveform file (see Part Eight) a sample of each of that chapter's voices. All you are trying to do is to test the compatibility of voices so you can see if they create a sufficiently diverse set of voices so that a listener would be able to distinguish between them.

Keep each VOICE TEST CHAPTER as a separate file.

Fortune's Promise by Sue Johnson - Leading Characters - Chapters 26 to Epilogue

Y = up to 30

M = 31 -60

0 = 60 plus

Chapters with page numbers below

Ages	Leading Characters	Sex	26	27	28	29	30	31	32	33	34	35	36	Epilogue
Y	Lucinda Beckford	F	156,157,158,164,165,				176,177,178,180,	182,	184,		191,192,	194,195,196,	201,204,205,	208,
Y	Hannah	F	159,160,161,163,164,165,			171,172,173,		181,182,	184,		192,		200,	207,
Y	Georgiana Milburn	F												
O	Lady Sophia Beeching	F											197,198,203,204,205,	207,
Y	Adam Lennox	M	163,164,	166,		170,171,172,				185,	190,192,	194,	202,203,204,205,	208,
Y	Giles Milburn	M			168,169,					188,		195,	197,198,201,202,203,	
Y	Oliver Gray	M											199,	
Y	John Beckford	M												
M	Josiah Beckford	M												207,
M	William Milburn	M												

Fortune's Promise by Sue Johnson - Supporting FEMALE Characters - All Chapters

Y = up to 30
M = 31 -60
O = 60 plus

Chapters with page numbers below

Supporting Characters

Ages	Supporting Characters	Sex	Pro	1	2	3	4	5	6	7	8	9	10	11	12	13	14	15	16	17	18
Y	Tilly	F		10			28	39,40											85,88	91	107
Y	Dead Amelia	F			12																
M	Ella Ivy's stepmum	F																			
M	Florence Temple	F																			
M	Mrs. Hoskins	F																			
M	Rose Dennett	F																			
M	Mrs. Parsons	F		8				39,40						71,72		73, 75		88			107
M	Dead Maria Milburn	F				23															
M	Caroline Beckford Mrs.	F						36,37												94	
M	Wife of injured reveller	F															79				
M	Farmers wife	F																			
M	Lady B's housekeeper	F																			
M	Landlady of Inn	F																			
M	Fairground farm wife	F																			
M	Jessie's mum	F																			
M	Temple's housekeeper	F																			
M	Market woman	F																			
Y	Temple's servant	F																			
Y	Dairymaid	F																			
Y	Runaway girl -Ivy	F																			
Y	Dora sulky	F																			
Y	Ella's maid	F																			
Y	Agatha grand daughter	F																			
Y	3 Fairground girls	F																			
Y	Lower Warren woman	F																			
Y	Lower Warren Jessie	F																			
Y	Sal Bishop	F																			
Y	One of Matilda's girls	E																			
O	Old Ginny	F				21,22															
O	Betsy Triggs	F					27,28			47											
O	Agatha Dixon old crone	F																			
O	Rector's wife	F																			
O	Matilda Marshall	F																			

Ages	Supporting Characters	Sex	20	21	22	23	24	25	26	27	28	29	30	31	32	33	34	35	36	Epi
Y	Tilly	F																		207
Y	Dead Amelia	F																		
M	Ella Ivy's stepmum	F	129,130,131,132, 136,138,139,140																	
M	Florence Temple	F						159,160,161,162,163	171											
M	Mrs. Hoskins	F															191,192, 194,195,196	200,203, 197,198		
M	Rose Dennett	F			147,149				166											
M	Mrs. Parsons	F																		
M	Dead Maria Milburn	F																		
M	Caroline Beckford Mrs.	F																		
M	Wife of injured reveller	F																		
M	Farmers wife	F																		
M	Lady B's housekeeper	F																		
M	Landlady of Inn	F																		
M	Fairground farm wife	F	139																	
M	Jessie's mum	F					151													
M	Temple's housekeeper	F					153					170,171,172								
M	Market woman	F						159					190							
Y	Temple's servant	F									167									
Y	Dairymaid	F																		
Y	Runaway girl -Ivy	F					151													
Y	Dora sulky	F	124,129,130	139,141,142																
Y	Ella's maid	F	124,125,126	140	145,146															
Y	Agatha grand daughter	F																		
Y	3 Fairground girls	F				146														
Y	Lower Warren woman	F					150													
Y	Lower Warren Jessie	F					153													
Y	Sal Bishop	F					153,154,155							181						
Y	One of Matilda's girls	E												182						
O	Old Ginny	F																		
O	Betsy Triggs	F																		
O	Agatha Dixon old crone	F				148												203,204		
O	Rector's wife	F																		
O	Matilda Marshall	F						154,155	156,161,164				173,174		175	181,182	184,186		

Fortune's Promise by Sue Johnson - Supporting MALE Characters - All Chapters

Y = up to 30
M = 31 -60
O = 60 plus

Chapters with page numbers below

Ages	Supporting Characters	Sex	Pro	1	2	3	4	5	6	7	8	9	10	11	12	13	14	15	16
Y	Farm boy	M																	
Y	Reuben Turner	M	4,6																
Y	Charlie Marshall	M												61,63,65,	67,		80,81,		
y	Dieing soldier	M				13,													
Y	Boy in Marchington	M					26,												
Y	Trio of army voices	M						30,											
Y	Stable Lad	M										52,							
Y	Gardeners boy	M																	
Y	Voice in cubicle	M													66,				
Y	Orderly Barracks	M														78,			
Y	Sergeant/Sentry	M															80,81,		
Y	Merchant clerk	M																	
Y	Shepherd	M																	
Y	One of Matilda's boys	M																	
Y	Pascoe	M				15.18.20.						52. 53.55.							
M	Digby	M					29,												
M	Pub landlord	M							41,										
M	Doctor	M									62,								
M	Bogus Fair Doctor	M												77,78,					
M	Commanding Officer	M																	
M	Coachman	M																	
M	Runaway girl's Dad	M																	
M	Daniel labourer	M																	
M	Matthew	M																	
M	Toll house keeper	M																	
M	Goose drover	M																	
M	Apothecary,	M																	
	Amos Jennings Parrot	M																	
M	Amos Jennings	M																	
M	Vicar Temple	M																	
M	Twister	M																	
M	Informant	M																	
M	Jenkins coachman	M																	
O	Ambrose Leitch	M																	
O	Farmer Braithwaite	M																	
O	Country doctor	M																	
O	Conversation in pub	M																	92,97,
O	Rector	M																	
O	Lawyer Craycombe	M							40,										
O	Men in Marchington	M											57,						

Ages	Supporting Characters	Sex	17	18	19	20	21	22	23	24	25	26	27	28	29	30	31	32	33	34	35	36	Epi
Y	Farm boy	M				142,143,																	
Y	Reuben Turner	M			134,																		208,
Y	Charlie Marshall	M																					
y	Dieing soldier	M																					
Y	Boy in Marchington	M																					
Y	Trio of army voices	M																					
Y	Stable Lad	M	108,																				
Y	Gardeners boy	M																					
Y	Voice in cubicle	M																					
Y	Orderly Barracks	M																					
Y	Sergeant/Sentry	M	110,111,																				
Y	Merchant clerk	M								152,													
Y	Shepherd	M															186,	188,					
Y	One of Matilda's boys	M																		204,205,			
Y	Pascoe	M																					
M	Digby	M																					
M	Pub landlord	M													180,								
M	Doctor	M																					
M	Bogus Fair Doctor	M																					
M	Commanding Officer	M	103,																				
M	Coachman	M		115,116,117,119,120,		124,125,131,132,		144,145,146,															
M	Runaway girl's Dad	M					140,																
M	Daniel labourer	M							148,											190,191,			
M	Matthew	M									156,												
M	Toll house keeper	M									156,												
M	Goose drover	M									158,					176,177,							
M	Apothecary,	M														177,178,							
	Amos Jennings Parrot	M														178,179,							
M	Amos Jennings	M									161,			173,		180,							
M	Vicar Temple	M									157,		168,169,	173,174,			186,						
M	Twister	M											168,										
M	Informant	M																			203,		
M	Jenkins coachman	M																			198,		
O	Ambrose Leitch	M								151,	158,159,					179,180,							
O	Farmer Braithwaite	M		119,120,			135,		136,138,	144,													
O	Country doctor	M							138,														
O	Conversation in pub	M																					
O	Rector	M																					
O	Lawyer Craycombe	M																					
O	Men in Marchington	M																					

Then as you go on, do that for every chapter. In that way you'll discover problems that you might not have realised, so you can make adjustments.

Whilst it is inappropriate for this project, because their accents are clearly established by the author, in another project where the voice actor has greater freedom, the differentiation can be made by a wider use of accents/dialects.

In that case use the internet and SEARCH for the wide ranging – **IDEA**: (https://www.dialectsarchive.com) International Dialects of English Archive where you can listen for FREE and mimic how your audiobook character might sound. It is extremely helpful.

So now you can begin to see what you are up against. This has been a real life example. It highlights where there are pitfalls, with any number of characters who come alive and go from one chapter to another, and from beginning to end.

The best way to avoid making mistakes is to do what they do in feature films. That is to record in "takes". So you could follow each character through all of their voice appearances in one go over several chapters, one at a time, taking care to follow the author's description of mood and setting, etc.

Each character would have a separate sound file, with gaps separating each speech waveform, each one having a (see later) Label track synced (Audacity screen bottom left hand corner – Labels track) to the words (which is important) so it could be copied and pasted into place in the narrators file along with the contributions from other voices.

In the whole book, the FEMALE LEAD characters make:

Lucinda Beckford (heroine).............. 90 speeches

Hannah (her best friend)................... 62 ....

Georgiana Milburn............................ 12 ....

Lady Sophia Beeching....................... 11 ....

(see sheets A–C covering 36 chapters)

In the whole book there are 33 FEMALE SUPPORTING characters making 101 speeches between them (see sheet D) – 13 are young; 15 are middle aged and five are old.

In Leading Character sheets A–C there are four female and six male leading characters. Three of those females are YOUNG and MUST sound different. This will be helped if one has a deeper voice than the other two. Of them, one might speak in a slow and deliberate manner, the other might be over-excited and talk quickly.

Lucinda with nearly 50% of LEADING FEMALE speeches has almost as many speeches as all of the SUPPORTING FEMALE characters put together. The same as all of the SUPPORTING MALE characters put together and almost as many as the LEADING MALE characters put together.

Lucinda is clearly the star of the show and the character with whom the listener will have the greatest empathy. If the narrator/voice actor gets her wrong, the whole effect is ruined.

A male voice speaking her part has to be particularly sensitive and softly spoken. He would have to speak convincingly with a higher register to suggest her soprano voice. Many men would not manage that. The author would be wise to centre on that for an audition piece. EVERYTHING DEPENDS ON THAT!

On the other hand, a female voice speaking all of the male parts might struggle with credibility on the baritone and bass registers.

At audition, the prospective narrator should question the author to get a thorough understanding of the total task, including an analysis like this which will reveal the extent of the time necessary to deliver a quality product. That in turn will determine the narrator's recompense.

Of the males in this story, four of them are young. One is the villain who fancies himself and is a bully who speaks aggressively. One dies early on and is of a lower social order. The other two are nice guys, so it will be possible to make one sound Welsh, as Wales is geographically near the story setting and feasible. The other two males are both fathers, but nowhere do they clash on the same page, but even so they must not sound the same. LISTENERS WILL REMEMBER!

Then there is the army of SUPPORTING characters (see sheet E) all of whom advance the story individually by their timely addition of snippets of information enhancing and lubricating the listeners' understanding and involvement as a close-at-hand onlooker.

As the analysis shows, they are interspersed here and there, at no time stealing the limelight. The narrator also, must ensure that their voices are equally unobtrusive. Even the parrot must be circumspect.

The task is to CONSISTENTLY maintain each voice over many hours and days of recording, with life's constant disruptions and interruptions and irritations, over several weeks.

The danger is of fatigue introducing errors which will be all too noticeable to the listener, 5–6 recording hours of intense concentration per day of a five-day working week is as much as I can manage and be happy with the quality of sound production, bearing in mind that recording is actually only a small part of the finished article.

Before you even attempt any audition where they might choose you, please practice extensively on any other novels where there is an interplay of voices. It requires intense concentration. If you don't you will panic, look a fool and embarrass yourself with your carefully built confidence taking a nosedive.

YOU being someone else

Consider these speeches (by an Italian male character with a shaky English accent) from *Apple Orchard Lemon Grove* by Sue Johnson:

A.

"Non ho capito. I don't understand."

There are 30 characters (words, letters and spaces) which records in 5.50 seconds.

B.

"Please can we go inside? It is very cold here"

There are 43 characters (words, letters and spaces) which records in 8.00 seconds

C.

"You must let me help you. I cannot stand zis cold weather any longer."

There are 68 characters (words, letters and spaces) which records in 9.00 seconds

D.

"You have candles?"

There are 16 characters (words, letters and spaces) which records in 2.00 seconds.

On the Audacity screen, above the wriggly waveform there is a timeline in minutes and seconds, so it is easy to relate to leaving "gaps" to the moving recording cursor. Gaps are created by the narrator being deliberately silent during recording, and by copy and pasting in slivers or slabs of pre-recorded speech or room tone silence after recording.

By now you have a sound file of the narrator's voice on a particular page in your Narrator's Script. It will contain gaps which you've deliberately left to accommodate speeches made by those fictitious characters which appear there. Now you must create sound files to contain those speeches.

YOU have to determine what each character sounds like. The author's words or notes will guide you. It's a good idea for the author, who knows the characters better than you do, to provide you with a potted biography of the main characters at least, and their voices and accents, or at least their background and social level, before you start. It is no good authors complaining afterwards or rejecting your finished work.

IT IS UNREASONABLE for the author to give his narrator an initiative test. If they won't give you that help, I suggest you turn them down rather than be involved in arguments later on, because anyone reading this *AUDIOBOOK HANDBOOK* will realise how much work there is involved.

It is possible, desirable, if not essential that that information is provided, ideally, on a spreadsheet. The example that I return to here is the 83 various voices in *Fortune's Promise – a Regency Romance* by Sue Johnson.

Voices vary. They should be carefully considered. For example, if there are two young women of the same age, who frequently appear together, like Lucinda and Hannah, how would a listener easily differentiate between them in conversations over a multi-chapter saga in 30+ chapters? One might be of a higher pitch or register than the other, or maybe one is a quick talker, a bit staccato and the other a slower more deliberate speaker, lazy-like or a drawl. One might be louder than the other. One might have a different accent to the other, maybe Welsh against English or metropolitan south east (Essex or Estuary) against the Midlands Black Country.

The voice has many components and variables, depending on age and sex, education, social propriety, evolution, misuse such as slang, precision in word choice and so on. All must be delivered clearly and consistently so that the listener is never left wondering what has been said or who is saying it. The listener will soon lose interest if he can't easily identify a character's voice.

With the silent reader in mind, as opposed to the listener, the author will have written words as grammatically correct as you'd expect them to be, but in bringing speech to life a bit of artists/actor's license can be used to make the words fit the character. In fact, if that wasn't so, it wouldn't sound right or real.

I record in such a way that every speech has its own coded label on a reference sound file which encompasses ALL of the chapters wherein that character speaks. That enables me to refer back to listen to exactly how that character spoke many chapters before.

It makes sense to leave gaps bigger than you need, especially between different characters labelled speeches for ease of copying and pasting into the main sound file. I'm going to show you step-by-step how this works. I'm going to re-record a random chapter from my published audiobook *Fortune's Promise – a Regency Romance* by Sue Johnson.

This is the third audiobook I've done with her. The previous ones are *The Girl with Amber Eyes* and *Apple Orchard Lemon Grove*, both available on Amazon Audible.com and through my websites www.audiobookhandbook.com. and www.martinhussingtree.com.

For simplicity I've chosen short Chapter 20. My original Narrator's Script and my annotated notes are given in this screenshot so you can follow it.

Mrs Parsons and Tilly hastened to light the oil lamps and bring more candles. Josiah gave a hiss of pain as they lowered him down onto the sofa and covered him with a rug.

"Tilly, you must go for the doctor," Lucinda instructed. Tell him he must come immediately."

Tilly began to whimper. "Miss Lucinda, I be afraid of the dark." Then she looked at the tall man in the dark blue riding coat and began to hurry towards the door. "You've let the Devil in, Miss Lucinda. That's the man I saw up on Longdon Hill the day after the February full moon."

"Don't be a fool, girl, or you'll be taken back to the workhouse where we got you from." Mrs.Parsons pushed Tilly towards the door. "Do as you're bid and no more nonsense."

Lucinda agreed with Tilly. If it wasn't for basic good manners she'd want this man with the insolent expression out of the house. She didn't like the way his eyes raked down her body as if he was undressing her with his eyes, one garment at a time. She shivered.

"You at least remember your manners, Lucinda," said Josiah. "Isn't there some refreshment you could offer these gentlemen?"

"All in good time, father," said Lucinda. "Will one of you gentlemen please tell me how this accident occurred?"

"Later, Lucinda," said Josiah, his face ashen with pain.

"He has Mr Milburn to thank for not being killed," said Lawyer Craycombe. "One of the horses went out of control and would've trampled him had it not been for his quick thinking."

Lucinda stole a quick look at Giles Milburn. Something in his demeanour made her feel uneasy. She knew without doubt that had her mother been alive, he wouldn't be sitting in their parlour.

**

Giles sat feasting his eyes on Lucinda Beckford, hoping the doctor would take his time. He liked the sight of her aroused with passion and the way her sapphire eyes flashed. His idea of doing something to one of the horses under the guise of going outside for some fresh air was a good one. He'd administered a dose of pepper to its rectum, something he'd learned from another unscrupulous gambler ………

The Narrator's Script of Chapter 20 covers 12 single sided A4 pages of double-spaced lines of words. There are approximately 25 lines and at roughly 300 words on each page, making that chapter 3,550 words.

The whole novel of 38 uneven length chapters set out that way has 290 Narrator's Script pages, so the narrator has to cope with something like 70,000–80,000 words and a large cast list of 83 + 1 various speaking voices.

There were 37 females of all ages and importance to the story and similarly 45 men. Their voices all had to be consistent throughout and differentiate themselves as they would in real life so that the listener is not confused.

Narrator's voice and character voice acting

There is a great deal written elsewhere about preparing your voice theatrically, exercises, breathing, drinks etc. for when you are rehearsing for performance in an auditorium before an audience, a crowd, where your voice needs to reach the people at the back. It sounds knowledgeable but in audiobook work, it really is unnecessary, just common sense. Just do it if it feels right to you. All you are doing is talking into a microphone about 18 inches or 50cm directly in front of you.

The **ONLY** thing that matters is that you speak **DELIBERATELY**, emphasising every syllable and pronounce correctly in character and **ENSURE YOU MAKE THE END OF EVERY WORD DISTINCT** and don't mumble … but if you must … mumble **CLEARLY** and coherently otherwise you'll lose your listener.

All you need to do to achieve this is to say aloud, repeating several times to yourself: **"I MUST SPEAK DE-LIBER-ATELY"**. Record yourself doing it. Get it into your head auto-matic-ally.

The practicalities of this, creating facial muscle memory in your jaw area, will become obvious when you come to edit and clean up the recorded waveform and deal with the gaps between words and cut out mouth sounds.

If you are new to this, you will probably be self-conscious, unsure of the pace that you should speak. Be guided ONLY by what it sounds like to you. Learn by listening to your own recording. It is not science. IT IS gut instinct. Like Goldilocks, choose what sounds "just right" to you. Comfortable listening. There's no such thing as "wrong". YOU are the painter painting sounds as you hear them. Creativity is a very personal thing.

Study professional actors and celebrities who have recorded audiobooks. Study TV announcers and Newsreaders. They are picked and trained to deliver their words clearly, confidently and at a pace which suits most people. Most of the time they are reading from an unseen rolling, pace controlled "autocue" at the side of the camera or microphone that they are talking into.

I am NOT a trained actor, but it has been said that I have a "nice voice". Authors accept that in asking me to narrate their precious work that they've spent months writing, that I will do so as diligently as them in accordance with this *AUDIOBOOK HANDBOOK*. At least in that way, authors know what they are going to get. It is my calling card, my sample book.

You must always be sensitive to the mood created by the author. Excitement and danger can be enhanced by slightly accelerating the rate of speech. Suspense and fear can be emphasised by slower speech.

Study the dramatic effect of silence, the creation of tension, of not knowing or being apprehensive of what is coming next. Getting that wrong can ruin everything. The relationship of narrator to the author's words is very much like that of a dancer and music. There must be harmony.

Let us consider YOUR voice as neutral. In other words, you might have a regional accent or not. Maybe a particular way of speaking, hopefully not too fast, nor harsh or piercing, the sort of comforting voice that you hear on the BBC World Service transmitted globally (the very epitome of everyday conversational English language) or one of their local radio stations. Those voices have been deliberately chosen by professional broadcasters as being friendly and neutral, almost unnoticeable, that is where the message is believable and far more important and more memorable than the messenger. So, it is with an audiobook narrator, who should be audibly almost invisible, where the story and the characters and the events happen as if he wasn't there.

On the other hand, some book publishers commission well-known actors at significant expense because their voices are a recognisable "brand", a sort of celebrity endorsement, all designed to remove the risk of purchase from a hesitant buyer. "It must be good because … .". It doesn't mean that they are better than you, merely that they are more familiar and likely to sell more audiobooks. With a celebrity voice, the listener is always aware that they are being read to, whereas with someone relatively unknown, they are more likely to be engrossed in the story itself.

The vast majority of authors are not rich, nor probably particularly well off and the cost implications of a commercial recording studio etc., are prohibitive. An alternative in recent years has been provided by Amazon's (Audible) ACX, who try valiantly to consider almost everyone's interests, but much is left to the author as commissioner of the service to provide their own specification to do justice to their previously published work.

This *AUDIOBOOK HANDBOOK* series was designed as an essential reference work to provide writers, authors and potential narrators with a mutually acceptable framework to safeguard the interests of both parties whilst conforming to the requirements of ACX and also Findaway Voices who provide the means.

Ideally you will separate your numbered Narrator's Script pages. Only ever use that one particular numbered script page at a time from which you are recording and hold it on a stiff clipboard.

The sensitive condenser microphone will pick up the slightest noise of rustling papers and any movement or fidgeting which will be translated into a visual glitch on the waveform recording your sound.

Depending on your preference in delivering air from your lungs, as singers or stage actors do, stand (in my case) or sit (if you prefer or are unable to stand) and by using a home-made "distance stick" ensure that you have a consistent distance between your chin and the pop screen. That is essential, because, when editing and patching together recorded segments, intentional or corrective, they must sound seamless as if they were recorded at the same time. The microphone is so sensitive, that the slightest difference in volume will be noticeable and ruin the illusion of make-believe.

Always record the page number. Say "page number 26" or whatever it is. Next, after a second or two, at the beginning of a chapter, say, "Chapter Six" or whatever it is. At the end of a chapter say "End of Chapter Six" or whatever it is.

It takes some getting used to, but audiobook work has no visual reference points, so it is easy to lose your bearings, like driving a car at night without lights which is why it is essential to speak page and chapter numbers and cross reference them with the Label track in editing.

This is essential, because when you get round to inserting LABELS on your sound recording, it will help you locate where you need to be. You will soon realise how important that is. If you don't do it, and you get into a mess, it might take you an hour or more to reorientate yourself. Not something you want to do often.

When using EDIT, it is IMPORTANT **NOT** to use CUT, as it removes the security of being able to retrieve a position if a mistake has been made.

It is IMPORTANT to remember that whilst a speech can be copied and pasted into its final position on the separate chapter sound file, its LABEL, with which it moves, expands and contracts, will not transfer with it even if it has been SYNC'd.

The LABEL track (see later), which mirrors it, is independent and works differently! It cannot be copied and pasted like a waveform can. You need to copy and re-enter it into the LABEL track of the receiving file.

The previously annotated Narrator's Script gives the all-important coded reference for EVERY characters speech. It is a discipline which forces YOU, the voice actor, to understand the story before you record anything. I do it this way:

Josiah – 3 – 45 – C

That tells me that the character speaking is Josiah in Chapter Three on Narrator's Script page 45, his third speech on that page.

His next involvement might be **Josiah – 3 – 48 – B** or **Josiah – 5 – 64 – A**. This method works well and mirrors how some professional actors contribute to a radio play or how they might learn their lines for a stage play.

It also enables YOU, who are going to be the voice of all of them, to consistently repeat their voiced speeches so that YOUR LISTENER recognises their individual voices as they would on the radio. Consistency is the key to maintaining credibility.

Having annotated your Narrator's Script, you will have a feel for who is the main character, appearing relatively frequently and a supporting character who appears anything from only once, to now and again.

Characters will be subdivided into men and women and youngsters. They are all equally important as they wouldn't be there if the author had not given them a job to do, setting the scene or advancing the story. Some only appear in one chapter.

How you choose to group them is up to you, but it's worth making a note of who is in which sound file so you can find them quickly. One example might be:

A name – Male adult leads, e.g. A – Josiah (Josiah – 3 45 – C)

B name – Female adult leads, e.g. B – Lucinda

C name – Male adult supports, e.g. C – Twister

D name – Female adult supports e.g. D – Old Betsy

E name – Villagers, etc.

F name – Country folk etc.

G name – Boys and girls etc.

It will save you a lot of time.

Part Four

Agreements with Audiobook Publishers
ACX and Findaway Voices

Agreements with Audiobook Publishers

Writing is a solitary occupation. For a self-published author, creating an audiobook is a different form of collaboration to that where a commercial publishing house is involved. In that case the author has some influence, however small, but no authority or control. His book no longer belongs to him.

Creating an audiobook himself with either ACX or Findaway Voices, or both or others, the author really does have total authority and control. As best he can, he performs all of the production and marketing roles that a professional publishing house would (see Part Nine – **Audiobook Marketing**). It can be time consuming, mostly frustrating, and jolly hard work. The potential commercial success of an audiobook is because it can reach an ever-growing wider global audience in a different form to the printed book upon which it is based, providing the distribution channel is chosen wisely. Sales is a numbers game. A matter of ratios.

Normally an audiobook is a creative collaboration with a third-party, a narrator, probably someone that the author has never met or spoken to. It is not in the narrator's remit to have read and studied the author's published book before being invited to audition. Much will depend on the extent of mutual communication where the author helps the narrator to do his or her job well. It should not be an initiative test or a guessing game. The narrator should not be expected to realise. He should be told. The narrator should not be surprised many chapters later with a detail which unravels all of his work up to that point. Both are on the same side as partners. The narrator's job is to bring the author's words to life as a storyteller in person would.

The creative artistic work of a narrator is an intellectual property in its own right. It can be seen. It can be heard. It can be transmitted all around the world. It is an identifiable physical commodity. It is the essential component of an audiobook.

A narrator is the creator of a physical audiobook recording. He has the equipment to do so and will have spent many happy hours making it. He owns the Rights to that recording if or until they are sold. It is his intellectual property over which he has legal authority until someone else actually buys it. Only when an author has bought that recording outright can that person legitimately say that they have the necessary legal authority that ACX or Findaway will recognise.

The narrator's recording, in the context of this manual, produced in his home studio, as described later, to their rigorous professional technical standards, is submitted currently to either ACX or Findaway Voices who are in business to make a profit, meet targets, and have practices and procedures to enable them to process externally submitted audiobooks in a timely efficient manner without contractual distractions.

The problem with their take-it or leave-it legalistic Agreements based in different and distant jurisdictions in the USA, is that due to their fired-up impatience and excitement, authors and others tend to never read them – although they should, even if they don't understand them.

Even if they begin to, in our case, they would get so bemused by the excessive legalistic jargon that they would just give up and hope for the best. The pitfalls are made worse with no cost effective alternative other than to accept, fingers crossed, whatever situation they are faced with.

Authors, especially, who are first and foremost writers concentrating on their words, from a myriad of backgrounds, perhaps with limited business experience, maybe sensitive or introverted, and probably not particularly well off, need advising and instructing rather than feeling as if they are being threatened with legal implications.

Both ACX and Findaway have been producing and distributing audio-books for many years. Their Terms & Conditions have probably had little or no revision in that time during which the world, their markets, have already changed and will continue to change. They've probably never asked for proof, by way of an invoice or receipt that the author has in fact bought the legal Rights to the recording. None of that probably mattered much until the introduction of split deferred ownership and split royalty payments which legally complicates what previously was a relatively, simple, cosy arrangement.

Both the ACX and Findaway Agreements presume, take for granted, from the required author's signed declaration, as supposed Rights Holder, that the author has bought, and therefore OWNS that intellectual property, the Rights, of the audio recording purchased or obtained from a third party narrator.

As far as I can see, neither ACX nor Findaway require evidence of a formal transaction defining the nature of that transfer of Rights, what the author has paid, if anything, whether it is for total or merely partial ownership of Rights, passing from the narrator to the author or simply a licence to use the narrator's work. At best it is a superficial Agreement simply based on "say-so". How it would fare in a Court of Law or arbitration is another matter.

If the author has not paid the narrator in full at the outset, or has not paid an agreed "incentive", and has evidence to prove it, he cannot be the Rights Holder, because legal ownership of the Rights has not been formally established. Until then, effectively, the successful narrator, perhaps not realising it, is granting the author a license to use his recording. So perhaps they are both Rights Holders and therefore both should be parties to the Agreements offered by ACX and Findaway in which case any Agreement signed might not be valid.

Nowhere, in either the ACX or Findaway Agreements is the narrator a party to those Agreements. The only one involved is the author, whereas, unlike a printed book, an audiobook would not exist without a narrator, whoever that might be.

It is difficult to see how the recently introduced concept of split royalty payments or part ownership can be valid without the narrator being part of any formal Agreement. Whilst that may not be contentious, it is by no means certain, where the narrator is no longer in the picture, the introduction of split ownership and royalties raises some questions. There are no adequate safeguards covering the narrator's long-term interests should circumstances change.

One such instance, which has happened to me twice, might be where, for whatever reason, unconnected with the narrator, ACX, for example, decided to no longer publish an audiobook denying the future income that the narrator might otherwise expect over several years. Currently it is a risky situation for narrators to find themselves in.

Setting aside situations whereby established corporate publishers have proper contractual relationships with authors and celebrity narrators where their respective agents and lawyers might be involved, situations involving private individuals might be less certain. It is that scenario which is the focus of this manual as the volume of self-published authors overtakes that of established corporate publishers.

For instance, has the author got "legal authority" as defined by the ACX Account Holder Agreement if there is no formal agreement with the narrator? If not, they say, the author MUST decline and NOT use ACX.

The ACX Account Holder Agreement says "If you are entering into this Agreement on behalf of an individual ... you represent that you have the legal authority to bind that individual, ... to this Agreement. If you do not have the legal authority ... you must select the "Decline" button and you may not use ACX".

The adoption of the **AUDIOBOOK HANDBOOK AGREEMENT** as promoted and described later in Part Five, between author and narrator alone, would go a long way to satisfying that legal authority. That is what this manual was designed for.

It would also tend to negate the dread of an author ending up in a US Court action. Anyone who has ever watched the frequent depictions of legal scenarios on American TV might shudder at the very thought of such involvement.

ACX Agreements

All of the detailed ACX Terms & Conditions can be found on their website. It is not easy reading. Their relevance is to authors alone, as none of the ACX Agreements involve narrators.

ACX documentation consists of:

ACX Account Holder Agreement 2021

ACX Book Posting Agreement 2017

ACX Audiobook Production Standard Terms 2019

ACX Offer and Acceptance procedures 2013

For clarity, this writer has done his best to paraphrase and condense that documentation into more commonplace language.

The purpose of the ACX Agreements are to insulate Audible (operators of ACX) from any legal action that might ensue in any dispute arising from their association with that individual i.e. the author, or any other Rights holding intermediary instigating production of an audiobook.

ACX Account Holder Agreement

In particular paragraph 14 relates to Governing Law and ACX Dispute Resolution Procedures. ACX make it abundantly clear that they do not get involved in resolving any disputes that might arise between author and narrator, but unreasonably – as they have made it none of their business – they have the nerve to attempt to stipulate where and how any resolution shall be achieved … . Nothing to do with us, mate!

In the real world, for most people, that suggestion is impractical. Inevitably lawyers will be involved. It will prove expensive, time consuming, barely satisfying and frankly probably not worth pursuing, unless you are obsessive, obstinate and opulent. ACX should know that.

It would be interesting to know how many disputes of this nature have actually been resolved in that way.

Hopefully after reading this manual an author will see the many shortcomings and risks by NOT formalising an arrangement with a narrator. Only then can the author honestly sign the ACX Account Holder Agreement.

It is convenient, if not lazy, for ACX to accept an author's assertion without proof that he has legal authority, when in all probability at that point, the author (Rights Holder) still hasn't got it, even though he may intend to do so, eventually (perhaps).

The ACX Account Holder Agreement only recognises one other party, namely the author who the Agreement assumes controls the subjugated narrator, the star attraction of the audiobook, who doesn't get a mention because ACX has no connection with him/her, and yet, until such time as the author compensates him/her, the narrator has as much legal authority as the author, maybe more so.

The conduct of the relationship between the author/Rights holder and the narrator does not appear in any ACX Agreement. Did ACX deliberately turn a blind eye or was it an enthusiastic oversight?

ACX Book Posting Agreement

The ACX Book Posting Agreement is between the author or whoever else legally holds the Rights to enter into that Agreement. That person is required to represent and warrant their full Right, power and authority to do so and that they alone will be responsible for and pay anyone else for royalties owed. In practice royalty payments are made by ACX.

What the ACX Book Posting Agreement does not do, is to consider the consequential effects for a narrator should ACX decide, for their own reasons, not to continue with publishing that particular audiobook.

A situation may arise, in a bipartisan agreement, where the narrator misses out on a worthwhile future income in an expanding maturing global market, where he might feel aggrieved at the author's on-going lack of effort in promoting their mutual venture or if the author's Agreement with ACX gets cancelled.

That involves a critical decision by the author without involving the narrator, although it is the first thing a narrator should ask if he is sharing royalties, or be told when auditioning, as the narrator may choose to withdraw if the arrangement is not to his liking.

The Agreement grants distribution rights to ACX on one of two possible bases. They are:

EXCLUSIVE – Where ONLY ACX can distribute the audiobook to its connections, i.e. Audible, Amazon or Apple (formerly iTunes) for a stated seven years. That provides the author with maximum royalties if the narrator is not involved or split equally between them if he is. Maybe not a good choice if sales turn out to be disappointing.

NON-EXCLUSIVE – Where others, such as Findaway Voices (Spotify) can also distribute anywhere across the globe. Findaway have far more potential outlets (including lending libraries) than ACX. It is believed that Findaway have a more attractive arrangement with Apple than ACX (Audible) do. This is a far more flexible arrangement, with a potentially far larger more diverse audience, but only yields half of the royalty income per sale, but potentially more of them.

ACX Production Standard Terms

All of these items should be scrutinised carefully and thoughtfully. They govern everything that happens from now on. There is a great deal of time and money at stake. You are not obliged to accept these terms when other alternatives are available.

ACX Deal Confirmation Page

ACX enables Rights holders (authors) to conclude agreements or "deals" to produce audiobooks with Producers (narrators) through the ACX Offer and Acceptance process and procedures. That Agreement will be set in stone in the resulting **Deal Confirmation Page** created by ACX and their Audiobook Production Standard Terms.

ACX will produce a schedule, somewhat like a car insurance agreement, covering all of the things that the author and the narrator/producer have committed themselves to, often without realising the consequences. It is a bit of a straitjacket where there is little flexibility. Take it or leave it!

Before the author makes an offer to a narrator, they should be certain of the terms proposed and ready to conclude a binding agreement on those terms. If they do that and the narrator accepts, the author and the narrator are legally bound by those terms and are in a binding contract with each other. Any other arrangements between the parties will be considered legally irrelevant.

The inherent negativity in the legalistic, adversarial ACX Agreement is displayed here. The whole philosophy of the *AUDIOBOOK HANDBOOK* approach is to proceduralise arrangements to AVOID the time wasting, inevitably expensive and inconvenient legal action which the ACX Agreement seems to encourage for the ultimate benefit of the legal profession.

For anyone currently in an EXCLUSIVE arrangement with ACX wishing to diversify their distribution in search of a much wider audience, the extra exposure afforded by Spotify's acquisition of Findaway, already with a more diversified distribution than ACX, would provide the widest global audience possible. The terms of an ACX Agreement permit that providing they receive a formal email to info@acx.com with the following message:

To whom it may concern, I have been distributing exclusively with ACX since [date] and I would now like to take my audiobook(s) from an exclusive distribution agreement to a non-exclusive agreement.

Please transition the following list of audiobook(s) all "Pay for Production" to a non-exclusive status.

[AUDIOBOOK TITLE];[AUDIBLE LINK]

Thank you [SIGNATURE]

When mailing ACX, be sure to send the email from the one associated with your ACX account.

Where split royalties are concerned with a narrator, BOTH must send the same letter individually.

Findaway work differently to ACX, consequently there is no direct comparison with their Agreements. They are not the same, although there are some similarities.

Now that Findaway are part of Spotify (since 2022), by the time that you come to read this, things might have changed somewhat, so you need to study their website.

The fundamental difference is that ACX, managed by Audible.com are effectively an in-house Amazon owned organisation operating within a clearly defined transatlantic zone, notably North America, the UK and Ireland.

ACX tend to lean to long term EXCLUSIVE Agreements in order to expand Audible.com's portfolio and to rely on long term income. Findaway Voices are the opposite, in that they favour NON-EXCLUSIVE deals to give them the greatest flexibility with their many distributors.

Another difference is that ACX cover their costs by paying authors and narrators less in royalties. Findaway require authors to make an initial payment.

Unlike ACX who sell audiobooks directly via the internet, Findaway operate through 40+ global distributors, their retailers and lending libraries, the Spotify streaming service as well as Amazon and Apple. In order to do that Findaway have to have Agreements with each of them, so Findaway's Agreements with authors are more flexible in that they have to reflect their other Agreements with their distributors.

Findaway's USP (unique selling point) is their global distribution through 40+ diverse distributors and now Spotify. Their audiobooks are sold across the world amongst independent booksellers as well as to lending libraries and public, educational, governmental and military institutions where they can be checked out (borrowed) and returned just like a printed book. It is an audiobook audience that ACX cannot easily reach.

Now that music giant Spotify have bought Findaway it will be interesting to see how things evolve. As from Autumn/Fall 2022, Findaway Voices audiobooks will also be available through their new owners.

Spotify are the world's most popular streaming subscription service. Currently (September 2022) they have 433 million monthly subscriber/ listeners around the world who will automatically now have the opportunity of listening to those audiobooks in Findaway Voices catalogue.

Authors may opt-out of being listed on Spotify, as they can do with any of Findaway's other distributors.

As of October 2023, as this manual goes off to be typeset their identity has changed to "Findaway Voices by Spotify" with a new website. Any changes to their operating conditions will be too late for this 2024 Edition, but see my website www.audiobookhandbook.com for clarification.

Findaway Voices Agreements

Unlike the more commercially driven self-contained Amazon subsidiary, Audible.com, Findaway is an aggregator and facilitator, or as some might see it "a middle man".

All of their detailed Terms & Conditions can be found on their website.

Findaway brings things together for others (mainly English speaking) making it happen all over the world or as much of it as westernised "progress" has influenced. For example, for anyone outside of its traditional northern hemisphere market, the only way to access it, say, from Australia, New Zealand, South Africa or Nigeria for example is to do it through Findaway Voices.

Findaway Voices Standard Distribution

Findaway Voices promotes flexibility. It has connections with many disparate distributors, retailers and libraries who in turn service the needs of their global regional audiobook listeners. It is a fluid but growing list prone to change from time to time and from which an author can pick and choose.

Findaway's list of approx. 40+ global distributors as of June 2022, was in alphabetical order:

3Leaf Group; 24 Symbols;

Amazon; Anyplay; Apple; Audible; Audiobooks.com; AudiobooksNow; Authors Direct; Axiell Media.

Barnes & Noble Audiobooks; Baja Libros; Baker &Taylor; Bibliotheca; Bidi; Bingebooks; Bokus Play; Books-A-Million; Bookmate;

Chirp; Cliq;

Downpour;

ESBCO; eStories;

Follett; Fuuze;

Google Play;

Hoopla; Hummingbird;

Instaread;

Leamos; Libro.fm;

Milkbox; MLOL; My Audiobook Library;

Nextory;

Odilo; Overdrive;

Perma-Bound; Pool;

Radish; Rakuten Kobo;

Scribd; Storytel;

Ubook; Ulverscroft;

Wheelers.

It is for the author to work out which are the most suitable for his story. If not all?

Findaway Voices STANDARD DISTRIBUTION is a NON-EXCLUSIVE Fixed Term Agreement whereby an author can place his audiobook with Findaway Voices and any number of distributors or retailers including ACX, amongst others, with whom a distribution might already exist.

Findaway Voices require an author to pay in full their quoted price, as well as the narrator's quoted price before they will manufacture and distribute the audiobook. In practice, from signing up, the author has several months to organise his finances during which time the narrator is recording chapter by chapter.

Once the audiobook is distributed Findaway Voices retain 20% of all royalties. The author (having paid the narrator in full) automatically receives 80% from Findaway Voices.

The Agreement is in force as soon as it is signed by the parties. Payment as described comes later. The Agreement can be terminated by the author in writing. Due to the potential numbers of distributors involved, and the disruption that might be caused to their operations, the Agreement formally ends after six months.

Terms & Conditions are set out in full on the Findaway website followed by three Explanatory Schedules C, D and E covering distribution royalties, Program policies and VoicesPLUS.

The audiobook can be withdrawn from distribution by the author at any time, by writing to Findaway Voices, but they cannot guarantee how promptly that will be enacted by each distributor.

The author supplies all artwork and any other promotional information in accordance with Findaway Voices requirements and sets the suggested nett retail price (SRP) and the suggested nett library price (SLP).

Findaway VoicesPLUS fixed term Agreement

The author may choose to take part in the EXCLUSIVE VoicesPLUS distribution programme.

As Findaway introduce new distribution partners, audiobooks will automatically be added to their list unless authors choose otherwise.

VoicesPLUS is an EXCLUSIVE Fixed Term Agreement (ONE year annually renewable, with options to opt out during the first six months, or with one month's notice) with Findaway Voices.

The author chooses which, if not all, of Findaway's distribution partners to whom the audiobook will be distributed, paying particular attention to any, such as ACX with whom a distribution might already exist. In those specific cases, it is effectively Non-Exclusive.

The author, having studied his competition, sets the list price given to distributors who then individually determine their particular selling price. It can be more or less than that indicated by the author.

Findaway Voices have no objection if an author sells his own audiobook. For example, as a CD through their AUTHORS DIRECT storefront or direct from the author's own website.

VoicesPLUS provides access to Findaway Voices sole-sourced global catalogue and, for what they are worth, offers inducements such as Piracy Protection; Enhanced numbers of promotional codes; Opportunities to take part on marketing and promotional activities; Previewing new features.

VoicesSHARE fixed term Agreement

To compete with ACX, Findaway have recently introduced what they call VoicesSHARE. The EXCLUSIVE programme lasts for ten years compared with the similar programme with ACX which lasts for seven years. In the case of termination requested by the author, where Findaway distribute to ACX, they will be unable to remove that audiobook prematurely if it violates ACX seven-year conditions.

Findaway Voices MARKETPLACE

Findaway Voices MARKETPLACE is a recent innovation which better allows authors and narrators to reach their preferred global audience with much greater freedom to produce an audiobook on their mutually agreeable terms. It is an ideal way to implement the contents of *THE Home Studio AUDIOBOOK HANDBOOK* described in Part Five which follows this. As you will come to see, it deliberately eliminates the disadvantages of existing alternative Agreements promoted by others.

Findaway Voices Master Production Agreement

As with the ACX Account Holder Agreement and their ACX Book Posting Agreement it is essential that you carefully study the terms under which Findaway Voices operate. On their website Schedule A provides the details.

The Findaway Voices Digital Distribution Agreement deals with how their arrangement works, which is DIFFERENT to how ACX works.

Their businesses are dissimilar, although the technicalities by which they produce audiobooks are much the same.

The fundamental difference between the two organisations being that there are NO UPFRONT or ONGOING costs with ACX however, the royalty income derived is less with ACX and you are tied in exclusively for seven years during which time you have no control over the selling price.

With Findaway Voices the benefits are of a much wider and larger potential global audience, and generally a more generous royalty income and some control over the selling price.

However, with Findaway Voices there are upfront costs which can be diluted by being tied in for ten years, as with VoicesSHARE but with an option to buy yourself out should you feel you could do better another way.

On their Schedule A I have highlighted these specific paragraphs to which you might give particular attention:

2. Production Services

3. Rights Holder Approvals for Production Services

4. Right to Produce Audiobook

5. Third Party Engagement

15. Miscellaneous

Findaway will provide regular Distribution Royalty payments incorporating sale/lending returns received from their distributors. Payments will be made in $USD unless alternative arrangements are requested.

All Agreements with Findaway Voices are subject to the Laws of the State of Ohio in the USA, and any dispute is to be dealt with in accordance with those Laws. However, as with ACX it is difficult to see how Findaway can stipulate the resolution of an argument which they deliberately distance themselves from and which is nothing to do with them. This compares with ACX who favour the State of New York.

Findaway has arrangements with some distributors which no-one else has, such as Apple and Chirp (a Bookbub company). That enables you to run advertisements for your audiobook which historically produces good sales amongst book-buyers (supposedly, providing the price is right). To access an audiobook buying public in this way is a huge advantage, so they say.

With Findaway's exclusive arrangement with Apple, they're able to offer a much better deal than Amazon's ACX.

Findaway's royalty rate paid to an author is more than that of ACX, although payment from ACX is usually quicker.

Findaway Voices has a more advantageous royalty rate deduction before you get paid (20%) than the much smaller Author's Republic (30%) for example and a more informative analytical reporting system.

Unlike ACX where there are NO UPFRONT COSTS, therefore no capital outlay, which appeals to cash strapped authors struggling with how to finance narrators, Findaway have a $45 fee, which is waived if the author's physical book has been produced by Digital2Digital (with whom Findaway have an association) an independent digital book publishing business (similar to Amazon's Kindle).

Part Five

Audiobook Handbook Agreement between Author/Rights Holder and Narrator

Audiobook Handbook Agreement between Author/Rights Holder and Narrator

In an ideal world this manual should not be necessary. You can happily ignore this Part Five if you're content with the Agreements put forward by both ACX and Findaway Voices as they currently stand.

The good thing is that neither of them insist on you using their Agreements although in reality you have no choice. Clearly they don't want to get involved if there is a dispute. However, YOU are at liberty to consider an alternative or supplementary Agreement to cover what they do not. Other than what this Part Five provides, I don't know of any other. So, who am I, you might reasonably ask, to suggest such an alternative which is this **AUDIOBOOK HANDBOOK AGREEMENT**.

As soon as anyone mentions "contract" immediately they become defensive, enter a mindset of things going wrong. So, they get someone "legal" to write a formal contract enshrining FAILURE as inevitable. DISPUTES as normal, and in some people's minds, to be enjoyed, one lawyer setting things up for TWO other opposing expensive competing lawyers in a sort of virility contest to find a winner. It gives the licking-their-lips "legal" minds a reason to exist, to get involved, to be judge, to feel important. Jobs for the boys?

Getting a lawyer to write a contract, is understandable but lazy, a blameless thing to do, passing the buck, abstaining from thoughtfully recognising and remedying what the problems really are. It demonstrates a complete lack of first-person empathy, and little experience of the interactive process in which they are not personally involved – what other people should do, all of which is explained in this manual.

Apart from formalising the obvious, a contract is a device detailing what to do when things go wrong. All the **AUDIOBOOK HANDBOOK AGREEMENT** does is to advocate a disciplined procedure TO AVOID things going wrong.

It is so ridiculously simple and easy to do using the workflows already in existence and which would give both author and narrator confidence in each other and a surety that things will turn out well.

For one thing, I'm NOT A LAWYER. There is no need for me to be, nor for anyone else to be. I was once an author of technical and management books and articles, amongst other things. Nowadays, apart from writing a novel, and whatever follows from this manual, I'll continue to be a multi-audiobook narrator so at least I know what I'm talking or writing about (in case you want to argue).

I feel somewhat self-conscious about telling you, but if you are to decide the relevance of this Part Five, then, I feel you should know a little about me. In any case, it is my book, and I would feel more comfortable with you knowing.

Much of my early career, when I was involved in complex construction project management, I became frustrated at the time wasted every day, in frustrating arguments about this and that. It seemed the norm. It had been that way for years. So, I researched the subject looking for a reason. I found it, and it surprised me that no-one else had realised what I had identified, nor had thought to do what I had done. As a result, I wrote a book *The Standard Form of Contract in Times of Change* which explained why. The basic founding principles and practices no longer applied as they were originally intended. They had evolved over time, seemingly without anyone noticing the gradual changes in practice, and deviated from presumed impartiality.

The "establishment", apparently, didn't want to know. Recently I discovered a copy of it, in a dust covered box on a high shelf – neglected. It is as relevant today, to the subject of this manual, as it was to the petty point-scoring days of adversaries from yesteryear.

Even today, the LAW as defined by EVERY English-speaking nation has its origin in the COMMON LAW of England from the 12th century. It is and continues to be based on and modified by localised case law and precedent in whichever jurisdiction it is applied. It is a lasting legacy of the former British Empire. It has been the framework of USA law before and since Independence, although nowadays it is expressed on a State-by-State basis. Findaway has theirs in Ohio and Amazon (ACX) has New York.

So why am I telling you all of this? Because trading practices across the English-speaking world are well established and well understood by OLD industries which have well tried and tested procedures. The parties are corporate bodies of technically trained, qualified and practiced personnel. I used to be one of them. Part of my training was in Contract Law.

The rapidly evolving, relatively NEW audiobook industry, on the other hand, is where the contracting parties are mostly private individuals, whose backgrounds and knowledge are inconsistent, less certain and somewhat unreliable, just as they were many years ago before impartial trade or professional bodies were founded.

The NEW audiobook industry is largely the product of two American commercial, predominantly sales, organisations, ACX – Audible – Amazon and Findaway Voices (Spotify), doing their own thing in their own way for their own self-centred benefit. They are not interdependent. There is no industry Code of Practice.

Both Findaway and ACX have evolved a process to make money through sales from a constant throughput of audiobooks upon which their commercial existences rely. They need authors and narrators. To do so they provide the means by which authors and narrators can come together to collaborate, providing them with finished recordings to sell.

Whilst their technicalities are similar and to some degree interchangeable, their business models and contractual arrangements are not. Neither Findaway nor ACX want to be involved to any great degree in the collaboration between author and narrator before they receive a product to sell, nor do they want to be responsible or involved if it doesn't go as well as they might have hoped.

In both cases they distance themselves from those situations by suggesting costly (to others) mediation or Court action in which they are not involved and which doesn't cost them any money.

Both organisations are American, so it is not surprising that their instinctive cultural knee jerk reaction is to involve lawyers. To outsiders, such as me in the UK, shuddering at watching American films, news items or TV depicting US courts in action, it is the last thing anyone with any sense or experience would want to get involved with.

One principle of the ancient Common Law, is that from the outset, such Agreements should be understandable by an "ordinary" person so that they can be held accountable for their understanding or lack of it. They should not be so complex that they need a third party to interpret what should be obvious.

From the way in which ACX or Findaway Agreements are presented, it is difficult to see how any "ordinary" author or narrator can make sense of what is being suggested in those Agreements without the assistance of an expensive lawyer or professional mediator. Hidden agenda maybe?

If you read my Introduction at the beginning, you might remember my comparison many years ago with William Tyndall who set out to make the Latin Bible (the almost exclusive language of the cliquish Catholic clergy) understandable to the least educated member of a congregation, a plowboy, who might have wanted to read it for themselves if they could.

The reality is that the legalistic contractual Agreements as put forward by ACX and Findaway are totally unnecessary. They try to do too much. A far more workable alternative is that of a mutually agreeable simple procedure which already exists, and if properly implemented makes misunderstandings and disputes almost impossible.

Both ACX and Findaway have dedicated, mutually accessible "workflow" computer screens allocated to each audiobook in production. They act as a scoreboard for recording and measuring progress and provide the means by which narrators and authors can communicate and gain confidence in one another.

The narrator uploads recorded, technically checked for sound quality, chapters for the author's approval. The author is informed throughout. They see the same screen so they both know exactly where they are. They can send each other messages. Get to know and respect each other, hopefully, to like each other and become trustworthy friends. Nowadays, they can even communicate through WhatsApp or several other means.

Providing both parties, author and narrator, thoughtfully do what they're supposed to do in a disciplined and considerate way, then there's nothing to argue about, nothing to dispute, no need for lawyers!

The premise upon which both ACX and Findaway work is author-centric which is perfectly understandable in the case of a published printed book where there is no narrator. Sadly, they perceive an audiobook, in its purest form, with the narrator as a hired hand, an outcast, a paid sub-contractor, a distant third party with no further interest, job satisfaction or recognition in its commercial or reputational outcome. Have they missed the point in a book that talks?

In the case of an audiobook commissioned by a large corporate book publisher a significant financial investment has been made. A recording studio and sound engineer are hired, plus publicists, cover artists and marketing people. A well-paid "celebrity" narrator is hired in the belief that the sales, based on his name, will boost their return to cover their extensive investment. It is that person's name which also appears prominently on the cover because they are using his or her familiar voice and persona as an endorsement – a safe purchase, not a risk – a trusted, familiar brand, like a packet of cereal on a supermarket shelf.

Ask yourself – in the case of a singer performing a song, who and what does the audience remember a few days later, and in what order? The singer? The song? The performance? Or the composer's name? An intriguing question. It's who they listen to, isn't it?

Those simplistic arrangements become more complex with the introduction of split-royalty payments, largely introduced to make upfront production costs more affordable to individual authors with far less cash than their corporate competitors.

The conundrum, without the publicity clout and contacts of a recognised book publisher, is who promotes it? Split responsibility without teamwork and trust is never satisfactory. It is fundamentally flawed. It is a naive concept, to pump prime their supply chain which both ACX and Findaway have introduced in a bid to get more printed books converted into audiobooks for them to sell and cover their overheads.

It is theoretically a nice idea but in practice difficult to work satisfactorily. Nowadays the competition for sales is fierce which means that the marketing effort is increasingly intense and time consuming. More of that in detail in Part Nine – **Marketing**.

By default, the job of promoting and marketing his audiobook has fallen to the (possibly publicity-shy, uninformed, disinclined, busy or preferring to do something else) author who may then become unhappy knowing that he's only getting 50% royalties.

Is he going to employ sufficient effort if the narrator (whom he might wrongly consider as a passenger) is going to get the other 50% for doing nothing, as he, or his nearest and dearest, might see it? Or more likely is he going to immerse himself in another book which would give him greater pleasure and satisfaction. What incentive does the narrator have if his name isn't on the front cover?

Audiobooks are an entirely different entity to traditional physical paper printed books. They are NOT normally retail sales in the traditional sense.

You don't normally walk out of a shop with one in your hand and read it on the bus going home, unless you've got one out of the library using a Findaway device.

With Findaway Voices their audiobooks are embodied in a single-use portable long-life battery-operated disc "player" device. Physically it is a different format to that of ACX and requires a different selling cover to be designed.

Other than that, Amazon audiobooks are essentially electronic ebooks sold and downloaded over the internet, one way or another. Technically they are either EPUB format which are reflowable, whereby the text rearranges itself for whichever computer screen or electronic device it finds itself on, or they are in Amazon's AZW language specifically for their Kindle devices.

For an audiobook to be commercially successful it has to be seen as a collaboration. Even more so when royalties are equally divided. Surely there has to be a better, more inclusive way of harnessing the talents of both author AND his narrator so that their individual contributions are recognised as well as rewarded.

The narrator's voice, tone and interpretation enriches the author's text. It becomes an entertainment, an entirely different experience, more so in the case of Findaway's portable devices favoured by libraries. If that were not the case audiobooks would not exist.

Children like to be read to by their parents. Usually the same story over and over again as they look at pictures together. It enhances their bond which they will remember for the rest of their lives, and when they grow up and have children of their own they will do the same.

An audiobook WITHOUT the otherwise unknown narrator's name on the cover might be seen as NOT being worth listening to, a second rate product, cheap and nasty. Shoppers buy "own label" essential or economy brands only when they can't get or can't afford the supposedly better or more familiar brand. Even more so if they've seen no advertisement or publicity on TV.

It doesn't matter if the narrator's name, his brand name, is not well known, it will seem as if it ought to be. After all, you can't know everybody can you? New previously unknown products are advertised remorselessly on TV so that their brand name becomes familiar.

The collaboration begins with the author identifying and choosing his narrator. Both ACX and Findaway have registers of potential narrators for the author to select from, or he can choose someone he already knows to audition or he can make the process competitive with others.

In most cases an author and his chosen auditioning narrator(s) are strangers. It is almost like an arranged marriage, full of risks and anxieties. In this day and age it seems ridiculous if they don't talk to each other over the internet, at least, in case they don't hit it off, before their arrangement is formalised. Chances are that if they don't talk to each other, to compliment and encourage each other, the relationship may flounder and become acrimonious,

It is crucial that the author carefully considers the audition test piece. The author MUST accept responsibility for making it clear beyond all doubt what he wants from a narrator. Only he can! He can choose/write the Audition Script in any way he likes. It is most important that he does. It is his only assurance that his audiobook "sounds right". He sets the challenge. A narrator is NOT telepathic. He should NOT be given an initiative test. The author should NOT assume anything, nor rely on what he thinks is "common sense", which he thinks is supposedly obvious. It is NOT a universal language.

The author has written a book. That is what he likes doing best. He is good with words. He knows how to use them. He has created characters and put them in situations. His words describe what they look like, sound like, how they speak, how they do things, what their mannerisms are, their idiosyncrasies. Certainly in the case of primary characters, all of those peculiarities are in a fictional biography notation in the author's possession before and during writing his book. It seems negligent NOT TO provide that detailed information to auditioning narrators.

The author knows the critical tension points which can make or break his story. If the narrator gets them wrong, then the audiobook fails.

Isn't it logical for one of those situations to be used as an audition piece whether it comes in Chapter 1 or in Chapter 12? The workflow enables recordings to be uploaded in any order.

There is no logic in saying that the audition test piece must be the opening lines alone, or the first chapter, or that it should only be of one character's voice or that of the narrator alone, or that it should be so many pages long or so many words or so many minutes duration. It should be created especially as a test embracing one or more crucial plot points. It should be as vigorous, ruthless and impartial as any professional stage play or movie. There is no logic in NOT directing the narrator to record chapters out of chronological order.

The author's last chance to confirm his choice of narrator is the 15-minute sample (it does not have to be precisely that length) which should be of a strategically important scene involving several characters. Why not do Chapter 12 first, say?

In movies they film scenes out of order to make best use of resources, weather, light and location. That's why they film those little clapper boards with references on them before the Director shouts "Action". The editing process can then rearrange them in the right order.

Why should audiobooks be any different? Doing things that way should eliminate any friction or abortive work, enabling author and narrator to gain confidence in each other.

The author is the only person who is in a position to complain at what the narrator provides. Once the narrator has been appointed, the only legitimate grounds for complaint should be those of mispronunciation, inconsistency and quality compared to the audition or lateness in providing recordings. By getting author approval on a chapter-by-chapter basis, all or any of those issues can be monitored and corrected quickly and amicably.

The question of lack of progress or "lateness" becomes a matter of tolerance. Provided the narrator has shown willingness to perform, and what he has provided to date, then any slippage should be tolerated, as it is often difficult to estimate accurately how long things will take, besides which, unavoidable external situations can get in the way. It happens! Impatience achieves nothing and if anything is counterproductive.

The author's justification for dissatisfaction can be proven or otherwise as necessary by comparing the evidence with this manual which was always intended as being the yardstick or specification against which ANY dispute could be quickly resolved.

The contents, text and format of this **AUDIOBOOK HANDBOOK AGREEMENT** is *FREE* for readers of this manual to use and adapt as a template. There is no cost. Its purpose is simply to facilitate a harmonious, mutually agreeable method of producing a recording, suitable for sale and distribution as an audiobook by ACX, Findaway Voices or by anyone else. It is provided here in this chapter and in the Appendix for photocopying purposes.

AUDIOBOOK HANDBOOK AGREEMENT
between
Author/Rights Holder & Narrator

Title of proposed audiobook:

....

This AGREEMENT is between the Author and/or Rights holder of a published book, the basis of the proposed audiobook:

....

And the appointed Narrator:

....

1. This Agreement is between these two parties alone and has no connection real or implied with any other Agreement connected to the creation of this proposed audiobook, its subsequent sale or distribution to others.

2. This Agreement does not prejudice or override in any way any other Agreement associated with this audiobook.

3. Both parties recognise and accept that the methods, principles and procedures laid out in detail in the latest edition of the manual *THE Home Studio AUDIOBOOK HANDBOOK* are the basis for their collaboration in producing the above titled audiobook.

4. In the event of any dispute arising which cannot be amicably resolved otherwise or by referring to *THE Home Studio AUDIOBOOK HANDBOOK* itself, the author Martin Hussingtree or his successors offer to mediate for a nominal sum based on written submissions appertaining to this manual by email or online to www.audiobookhandbook.com.

5. Both parties accept the conclusion of such mediation, which will be given in writing, will settle the matter and that the unsuccessful party will bear the total cost. There will be no appeal.

6. The contents, text and format of this **AUDIOBOOK HANDBOOK AGREEMENT** is FREE for readers to use and adapt as a template. There is no cost. Its purpose is simply to facilitate a harmonious, mutually agreeable method of producing a recording, suitable for sale and distribution as an audiobook by ACX, Findaway Voices or by anyone else. It is provided here as Appendix Five for photocopying purposes.

7. **The Author/Rights Holder accepts that they are totally responsible for:**

a) The decision to choose and appoint the Narrator. The conduct of any auditioning process involving one or more potential Narrators which will include selecting those available and willing, and providing Narrators with a detailed synopsis of the story, number of chapters, including the front and back statements and retail sample, total word count and a listed number of characters and their detailed biography, accents, characteristics and idiosyncrasies of ALL main and numbers of supporting characters (ages and sexes) whose voices the Narrator will be expected to consistently replicate throughout the recording. That will enable a Narrator to estimate how long it will take him and bid for the PFH (price per finished hour) of workflow measured listening time that he should be paid for doing his work. That is *NOT* the same as the recording and editing time including all research and production time which will be much longer).

NOTE: Failure to do this thoroughly may entitle the Narrator to ask for an increase in PFH!

b) A carefully thought out, representative audition script sent by email, typed text, to each potential Narrator, double-spaced with wide margins for the Narrator to annotate and work from and also comprehensive biographies of those characters who appear in the audition script and any other relevant information which the Author/Rights Holder might require to enable him/her to make a judgement of the most suitable Narrator for bringing their words to life.

NOTE: Failure to do this thoroughly is a recipe for disaster!

c) The review and approval of any initial sample of the Narrator's recording.

d) Keeping the Narrator informed of any indisposition, holiday or absence which might delay the Narrator's work.

e) The Author/Rights Holder will advise the unsuccessful Narrators as soon as possible after reaching their decision.

f) Once the Narrator has been appointed, the timely (within a week), formal approval or otherwise of EACH AND EVERY submitted recording on a Chapter-by-Chapter basis. The Author/Rights Holder CANNOT change their mind or quibble over minor details on matters which they have already supplied and/or approved or sought to incorporate as an afterthought. The Narrator cannot continue without that formal approval, and has grounds for complaint if the author's approval is unreasonably slow or repeatedly so.

g) The Author/Rights Holder and Narrator may negotiate a private reimbursement regime beyond the scope of any other Agreement. Upon approval of each recorded and uploaded chapter or finished piece, the Author will pay into the Narrator's bank account money by electronic transfer calculated on that chapter or piece's PFH x the workflow stated time as requested by the Narrator. The Author/Rights Holder will message the Narrator confirming that that has been done.

h) The Author/Rights Holder CANNOT re-write or revise any chapter's text which the Narrator has already begun recording or has been recorded unless to correct an error or oversight not previously identified, in which case the Narrator may claim an additional payment.

i) The Author/Rights holder will properly manage their own tax affairs. All payments from ACX or Findaway or any other paid directly to them should be declared in whichever tax regime they abide. No-one else will be responsible for that.

Failure to comply with these responsibilities will discharge the Narrator from their responsibilities and entitle them to seek recompense as they think fit in a civil Court.

8. **The chosen Narrator accepts that he/she is totally responsible for:**

a) Providing the Author/Rights holder with evidence of their previous similar work and any references from third parties, as well as information about their availability and ability to undertake the proposed project.

b) Diligently and purposefully applying their knowledge, experience, ability and technical competence to the audition script provided to him. To use his best endeavours throughout all chapters to faithfully and consistently reproduce their audition performance and apply it to all and every situation not covered by the audition.

c) If successful at audition, based on the comprehensive information as described and provided by the Author, the narrator is to give his best and realistic time ESTIMATE in calendar weeks (including statutory holidays) of approximately how long the Narrator might take to totally complete the whole recording excluding time taken by the Author/Rights holder to give approvals. This is indicative only. It is NOT a guarantee! However, the Narrator's monetary quotation of total cost per finished hour (PFH), as measured and shown by the workflow IS GUARANTEED and cannot be varied.

d) Providing recordings of the Author's text on a chapter-by-chapter basis to the technical standard specified by ACX and/or Findaway or both or any other and a request for payment of that item calculated on that chapter or piece's PFH x the workflow stated time. It is for the Narrator to advise the Author each time by way of an invoice message on the workflow and for the Author to check and provide payment under a private arrangement.

e) Alerting the Author by email, as well as through the workflow, that the latter's attention is required to listen and approve recordings on a chapter-by-chapter basis as well as any re-submitted chapters and any proof-reading oversights and inconsistencies identified by the Narrator which might require correction.

f) Advising the Author by workflow message and email if, for whatever reason, he is experiencing difficulty in maintaining progress against his original time ESTIMATE together with his proposals for recovering his schedule or extending it.

g) As appropriate, where the audiobook is sold on a split royalty basis, the designated and acknowledged (on the front cover) Narrator shall use his best endeavours, in consultation with the Author/Rights holder, to contribute to any on-going marketing effort.

– 4 of 6 –

h) The Narrator will properly manage his own tax affairs. All payments made for their services should be paid directly and declared in whichever tax regime they abide. No-one else shall be responsible for that, nor will anyone else be responsible for any obligations they may have to any associated trade union or trade body.

i) If during the course of recording, which potentially might take several weeks or even months, the Narrator chooses to abort his contribution for whatever reason, repaying the Author all monies paid to date. That will be the limit of their liability as it was up to the Author in the first place to evaluate the risk of him/her doing so. Failure of the Narrator to do so may permit the Author to recover that money with costs through a civil Court action.

j) Keeping the Author/Rights Holder informed of any indisposition, holiday or absence which might delay the Narrator's work.

9. Split royalty payments:

a) Where such situations occur, both ACX and Findaway have provisions for remitting royalty payments direct to both Author and Narrator usually on a monthly basis providing numbers of sales warrant it. That is governed by a separate Agreement with whichever publisher/distributor is involved.

b) In the unlikely event that the publisher/distributor, ACX, Findaway or another, terminates their Agreement with the Author so that the audiobook is withdrawn from their list, meaning that split royalties cease and that the Author cannot get it re-listed with another of equal standing, if any, then the Narrator may have grounds for suing the Author in a civil Court for loss of expected income unless an amicable agreement for compensation can be agreed between them.

c) In the unlikely event that the Author, at any time in this Agreement, chooses to divorce the Narrator, and providing the chapter-by-chapter stage payments are up to date at that time, the Narrator is entitled to keep what he has been paid then the Narrator may also have grounds for suing the author in a civil Court for loss of expected income unless an amicable agreement for compensation can be agreed between them.

10. Cover art:

   a) Where the Author is the sole Rights holder, or the Rights holder alone, and the Narrator has no commercial interest in ensuing royalties from sales, the Narrator has no automatic right to have their name on the promotional front cover. THAT is not good practice. However, the Narrator MUST be given the OPTION, at no cost, to have their name on the front cover prominently and proportionately displayed.

   b) Whether or not the Narrator has a commercial interest in the sales of the audiobook, they will have an on-going reputational interest, which at the outset may influence their decision whether or not to provide their services.

   c) The design of the proposed front cover matters as it is influential in the audiobook's commercial success. It is the prerogative of the Author and MUST be established and openly displayed before the Narrator is appointed at which point the Narrator has the discretion to withdraw.

   d) The design shall be produced both in a portrait and in a square formats suitable for use in either an ACX format or a Findaway format in accordance with their requirements.

   e) Where the Narrator is to have a commercial interest due to the Author/Rights holder electing to employ split royalties, which will impact the on-going royalty payments and reputational interests of both, the Narrator will have the power of veto on the cover design offered by the Author/Rights holder. If a satisfactory compromise cannot be reached, the Narrator must withdraw.

11. Territories:

   a) With differences between ACX and Findaway, the Author/Rights holder and the Narrator must discuss and agree on where sales are best targeted.

   Signed this day:..

   Author/Rights Holder:...

   Narrator:...

END OF AUDIOBOOK HANDBOOK AGREEMENT

Part Six

Your Home Studio

My Home Recording and Writing Studio

This segment takes you from simply thinking about having a recording studio of your own, to obtaining the equipment and creating a working environment in which you can produce professional quality results to satisfy the world's largest publishers of audiobooks for commercial and other purposes.

Welcome to *MY* home studio. This is where I'm writing and illustrating this book. I hope you're finding it enjoyable and useful. It is in the spare guest bedroom of the house where I live in a village in the middle of England.

Yours may not look like mine, I'd be surprised if it did, but if you are serious, then yours will need to have the same or similar component parts.

If ever you are mystified by the elitist use of the initials DAW, it is simply techie speak for Digital Audio Workstation. All that means is what I am describing here with appropriate software added.

From the following photographs A, B and C you will see how I have taken over a guest bedroom and converted it into a very effective and relatively inexpensive Home Studio. Central to that is my home-made acoustic alcove made from a pack of 6 no. 100mm x 1200mm x 400mm mineral wool acoustic slabs from a local DIY store or builders' merchant; old bed sheets to cover the itchy fibres; wooden dowels; glue; duct tape and carpet tiles. It is effective but not sophisticated. See Appendix Part Six at the end of this manual for details of how to make one for yourself. It's not difficult.

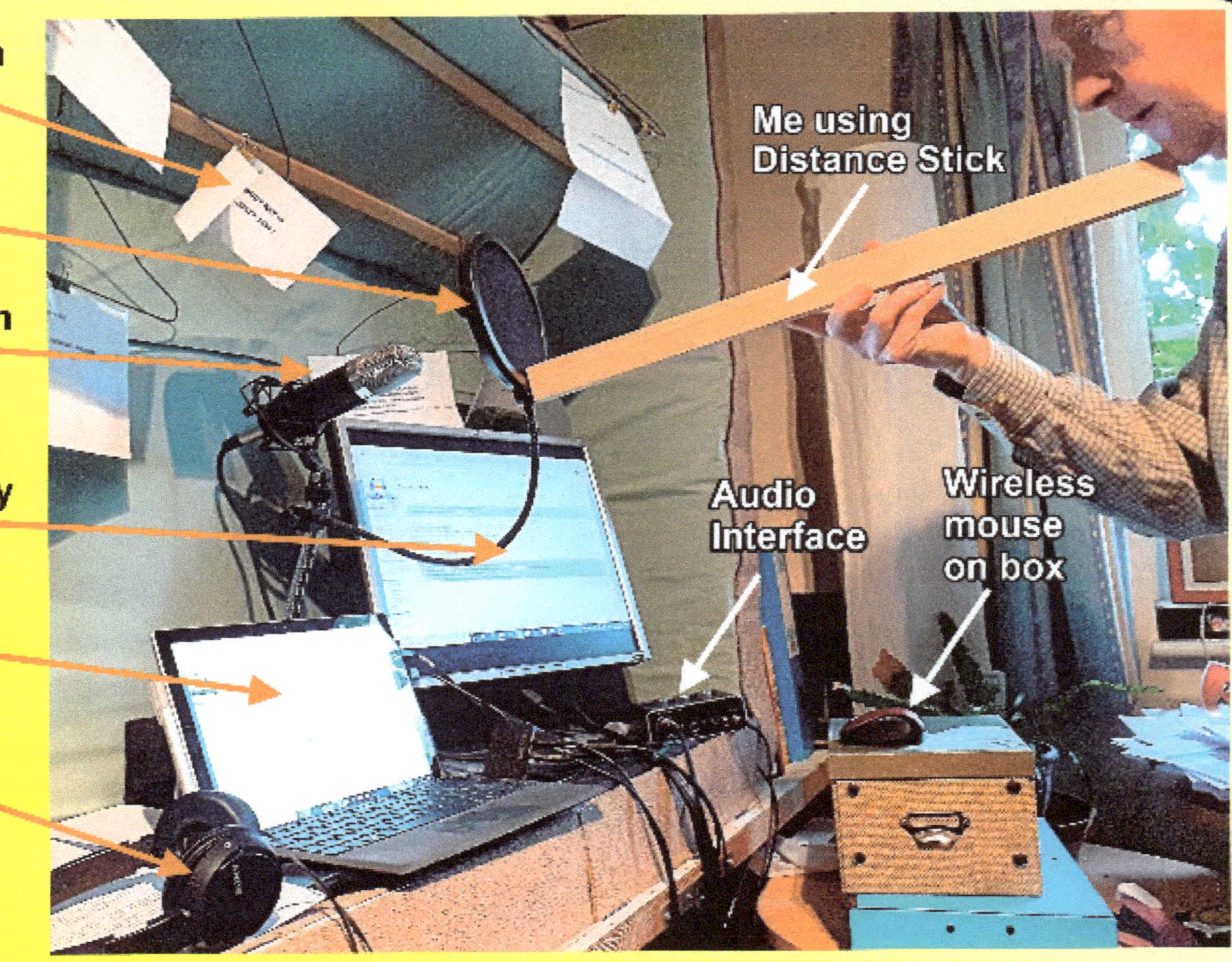

Reminders on wire-coat
Popscreen
Condenser microphone on stand
Larger second screen to study small details
Surface Pro laptop
Headphones
Me using Distance Stick
Audio Interface
Wireless mouse on box
A

Prototype acoustic alcove
Portable
wallpaper pasting
table
B

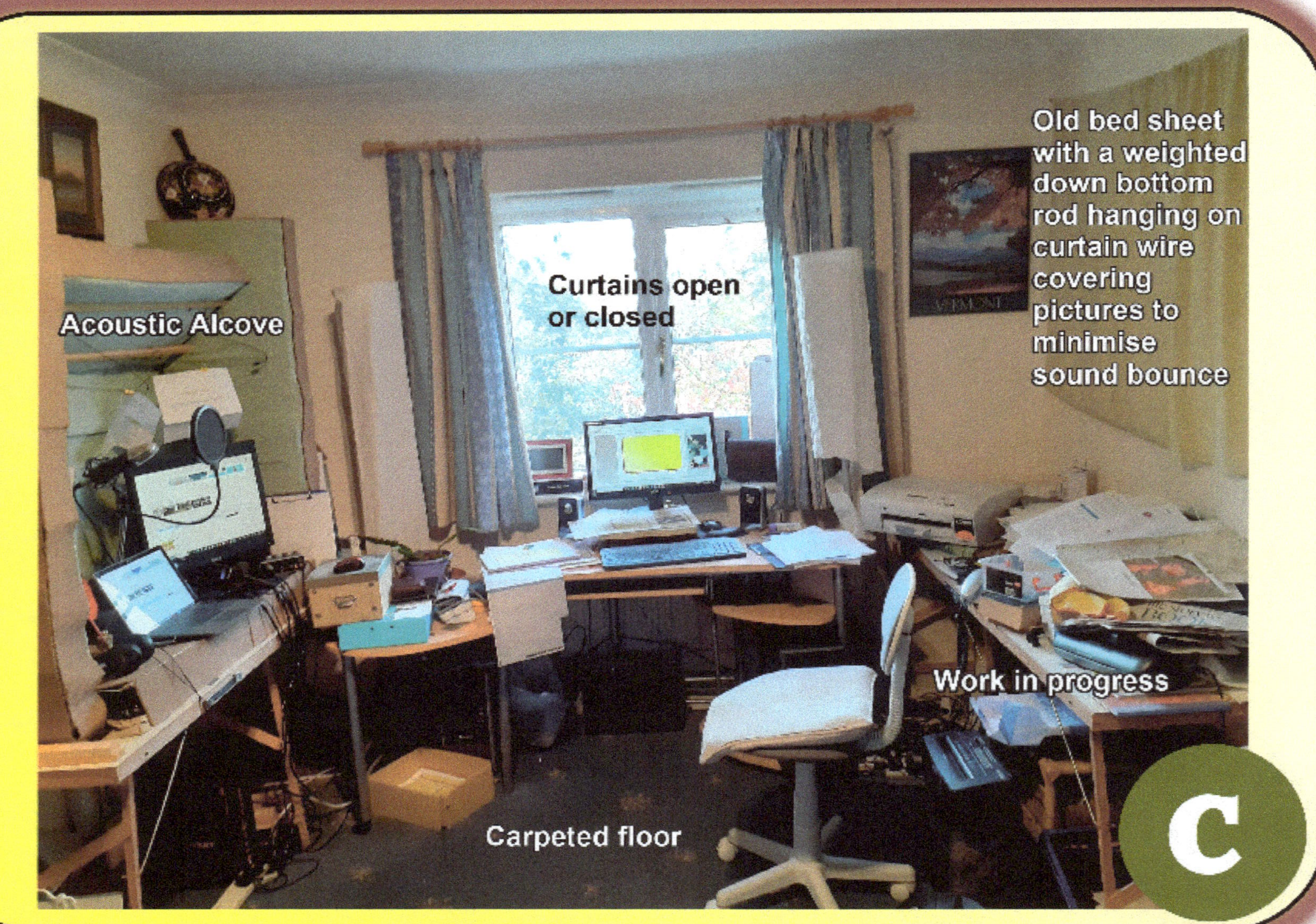

Acoustic Alcove
Curtains open or closed
Old bed sheet with a weighted down bottom rod hanging on curtain wire covering pictures to minimise sound bounce
Work in progress
Carpeted floor
C

Because the microphone, pop screen and bench stand, are, for all intents and purposes housed in a sound absorbent acoustic alcove there is virtually no sound bounce back. For what little there is, hanging curtains at the window and one on the back wall make surrounding vertical surfaces "soft".

Also in the alcove are wire coat hangers for attaching prompt notes, aides-memoire, etc.

My laptop computer is a Surface Pro connected to a large re-purposed older screen for a more detailed view.

All of this is supported on a cheap, fold-up DIY wallpaper pasting table to form a workbench. It makes the whole set-up portable in case you need to change locations or you need the room for another purpose.

A wireless mouse is mounted on a rigid cardboard box lid to provide a convenient and comfortable height for my right hand.

To one side, by the window, is a proper computer desk (second hand) housing a traditional older desktop computer with a nice wide keyboard and screen in the conventional way. More my style! That is where I am writing this.

On the window sill is the house router and on either side are two standard lamps from IKEA to mitigate shadows. The printer, landline telephone and an untidy heap of "stuff" rest on top of another fold-up pasting table, in and around which are many forgotten things which one day I will rediscover. I am a man, after all.

Behind this camera position, at the other end of the room is a pull-out sofa bed, lots of books and some treasured water colour paintings by my father and grandfather, both architects, from many years ago.

Much has been written elsewhere about the "sound environment" most of which relates to those who want to record and manipulate music. I don't! All I want to do is to write and narrate books, my own and those of others sold notably on Amazon and Findaway, which represents by far the largest global market for such works and to any others in due course who may offer a similar service.

To do that requires meeting the stated technical requirements of ACX, and Findaway Voices. My only interest is to satisfy them. This manual will show you how.

ACX, for example, have three requirements relating to the sound recording that you make. One of those is to virtually eliminate Noise Floor the name given to any otherwise imperceptible interfering background noises picked up by the sensitive condenser microphone which are not part of the words spoken by the narrator, or the characters conveying the action, and consequently ruins the engrossed listener's concentration.

Your priority is to achieve that, because if you do, you will have quickly achieved 33% of what ACX require, which is the same for Findaway.

Get used to sitting still and quietly doing nothing whilst you record acceptable, hopefully imperceptible, background "nothing" noise known as Room Tone. It is both useful and essential. It is NOT the same as computer created "silence" which is to be avoided unless desperate.

Hopefully you will hear nothing on playback, or at least you will think that is the case. Maybe one way of describing Room Tone is in domestic decorating terms. If you can imagine cans of apparently white emulsion paint, room tone is effectively a "warm white", barely discernible, like a scent, but definitely different and more pleasant.

On Audacity's screen on the Surface Pro there is a topic in the menu at the top of the page called Generate which if you click on it, will give you the option of instilling "silence". It is dead, lifeless and only to be used in desperation in small doses. However, contrasted with "room tone" it will be noticeably different and may be picked up and disqualified by the ACX quality check.

At the beginning and end of a submitted chapter, ACX and Findaway require there to be stipulated periods of "room tone" which their equipment will expect and recognise.

Microphone, Audio Interface and Headphones

Together with your voice, these three pieces of kit make the sound that your listener hears. Their experience of listening to the author's words spoken and continuing to do so depends entirely on them.

Your voice is what you make it and costs you nothing other than time and effort in improving it.

The microphone MUST be a studio condenser microphone as in the photograph. It will have the necessary clarity, fidelity and sensitivity that you need. Nothing else or less will do and nothing more is necessary.

It doesn't matter if it is vertical, up or down, or horizontal, but what does matter is that it is STILL and suspended in one position in a "shock mount", a purpose designed cradle and stand.

It can be bench/table mounted with a stand like mine in the photo. Or it can be more expensively floor, wall or ceiling mounted to suit your intended recording position.

The technical specification of my Studio Condenser Microphone is:

Features:

✓ *18mm aluminium diaphragm for rich and accurate recording

✓ *Low noise electronics

✓ *Ideal for home and studio recording

✓ Capsule: 18mm aluminium diaphragm

✓ Transducer Type: Condenser

✓ Frequency Response: 20Hz–20kHz

✓ Pick-up Pattern: Cardoid

✓ Sensitivity: -38dB±3dB at 1 kHz

✓ Impedence: 200Ω at 1kHz

✓ Phantom Power: 9–48VDC

✓ Cable: 2m long XLR to XLR cable

✓ Connector: XLR on Mic, XLR on cable

A vibration resistant Shock Mount which holds the microphone still, normally comes with a stand, of which there are a number of designs and complexity. Likewise, the circular "pop screen" which is essential to combat natural sibilance (spitting and splashing) and plosives of words spoken near to the mic.

REAR VIEW
AUDIO INTERFACE
U-PHORIA UM2
OUTPUTS
2 (R)   1 (L)
USB
+48 V
OFF   ON
USB cable from back of Audio Interface to computer through ISOUL 2.0 Hub with connectors to wireless mouse and Seagate basic portable drive storage
2 no. lights - red & orange show that it is connected properly
U-PHORIA UM2
behringer
INST 2
Cable from back of microphone to Mic Line 1 with special connectors
FRONT VIEW
Headphones lead might require an adapter like this to fit snuggly into the Behringer Audio Interface
E

An Audio Interface is the essential "clever bit" between the sensitive Studio Condenser Microphone output and your sensitive headphones input whilst at the same time taking power via your computer providing an input to the Audacity software.

There are many varieties of Audio Interface equipment at various price points for differing purposes. Almost all provide the technical function that I have described. It is a very technical subject (beyond my comprehension) which is not discussed here as it also concerns music recording, broadcasting and concert performance.

Having taken technical advice about the specific use described in this manual, I ended up buying a reasonably priced Behringer U-PHORBIA UM2 (as illustrated below) and I'm delighted that I did. It does a good job. It really is of a technically state-of-the-art professional industry standard. Its technical description is an:

Audiophile 2x2 USB Audio Interface with XENYX Mic Preamplifier

It is as versatile and compatible with standard cables and my Microsoft Surface Pro4 laptop as it is with others including Mac.

It creates an efficient, effective and simple solution and is more than adequate to facilitate the consistency and quality required to satisfy ACX and Findaway technical requirements.

USB cable from the back of Audio Interface to computer through ISOUL USB 2.0 Hub with connectors to wireless mouse and Seagate basic portable drive storage (for back-up).

The jack (pointed end bit) into the Audio Interface may need an adapter (see photo) and a lead length of about 1.0 metre or 3 feet.

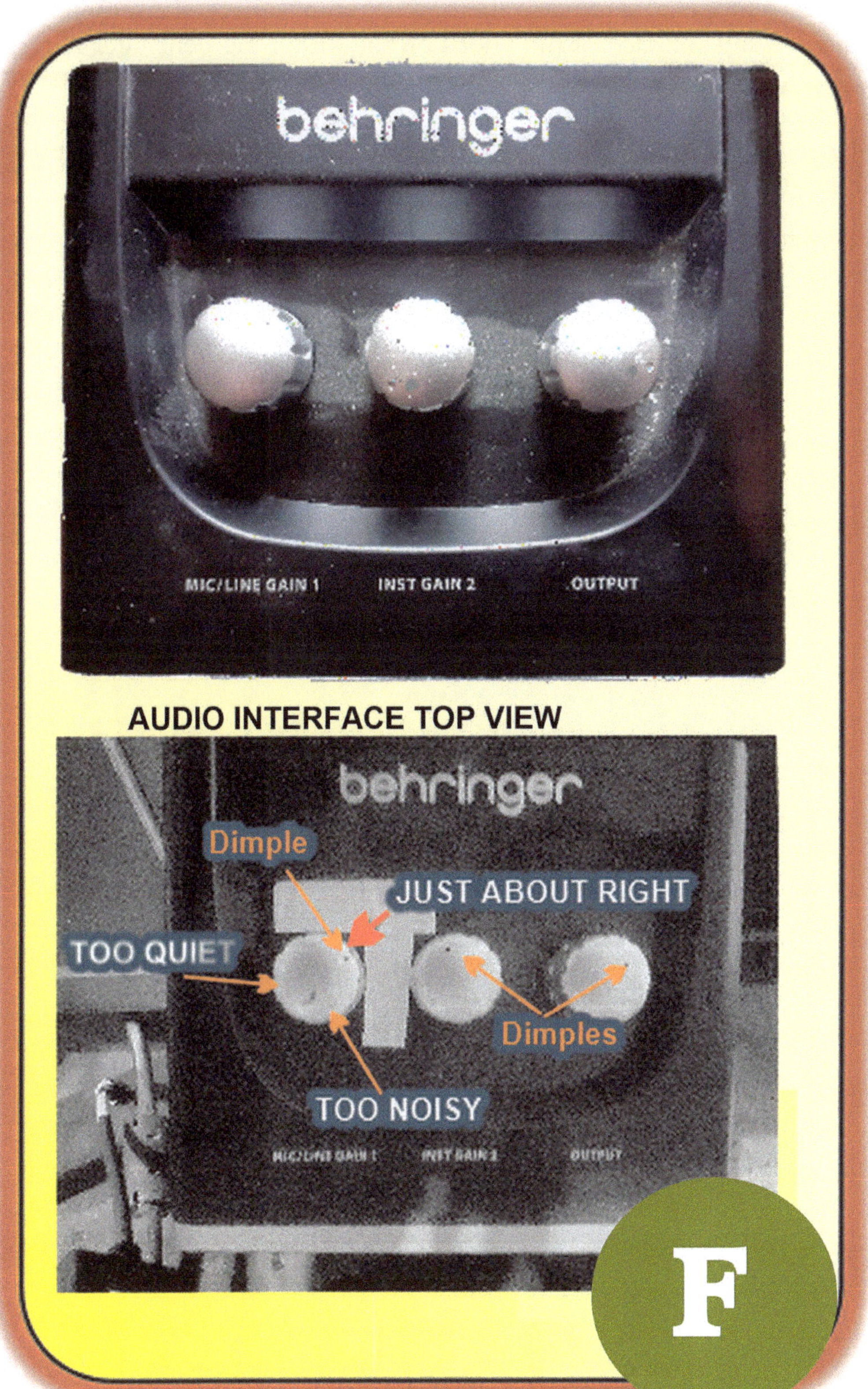
behringer
MIC/LINE GAIN 1   INST GAIN 2   OUTPUT
AUDIO INTERFACE TOP VIEW
behringer
Dimple
JUST ABOUT RIGHT
TOO QUIET
Dimples
TOO NOISY
MIC/LINE GAIN 1   INST GAIN 2   OUTPUT
F

The only thing I would criticise about this fabulous piece of equipment is that the settings of each of the knobs on the top of the Behringer Audio Interface are governed by barely discernible "dimples". In order to ensure that the all-important GAIN (loudness) knob is where it should be I have cut up and stuck two sticky labels onto the casing with a red arrow pointing to where the "dimple" should be.

On the other two less critical knobs, keep them more or less where I have indicated. Make sure you do this. If there are children or "well-wishers" fascinated by what you do and fancy having a twiddle with your knobs when you're not there, it is difficult to be aware of tampering when the dimples are difficult to see. You could waste hours bewildered by this.

Distance Stick is 21
inches long (53cm)
Sony headphones
G

Here you will see my own invention – the Distance Stick! A cheap piece of wood from a DIY store which saves hours of time-consuming frustration.

I record standing up, like they do in radio plays. For that reason, experience has taught me to use my Distance Stick. Every time, just before I record, I place my 54cm (21 inches) long piece of planed softwood (nom. 3.5cm x 1.8cm or EX 1.5 inches x 0.75 inches) on my chin and touch the frame of my pop screen as you will see in the photo.

Recording a novel is a lengthy process. For one person working alone it takes place over many days and weeks. The finished recording has to maintain a sensitive consistency of "loudness" throughout that time. At all costs it has to preserve a sense of location and continuity.

To be believable to its audience, any "performance" has to suspend that belief in reality in the mind of its audience, in our case, your listener. They are there as an onlooker – watching, listening, concentrating intently. The slightest inconsistency will shatter the illusion and their attention. The narrator's distance from his microphone is critical in maintaining that belief. Any variation will be noticed. Any mistakes will have to be rectified later and that can take a long time, quite possibly needing you to start again and re-record whole passages.

There is an enormous range of headphones. We are only concerned here with this purpose only – listening to your own recording. No other. NOT music! Your choice!

Mine are inexpensive (not cheap) Sony, fully adjustable over the head, soft comfortable fit, cushioned over the ears to cut out distractions. Angled to suit each ear (marked L and R – I have a red sticker to tell me which is right).

Always go for a well-known named manufacturer – they are all good, and may differ slightly, and read reviews. Try listening to your voice if you can. Everything depends on your listener liking that, as if you are with them in person, captivating them with your story. Expensive is not necessarily the best choice.

Part Seven

Audacity®

Audacity®

Audacity® is the registered trademark of Dominic Mazzoni. Audacity software is copyright 1999–2021 Audacity team.

Audacity have kindly given this author permission to use images of their software in the production of this manual.

Audacity is free software, developed by a group of volunteers and distributed under the GMU General Public License (GPL). It is an easy-to-use, versatile editor and sound recorder for Windows, macOS and some other operating systems. It has been translated into more than 30 spoken languages. It has been going for over 23 years and has been downloaded more than 100 million times. It is truly tried and tested, and to my way of thinking, may be described as *THE* global standard.

Free software is not just free of cost. Free software gives you the freedom to use a program, study how it works, improve it and share it with others. For more information, visit the Free Software Foundation.

Programs like Audacity are also called open source software, because their source code is available for anyone to study or use. There are thousands of other free and open source programs, including the Firefox web browser, the LibreOffice or Apache Open Office suites and entire Linux-based operating systems such as Ubuntu.

Audacity welcomes donations to support Audacity development. Anyone can contribute to Audacity by helping them with documentation, translations, user support and by testing their latest code.

There are of course other software producers, and all of what is described here, in this manual, can be used with them. But as the target readership of this *AUDIOBOOK HANDBOOK* is perceived as non-technical, those other alternatives are purposely not discussed here.

As well as for music, which it its prime function, you can use Audacity to record live spoken audio, and to cut, copy and paste, splice recorded sections together whether or not you use simple or sophisticated equipment in a commercial studio, or in our case, your own home studio.

Audacity software can be found and downloaded from https://www.audacityteam.org/. It is a well structured, comprehensive website. However, the volume of technical information might overwhelm and confuse you. Most of it is not dedicated simply to audiobook production, which is one of the reasons why this more limited manual was written in less technical language.

Audacity® Project Screen

In the following screenshots, all being well, this is what your downloaded Audacity blank screen will look like.

Like learning to drive a car, or use any machinery, equipment or computer software, you need to familiarise yourself with the controls, levers, knobs and buttons that make it work.

There is NO START button. Make sure that all around you is
QUIET. Then click on the round RED button to begin recording

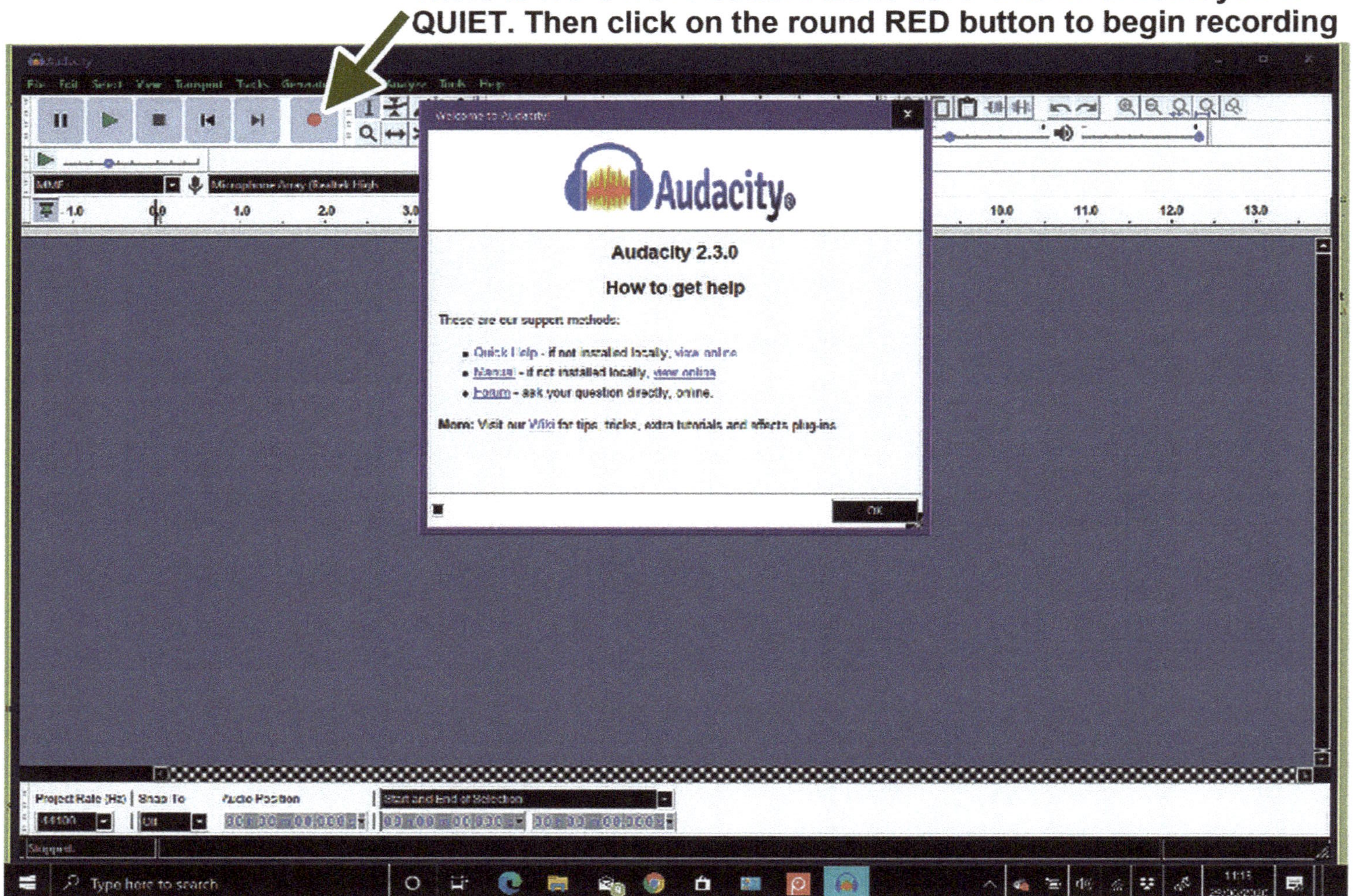

This is how the AUDACITY screen opens.

Before you begin, use your mouse to move the square white "welcome to Audacity" screen into the middle of the grey area so you can see the top of the screen more clearly. On that white square it tells you what version of Audacity you have. The Audacity team of incredibly clever and helpful enthusiasts are constantly updating. Their latest update (now [July 2023] ships as version 3.3.3) to suit their breadth of applications. I'm content with version 2.3.0 which does all I, and you, need. I have no compelling reason to update mine which I have happily used over the past three years of writing and illustrating this work, as are probably many other existing users.

ALL of the screenshots in this manual are version 2.3.0.

The white square reassures you of where you can look for HELP and inspiration whenever you need it. The best time to look at what Audacity offers in that respect is NOW to reassure yourself, rather than wait until you are confused, frustrated and panicking, which you will be sooner or later. If you want, you can always tick the little box in the bottom left-hand corner if you don't want to see the white square again at start-up.

The latest 3.3.3 version, as are all previous versions, is supported by easily accessible comprehensive visual tutorials. That is one of the reasons why it is intended to produce newer, print on demand, versions of this the 2024 Edition of *THE Home Studio AUDIOBOOK HANDBOOK* every year or so to accommodate such changes and to keep up to date as far as that is practically possible.

The Audacity project screen is a collection of individual TOOLBARS and SLIDERS, some of which you use to make things happen and two RECORDING/PLAYBACK METERS which show you what has happened as a result. Primarily designed for music production, the Audacity controls can all be unhinged and moved around your screen to allow you to configure your own control panel as you wish. Personally, not wishing to tinker, I leave things as they are.

The top left-hand corner, so-called TRANSPORT toolbar houses the major controls of motion – individual distinctive buttons for Start; Stop; Pause; Skip forward and back making it difficult to go wrong.

In audiobook work there is only one microphone. It is not stereophonic. So where L and R appear, only one of them is working. That is automatic and doesn't concern you even if it might be disconcerting to start with.

Anything with a microphone symbol is for recording.

Anything with a speaker symbol is for listening.

Recording Volume Slider showing 0.29

At the bottom of the screen is the Mixer Toolbar with the Recording Volume slider which you set for your voice. This is set for me at 0.29. You will need to experiment where that volume is most appropriate for your voice, but if you aim for where I have mine – a baritone middle-aged, older man (see blue circle), and adjust for yours, you won't be far off.

Understand that this should be a FIXED SETTING, which you don't change once you have decided its best position. It is not dynamic, it doesn't move automatically, so it doesn't compensate. That is why a DISTANCE STICK is essential to keep your mouth in a fixed position relative to your microphone for consistency in editing and correcting mistakes.

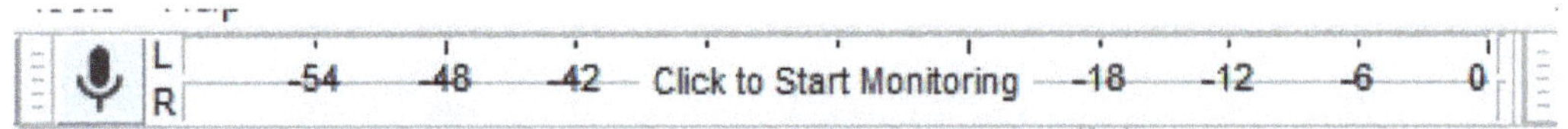

Recording Meter measuring loudness in

Visual loudness warning

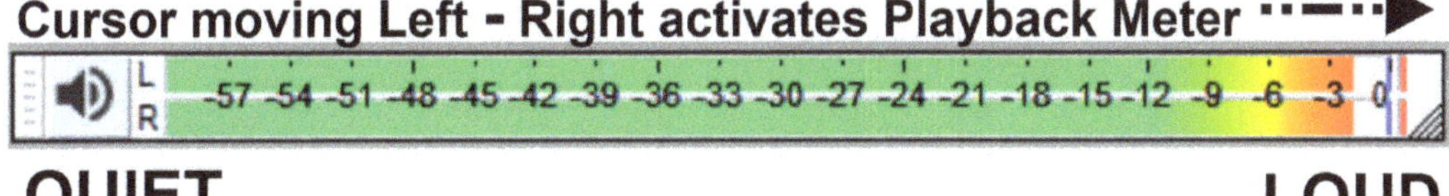

The RECORDING METER TOOLBAR in the centre at the top of the screen with a single microphone symbol, is a way of monitoring the RECORDING VOLUME. It has a direct impact on the PLAYBACK METER TOOLBAR and keeping the recording within acceptable limits avoiding the yellow/amber/red warnings.

The centre/left hand RECORDING METER identified by a single microphone symbol MEASURES microphone real-time LOUDNESS or VOLUME in decibels as you speak. It becomes active automatically when the RED START button is pressed so that recording takes place. It is calibrated in decibels (dB) from RIGHT to LEFT, i.e. DOWN from 0.00dB which is theoretically the limit of ULTIMATE LOUDNESS (-6dB is the effective limit) UP to the ALMOST SILENT -60dB.

As audiobook recording is in MONO there are no L and R speakers. The yellow/amber/red clipping warning means that it is unlikely to PASS the ACX-Check (see later) and subsequently be rejected by ACX and/or Findaway Voices.

Cursor moving Left - Right activates Playback Meter ··━··▶

QUIET   LOUD

The amber (orange) displayed here in this played back recording warns that the sound is getting "too hot" or getting too near to 0dB. The red colour at the end indicates that clipping has occurred, adversely affecting the whole recording which will NOT PASS ACX-Check

The PLAYBACK METER TOOLBAR next to it with a single speaker symbol, simply monitors the volume that YOU listen to, preferably through good quality headphones. That is what your listener hears. It does not affect the volume or quality of what eventually gets exported to ACX and/or Findaway Voices. Best keep the volume low for your own comfort.

When recording takes place, the vertical black line cursor moves the opposite way, i.e. from LEFT to RIGHT. The RECORDING METER shows "good sound" in GREEN between -60dB and -12dB.

"Questionable" sound (from -12dB to -6dB) is shown as YELLOW/ AMBER and RED beyond which is "Unacceptably TOO LOUD" as clipping will have taken place.

The analogy of a roadside traffic light warning of danger is worth remembering. OK to carry on; Caution – be careful; Danger – you might get killed (or worse).

"Clipping", like trimming the top of a hedge or bush in a straight line, will automatically chop off the top extremities of the unacceptable sound of the undulating waveform which will seem unnatural and effectively ruins the recording. CLIPPING IS TO BE AVOIDED AT ALL COSTS if you are to get an ACX-Check (Part Eight see later) PASS and meet technical requirements imposed by both ACX and Findaway Voices.

Different narrators have different voices, so depending on the "loudness" of their voice relative to its closeness to the microphone which might create CLIPPING, the individually designed indispensable Distance Stick keeps that voice nearer or further away from the pop screen. Its length is determined by trial and error to suit the individual narrator. It is instrumental in keeping your sound within acceptable (PASS-able) limits. The Audacity software also provides two volume control sliders to make further adjustments. The only problem of relying on them is that they can be accidentally moved, however slightly, which is very difficult to detect.

That is IMPORTANT for when you are cutting and pasting, slicing speeches together when recording has finished. The same voice at different distances from the pop screen will be noticeable to your listener and may ruin their experience.

Above it, the third slider is the PLAYBACK play-at-speed SLIDER. It has little relevance to audiobook work and is best left somewhere in the centre after you've had a couple of trial runs to see what it does.

NOTE: On the meters there are NO positive (+) numbers only minus (-) numbers which indicate progressions of QUIET away from ZERO (0) which is TOO LOUD.

To the uninitiated beginner this all takes a bit of understanding. It seems contradictory, but it's not. Pause and concentrate until you understand.

As you will see in the example of *Fortune's Promise,* there are 83 different character voices, all of which must be consistent and distinguishable wherever they occur in the final recording. If a character sounds different, the listener will know and may even give up. It makes sense to do them in "takes" as if they were appearing in a movie, bringing them together in the "cutting room" where the final editing takes place.

Amongst those controls that we have discussed, there are also several self-explanatory pictorial symbols for you to use if you find them relevant.

Below those controls there is a shaded line of four CRITICAL options which you must complete, from left to right they are:

A box for you to choose your **AUDIO HOST** or interface and their alternatives.

MME (which I use) is Audacity's default and the one most compatible with many other audio devices.

WINDOWS DIRECT SOUND is newer than MME, with arguably less latency. In my view this is an unnecessary technical subtlety for audiobook work. May be beneficial for music.

WINDOWS WASAPI is the newest alternative, but again is a tweak that will only appeal to technical purists and knob twiddlers.

A box for your **RECORDING DEVICE** signified by the single microphone symbol. Only an independent professional microphone with an audio interface can produce the necessary sound quality. A laptop cannot. Of the choices given, Microsoft Sound Mapper-Input or in my case Microphone Array (Realtek High Definition) are suitable.

A box for the **RECORDING CHANNEL** As all audiobook work is MONO, the stereo alternative is unsuitable.

A box for the **PLAYBACK DEVICE** is signified by the single speaker symbol. Of the choices given for headphones, Microsoft Sound Mapper-Input or in my case Microphone Array (Realtek High Definition) are suitable for the professional quality headphones necessary. On no account use independent speakers which are best for music applications.

IMPORTANT:

Occasionally ghost-like "gremlins" cause settings to mysteriously change, when updates and the like happen. So, every day remember to consciously check that nothing has changed.

One last thing to remind you of is at the bottom of the Audacity Screen is a row of numbers. It is critical that you ensure that the **Project Rate (Hz)** is showing **44100** and that **Snap-to** is showing **OFF.** Leave the rest as 000000000000000 in each case and forget about them.

AND EVEN MORE IMPORTANT:

Whatever you do, don't let ANYONE "play" with your settings, or even get near to them, otherwise you can lose any amount of finished work, and you might never get to know why you have got problems.

It's a good idea to photograph ALL of your controls as a damage limitation exercise so you can always get back to where you were.

Dropdown Menu to edit Track:- name waveform; colour etc..

Use the Gain Slider to slightly adjust volume up or down to get the waveform within acceptable limits. Use ZOOM to get a more detailed view.

Delete Track

Keep central as L&R only applies to Stereo

This vertical scale measures recorded sound intensity or volume in decibels dB

Keep the volume of recorded sound (the wiggly waveform shape) as far as possible within these boundaries to get a PASS from ACX- Check

The all-important Labels Track appears once you click on EDIT>Labels>Add label at selection

Move horizontal yellow dividing line up or down to suit layers of Labels below

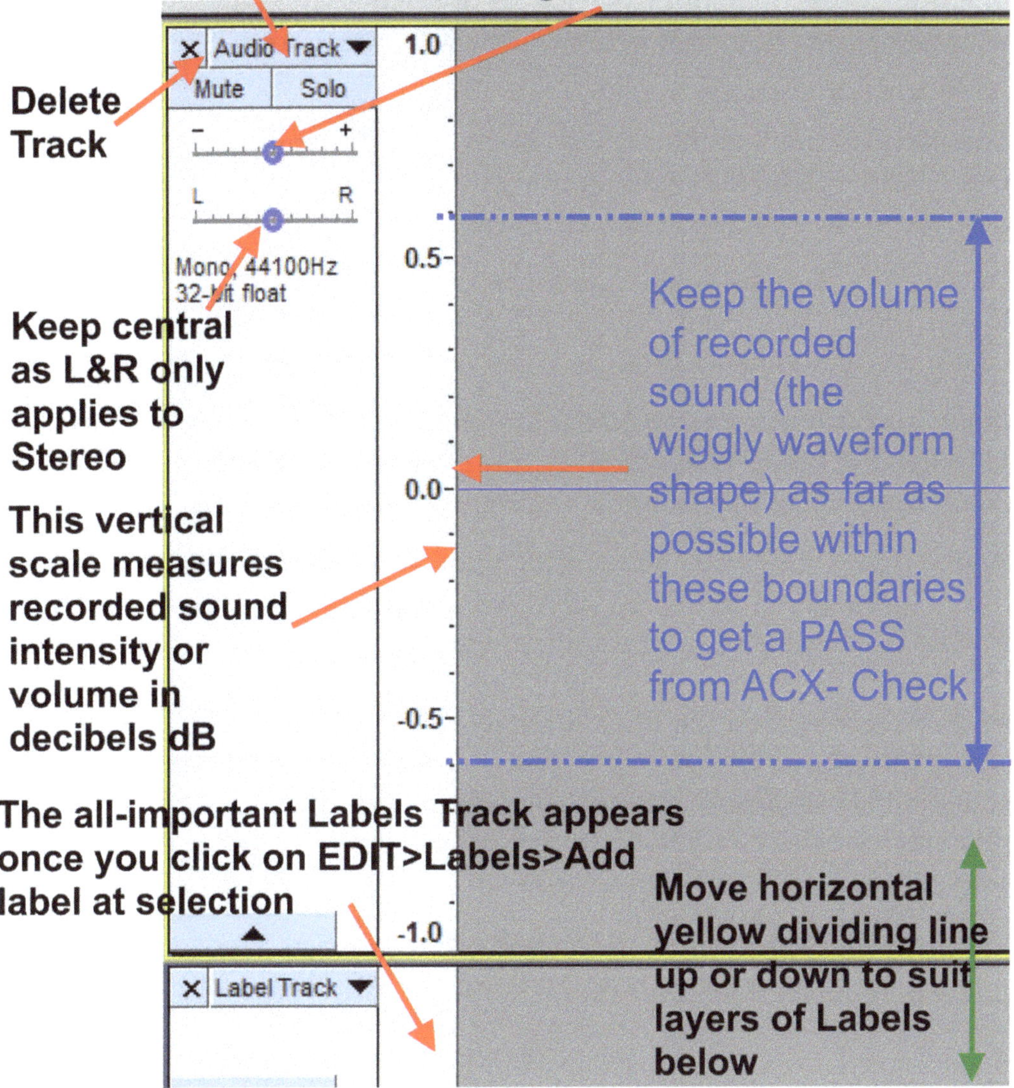

As soon as you press the RED round record BUTTON, the AUDIO TRACK CONTROL PANEL appears on the left of your screen. Before you attempt to record anything, after a few seconds press the BLACK square STOP button. Then use your mouse to move the horizontal yellow dividing bar up to about three quarters of the way down the page. This will enable you to gain a better view and understanding of how things work.

You must ensure that the TRACK in the top left-hand corner has a name. Use AUDIO TRACK or whatever you wish to call it. If it is not, click on the little black triangle on the right and find it on the drop down menu.

DO NOT click on the small **X** on the left, as it will delete the control panel. If you click it by mistake go to EDIT at the top of the screen and click UNDO to get the panel back.

In the Audio Track column on the left-hand side, there are two sliders, the LOWER one L–R is redundant as you are recording in Mono, not stereo. So, the blue circle should remain in the middle.

Above that is the GAIN slider which you can use to make slight adjustments up or down to the recording volume. Ideally it needs to sit in the middle of the plus (+) and minus (-) symbols. You won't know whether you need to use it or not until you've recorded something as a test piece to see how it shows on the RECORDING/PLAYBACK METERS. Spending time getting your DISTANCE STICK a comfortable length and the GAIN slider in balance and an acceptable reading from the ACX-Check read-out (see later) will pay dividends in the long term and allow you to concentrate on your story and characters.

Press the RED round START button again to get the vertical cursor moving so that the thin blue horizontal TIMELINE records whatever sound it detects through the sensitive condenser microphone. The line then deforms step-by-step into a WAVEFORM as you record speech and apply different EFFECTS.

Once you eventually become comfortable with all of this, there may be a good case for you recording different characters on different tracks, or as you might do with different instruments or sections of a band or choir. Then you could use the drop down menu to colour each waveform in a different colour to help you identify them before you copy and paste them into their final positions.

Under EDIT (see later) there is a separate section on LABELS and SYNC-LOCKING them to their respective characters and speeches in order to manage compiling the different inputs.

Make sure that the horizontal yellow dividing bar which you previously repositioned has sufficient space below it to accommodate a stack of several rows of LABELS, one above the other.

Nothing happens until and unless you press the round RED BUTTON. Recording begins. The vertical thin black cursor leads the thin blue horizontal TIMELINE (before it deforms into a WAVEFORM) across from left to right as it picks up the slightest sound from the microphone – so keep quiet for 20–30 seconds. To stop it press the BLACK square button.

You now have a recording of "nothingness" in your Home Studio, apparent silence. That is what is called NOISE FLOOR or ROOM TONE visually and audibly. It is the consistent sound of those surroundings which are captured in the momentary gaps between every word, every breath and at the end of every speech and every sentence. It is NOT the same as the computer created sound of "dead" silence, which is to be avoided.

SAVE (PROJECT) that 20–30 seconds of apparent silence recording as AAARoomTone (so it always goes to the top of any list making it easy to find, as you will copy and paste it often). Do it again at the start of every chapter and SAVE (PROJECT) it, which always overrides the previous one. Then go back up to **FILE>Save Project <u>As</u>** .... . Click on that and you'll see a small window inviting you to fill in blank spaces.

Audacity® Menu Bar

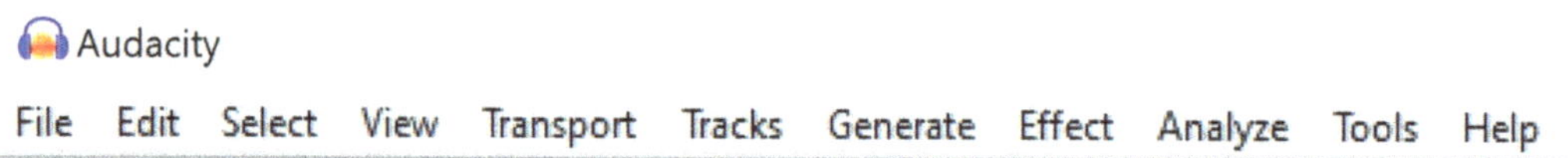

Along the top of the Audacity Screen there is a row of column headings. Each of those headings has a separate drop-down menu. Everything that you need to do in Audacity® comes from those columns.

For ease of understanding, Firstly, I've described those main column headings in general terms, and then secondly in specific detail.

File: START HERE> ESSENTIAL for project managing before, during and after recording.

Edit: ESSENTIAL for enabling you to do things AFTER recording and adding **LABELS**.

Select: Not applicable to audiobooks.

View: Useful in examining the waveform in more detail.

Transport: ESSENTIAL CONTROLS for recording and listening –

Start; Stop; Pause; Playback; Skip forward and back.

Tracks: ESSENTIAL to automatically **SYNC-LOCK** labels to speeches after recording.

Generate: Only useful if "dead" silence is needed other than room tone.

Effect: IMPORTANT in converting recorded speech into the waveform necessary for creating an audiobook. There are eight ESSENTIAL Effects and another 35 which are not suitable for audiobook work.

Analyze: ESSENTIAL for accessing the all-important **ACX-Check** (see later).

Tools: Apart from the moving vertical cursor recording speech, the others are only useful for non-recording purposes.

Help: ESSENTIAL for if you don't understand anything

FILE

File has a drop-down menu of:

New / Open (*an existing file*) / Recent Files / Close / SAVE PROJECT / Export / Import / Page Set-up / Print / Exit

NEW: Everything starts from here. Click New and a second screen appears, just like the one you just clicked on. This will be your everyday workbench for recordings that you will be working on prior to exporting as an MP3.

This is where your recording starts as a thin blue line as it morphs onto a wiggly waveform of sound.

All of the other options are standard commands on any computer system.

EDIT

Edit has a drop-down menu of:

Only these in BOLD are of use to us here in audiobook work.

UNDO / REDO / CUT / DELETE / COPY /PASTE / Duplicate / Remove / Special / Clip Boundaries / LABELS / Labelled audio / Metadata / Preferences

UNDO: In the absence of a conventional **BACK BUTTON**, this is what you use to correct **MISTAKES,** going back and back (no limit) as far as you need to.

REDO: Use this to restore last action after you've made an alteration.

CUT, DELETE, COPY, PASTE command functions are as most other computer programs.

LABELS: This is **MOST IMPORTANT** in identifying your characters and enabling the narrator to maintain control. A **LABELS** track automatically appears under your Mono track recording when you click Edit>Labels>Add Label at selection (see Part Eight – LABELS – your management system).

SELECT has a drop down menu of:

Only these in BOLD are of use to us here in audiobook work.

ALL / None / TRACKS / Region / Spectral / Clip Boundaries / Cursor to Stored Cursor Position / Store Cursor Position / At Zero crossings

ALL: Works like any other software in order to shade highlight any number of items requiring the same treatment.

TRACKS: Audiobook work only uses **ONE TRACK (Mono)** for recording. However, a sympathetic accompanying non-audible **LABELS TRACK** is a godsend in managing and organising (non-recording, none audible) contributions or stage directions that you cannot see or hear. **Always ensure you create a Label Track to work with**, below your Mono soundtrack.

VIEW. has a drop down menu of:

Only these in BOLD are of use to us here in audiobook work.

ZOOM / TRACK SIZE / Skip to / History / Karaoke / Mixer Board / Toolbars / Extra Menus (on/off) / Show Clipping (on/off)

ZOOM: Does what it says. It makes things visually bigger. It does NOT make sound louder. It enables you to be more precise if you are deleting something, separating or splitting up the waveform to enable an insertion between already recorded words.

Zoom in and then Zoom-in again as necessary. Zoom Normal clicked once, takes you back to the original track. Zoom Out has little purpose in audiobook work.

TRACK SIZE: Is mostly relevant to musical applications, where several microphones need to be seen on the same screen.

In Mono audiobook work, recording begins with one default size, the track width of which can be dragged down the screen to get a better view of what is going on.

TRANSPORT: Has a drop down menu of:

Playing / Recording / Scrubbing / Cursor to / Play Region / Rescan Audio Devices / Transport Options

More suitable to use in music recording and editing.

TRACKS: Has a drop down menu of:

Only these in BOLD are of use to us here in audiobook work.

ADD NEW / Mix / Resample / REMOVE TRACKS / Mute & Amp; Unmute / Pan/ Align Tracks /Sort Tracks / SYNC-LOCK Tracks (on/off)

ADD NEW: In this Mono Track context, the track is automatically triggered by the *RED* record button. As previously discussed, a **LABEL TRACK** is automatically set up by clicking **Edit>Labels>Add label** at selection. So, with multiple labels stacked up in one wide track, there is little point in having a spare track unless you specifically want one.

REMOVE TRACKS: Occasionally by mistake, a new track appears on the screen – it's electronic. It happens! So, this enables you to get rid of it, and breathe a sigh of relief.

SYNC-LOCK Tracks: THIS IS IMPORTANT. This is useful in keeping a LABEL and its speech together, but don't rely on it too much as it easily comes undone. You need to keep checking it.

GENERATE has a drop down menu of:

Only these in BOLD are of use to us here in audiobook work.

ADD/REMOVE PLUG-INS / Chirp / DTMF Tones / Noise /SILENCE / Tone /Pluck / Rhythm Track / Risset Drum

ADD/REMOVE PLUG-INS: This is useful in reducing the large number of superfluous **EFFECTS** provided in the Audacity shipped software. This saves time, increases your output and reduces mistakes. It also enables you to add any others such as **ACX-Check** that you may wish to use or to re-introduce previously discarded ones.

SILENCE: This is NOT the same as **ROOM TONE.** Computer generated silence is dead, lifeless, and if used for anything other than in sheer desperation, it should not be used to any degree as it will be adversely noticeable. **ROOM TONE,** on the other hand is REAL! It is what should fill the gaps between anything which is an audible sound.

EFFECT: This is shipped with an extensive drop down menu which is confusing and unhelpful to us as the majority of options are of no use in audiobook work.

Use **ADD/REMOVE PLUG-INS** to clear away out of sight all of those on the list EXCEPT the ones shown in BOLD below. If at some future point you decide to reintroduce them, you easily can, but not now.

For now you simply need a workable drop down menu of:

Amplify … **COMPRESSOR** … **EQUALIZATION** … Noise Reduction … **NORMALISE** … **LIMITER** … Low Pass Filter … High Pass Filter

The capitalised **EFFECTS** are well illustrated in the **FIRST AND SECOND PROCESSING SEQUENCES** once you have made a recording.

The NON-capitalised **EFFECTS** are only necessary if you have difficulty in getting 3 PASSes on **ACX-Check**.

ANALYZE: This has a drop-down menu, which when shipped DOES NOT include the ESSENTIAL **ACX-Check** (see below). That has to be downloaded separately, and hopefully, if you have followed the instructions carefully, **ACX-Check** will appear here.

TOOLS has a drop down menu.

Some of these are dealt with elsewhere. None are dealt with in this Edition as they are not applicable to audiobook work.

Add / Remove Plug-ins /Macros / Apply Macros /Screenshot / Run Benchmark / Nyquist Prompt / Regular Interval Labels / Sample Data Export / Sample Data Import

HELP: Has a drop-down menu for:

Quick Help / Manual / Diagnostics / Check for Updates / About Audacity

All are enormously helpful for general reading and when you get stuck, which you will, frequently. However, you might find the volume of inter-related information overwhelming, time-consuming and often puzzling. Make it your friend.

ACX-Check

For legal reasons, you will need to separately download Audacity's own *FREE* **ACX-Check** plug-in. Originally it was only intended as a useful aid, which it still is, and in my view INDISPENSABLE in meeting ACX (and by default Findaway Voices) technical requirements. Although it is not formally recognised by those two publishers, it is, in my opinion, essential and does the job well. On its own it does NOT GUARANTEE acceptance by either publisher, whose approval processes are always subject to change without notice.

By updating this manual annually or in bi-annual editions any changes will be covered.

At the top of the Audacity® screen in the MENU BAR under the **EFFECTS** column, there are many plug-ins written in the Nyquist programming language (written by Roger Dannenberg, Audacity® co-founder) with support from Yamaha Corporation and IBM.

Harry Nyquist, a Swedish physicist and electronic engineer who made important contributions to communications theory was a contemporary of the birth of Audacity. Essentially it is Audacity®'s own customer plug-in format.

To download **ACX-Check** automatically so that it ends up in the **ANALYZE** column, at the top of the screen, where you want it, carefully follow this sequence:

Go to the adjacent **TOOLS** column>Add/Remove plug-ins>Download Nyquist Plug-in installer from the Audacity Manual. From the Browse box drop down menu click on **ACX-Check**. This should then appear in the **ANALYZE** list.

Part Eight

Recording, Editing, Labelling and Submitting

Recording

Even if I said, don't be apprehensive, you will be. Anxiety is natural. Just for a moment, think of recording an audiobook this way. Each recorded speech waveform is copied onto a playing card, one of many in a pack or deck in a traditional game of cards. The pack is contained in a packet, carton or small box, just fractionally bigger than all of the cards put together. The box or packet has to be a bit bigger, let's call it tolerance, so that when you collect up and shuffle all of the scattered cards to put them away for another day, they just fit in snugly without moving about.

No need to be scared by them, waveforms are no different from each of those cards. All that Editing and the Audacity EFFECTS do is to manipulate them, one by one, to ensure that they are in good order so they all fit neatly back into their box, so that ACX and Findaway can process them without much effort and send them to whoever asks for them.

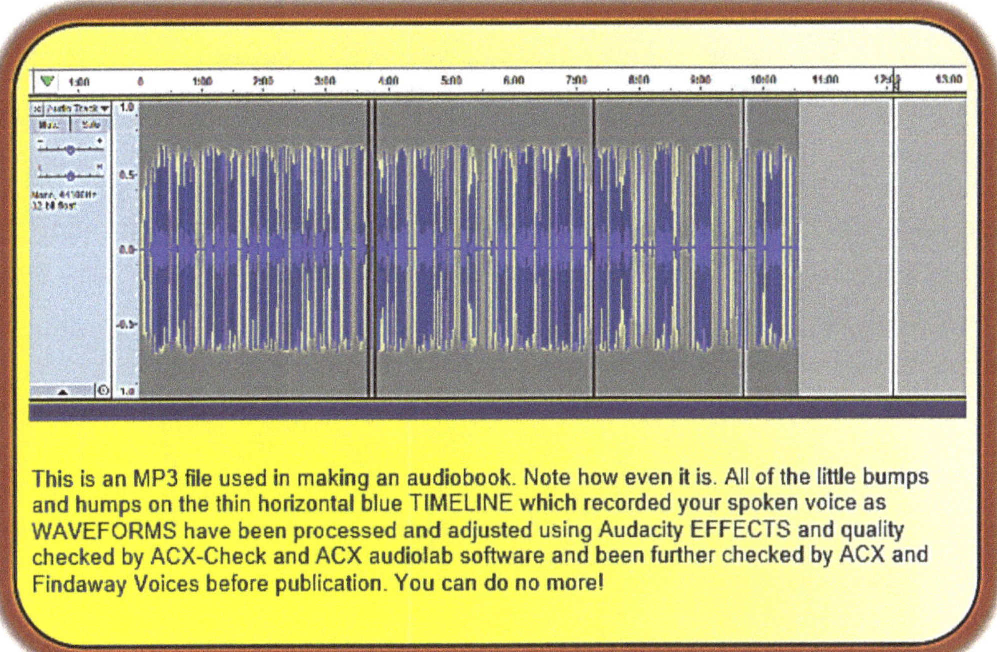

This is an MP3 file used in making an audiobook. Note how even it is. All of the little bumps and humps on the thin horizontal blue TIMELINE which recorded your spoken voice as WAVEFORMS have been processed and adjusted using Audacity EFFECTS and quality checked by ACX-Check and ACX audiolab software and been further checked by ACX and Findaway Voices before publication. You can do no more!

This image of the tightly packed processed waveforms, just like those playing cards is what we're aiming for once all of the Audacity EFFECTS have been applied, and the whole recording has received an ACX-Check PASS and ACX audiolab approval in an MP3 format.

Simple really, so let's get on with it! This is how you begin.

Raw Recording – First attempt!

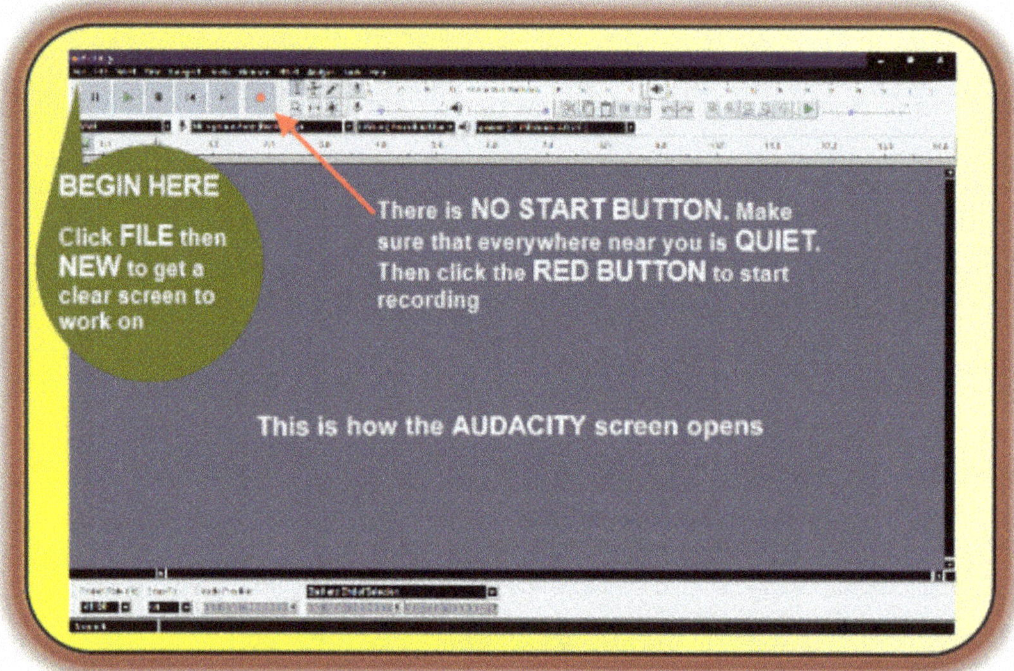

Before you record, you should have analysed the task before you on a spreadsheet and created a Narrator's Script, all as explained in detail in Part Three.

Depending on your preference, and the complexity of the scene, you can either record a page as the narrator, with just one or two character voices, say, or you can create a "palette" of voices, some or all, on one or more separate recording files, each with a different, easy to find, name, which in due course you will copy and paste into suitable gaps (see LABELS later) left in the previously recorded narrator's page.

Whichever way you record, for ease of management, ideally use one Narrator's Script page at a time, otherwise you'll end up with lots of unidentified wriggly waveforms with or without intended gaps left for copying and pasting in later. It's very easy to get distracted and lose your place with nothing visual to help you. It can be like trying to find your way blindfolded.

All of this section relates to one typical Narrator's Script page. The successful recording, along with other pages, will be converted into a Chapter MP3 file so that it can then be shared with the author for approval. All of the approved Chapter MP3 recordings are collected together at the end and forwarded to either ACX or Findaway for publishing and distribution.

A label box, (discussed later) maybe inserted in a different colour, saying START HERE is a good discipline at the end of a session and saves you asking yourself where you had got to on the following day or if you don't come back to it for a few days or after a holiday break.

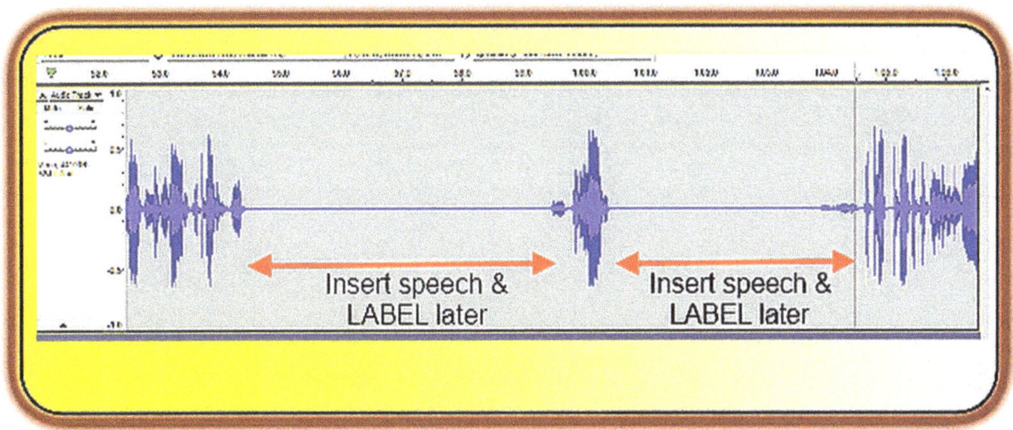

This screenshot is a continuation of a previous waveform. Note how gaps have been deliberately left for subsequent copy and pasting of characters speeches. The gaps are of approximate durations judged from the number of words on the Narrator's Script. It is easier to leave wider gaps than necessary and delete excess space afterwards than it is to leave inadequate space which means shuffling about, takes far longer and encourages mistakes.

So, depending on the duration of speech to be inserted, excluding exceptions, standardise your gap "length" to be say 5 seconds, 10 seconds, 15 seconds, 20 seconds or more. Your choice. Nothing complicated, just slow silent counting. That will cover most of the speeches you will need to paste in later.

When preparing your printed Narrator's Script, write 5, 10, 15 or 20 say in a circle or different colour so it is easy to see out of the corner of your eye so as not to disrupt your concentration. After you have done that a few times it becomes automatic.

If you are new to this, you will probably be self-conscious, unsure of the pace that you should speak. Be guided ONLY by what it sounds like to you. Learn by listening to your own recording. It is not science. IT IS gut instinct. Like Goldilocks, choose what sounds "just right" to you. Comfortable listening. No such thing as "wrong".

Study professional actors and celebrities who have recorded audiobooks. Study TV announcers and newsreaders. They are picked and trained to deliver their words clearly and at a pace which suits most people. Much of the time they are reading from an unseen rolling, pace controlled "autocue" machine at the side of the camera or microphone that they are talking into.

In addition, study websites, podcasts, webinars, foreign voices and accents to see what you don't like and don't rate. Nowadays, many who appear on them do not enunciate clearly, gabble at breakneck speed with their teeth together so that their sound is muffled and frequently incoherent. Avoid those who constantly say they are "excited". Speaking to a wide and varied audience is NOT the same as having a cosy chat with your best friend who might have a similar affectation.

I am NOT a trained actor, but it has been said that I have a "nice" voice. Authors accept that in asking me to narrate their precious work they have spent months writing, that I will do so diligently in accordance with this *AUDIOBOOK HANDBOOK*.

Authors value narrators who are reliable and keep them informed. They get anxious too.

You must always be sensitive to the mood created by the author. Excitement and danger can be enhanced by slightly accelerating the rate of speech. Suspense and fear can be emphasised by slower speech.

Study the dramatic effect of deliberate silence, the creation of tension, of not knowing or being apprehensive of what is coming next. Getting that wrong can ruin everything. The relationship of narrator to the author's words is very much like that of a dancer interpreting music. There must be harmony.

If on your first listen through, you feel that you need more or less of anything such as silence, just write a REDO label, e.g. slower: more silence, etc.

You can always shade highlight your work and delete it. Similarly you can always shade highlight a blank space, copy and paste it where you want to give yourself more room or more silence.

If you get it wrong you can always correct it (Audacity>Edit>Undo).

Never be scared of gaps in a waveform. They are natural, important and necessary. Words are written with space in between them, otherwise they would not be understandable. It is important to realise that often words spoken "tail off", fade, whereas words written also stop abruptly. Words that end with –s; -t; -ed; -ing; are just common examples.

Always listen to what you have done in editing in case you've been careless by over zealously chopping off the end of a word. Easily done! I have, lots of times.

When you first listen through what you've recorded, you stop at the first deliberately left "speech gap", so you can later copy and paste in a character's previously recorded speech along with its coded reference and label. Alternatively, you may record a speech, there and then, and copy and paste the speech to the reference file later. By "speech" I mean just the spoken words, nothing else, even if it's just a one word exclamation.

The narrator doesn't need a label. If there is no label, then it is given that the narrator is doing just that, narrating, setting the scene. If for any reason the narrator needs to say something, he then becomes a character.

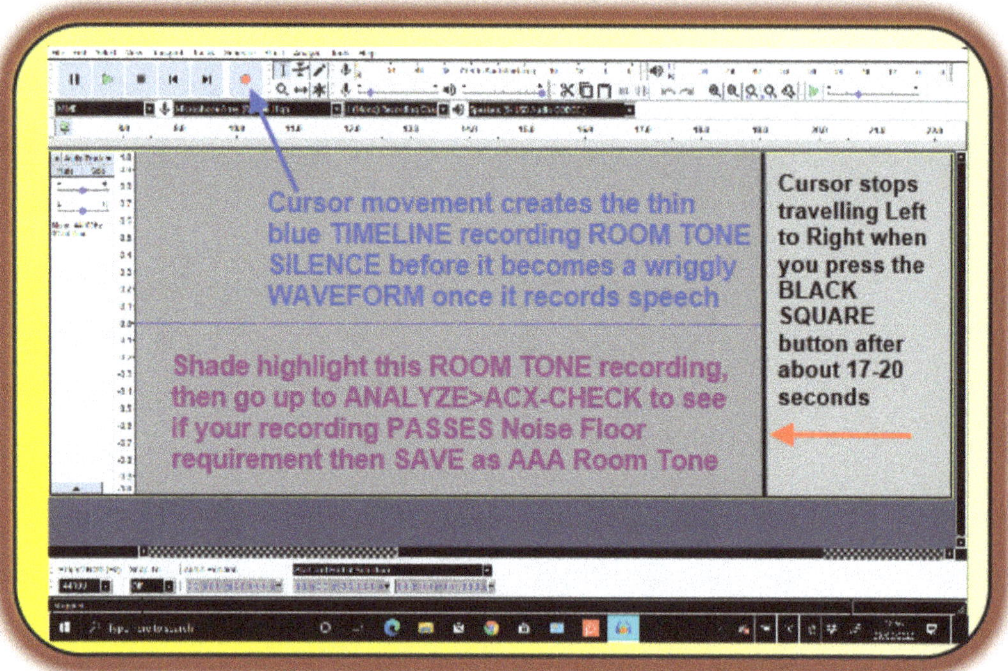

Cursor movement creates the thin blue TIMELINE recording ROOM TONE SILENCE before it becomes a wriggly WAVEFORM once it records speech
Shade highlight this ROOM TONE recording, then go up to ANALYZE>ACX-CHECK to see if your recording PASSES Noise Floor requirement then SAVE as AAA Room Tone
Cursor stops travelling Left to Right when you press the BLACK SQUARE button after about 17-20 seconds

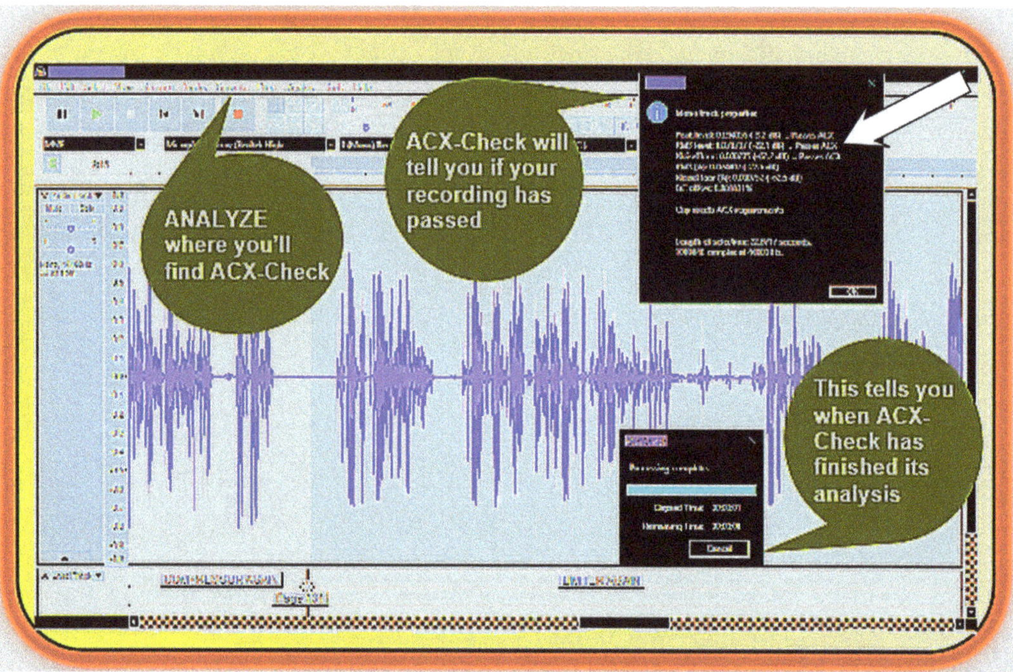

ANALYZE where you'll find ACX-Check
ACX-Check will tell you if your recording has passed
This tells you when ACX-Check has finished its analysis

I use the term TIMELINE to mean the timed progress of the thin horizontal blue line across the screen before it gets distorted into wriggly WAVEFORMS as it detects sound.

At this point it is important to shade highlight the whole of the Timeline that you have created. Go to MENU TOOLBAR top line options and find ANALYZE. If you have installed it correctly you should see ACX-Check in the drop down menu. Click it! Do it frequently. What you are waiting for is to see if you get a PASS on each of three tests, particularly the third one which relates to NOISE FLOOR or non-spoken detectable interference sound.

At this stage, that is all that matters. The other two don't matter yet. If you do get a PASS you are well placed NOT TO HAVE any problems, unless you encounter extraneous noise as you go on.

The first thing to do is to create a file of AAA Room Tone. Make sure you save it. That is the essential background of apparent "silence" which the recording software recognises as NOISE FLOOR and must meet certain criteria. Get that wrong and everything else is a waste of time and energy.

If you don't get a NOISE FLOOR PASS before you speak, you certainly won't get one once you do. The problem is your noisy environment. You must attend to that before you do anything else, or simply wait until it is quieter.

The thickness of that horizontal thin blue line indicates how consistently quiet the recording is. The thicker it is, the more likely you are to having a problem. Equally, if it has any knots, spikes or bumps, then you may have a bigger problem.

To look at it more closely to view any imperfections, go to top toolbar View>Zoom>Zoom in>Zoom in again. To come out of it > Zoom Normal.

Once back to Normal, hold down the Shift Key, and move your cursor over as much of the blue line as you can, to shade it, and press File>Save Project As>File name (suggest you use) AAA Room Tone. It is indispensable. Your audiobook will never be accepted without it, at the beginning and the end. That will then always be available at the top of your list (which is why it is AAA) and easily findable for whatever project you are working on in that session. Whenever you start another session do it again.

If, however, you don't get a PASS on your Noise Floor element, the screen will indicate by how much you need to adjust your environment.

Once you start recording you'll see how your voice distorts the horizontal Timeline into an undulating wriggly waveform.

ACX Check

BEFORE you can find out if your recording gets all three PASSES from ACX-Check software it is necessary to prepare it for that technical scrutiny by applying certain EFFECTS from the menu at the top of the Audacity screen. The recording to be tested should be shade highlighted so that chosen Effects can be applied.

Once you have established AAA Room Tone you can then begin recording proper. After your first listen through of your spoken recording the next thing you must do is to run an ACX-Check, as discussed earlier, to make sure that technically nothing is amiss. Firstly, attend to any discrepancies such as mouth noises, unnoticed ticks and clicks, pronunciation.

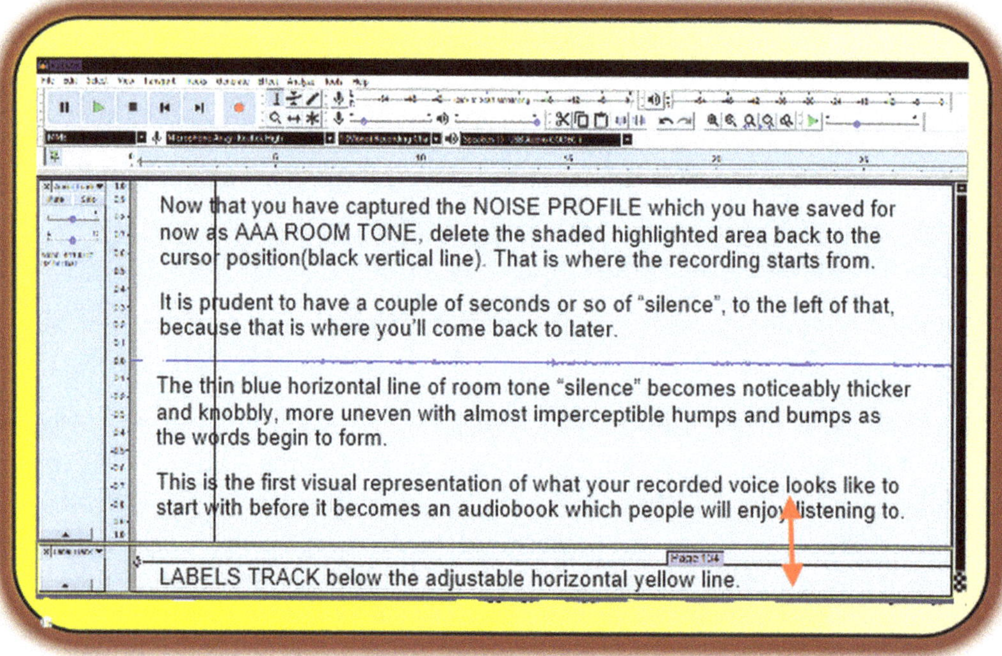

The wriggly waveform may only have recorded your voice as narrator. In between, there may be straight line gaps, deliberately left as spaces for speeches by characters to be recorded, copied and pasted/inserted into the narrator's master recording later on.

In your first listen through, you will be listening to the recording whilst at the same time reading your Narrator's Script as you listen for things you need to change and correct such as unwanted noises.

One such is unavoidable "mouth noises", the sound of sucking in air, inhaling through your mouth to inflate your lungs so you can speak the words that you are recording.

Left unedited out the listeners will be constantly reminded that they are being "read to" – listening to a recording, like a dripping tap, whereas the reason why they are listening is for their private "escapism" from immediate reality, their headphones block it out, the pleasure of being transported into another life, time or world, as if they were there, on their own, imagining and listening as a bystander or voyeur might.

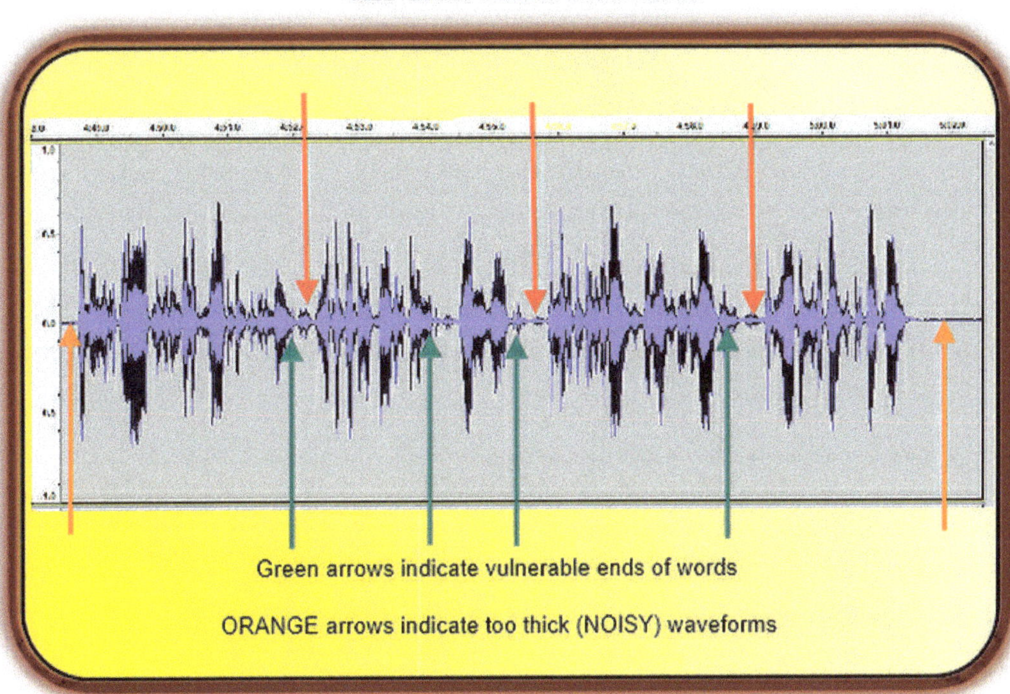

Logically, inhaling mouth noises almost always occurs before words are spoken. With practice you will recognise them visually. On the thin blue horizontal timeline they usually appear as a round shape, circular or elongated like the shape that your lips make. They occupy time, a disruptive second or so, thus they can be safely shaded and deleted without adversely affecting anything.

This benefits natural continuity. Sneezing or nose blowing can be dealt with in the same way.

Unintentional "machine noises" like ticks and clicks are usually short sharp split-second spikes on the waveform. More often than not, they can be tolerated, unless they become "noticeable" affecting the listener's concentration, in which case they need to be deleted in the same way.

There will inevitably be other unwanted noises caused by rustling papers, external noises, expletives and so on. These can be deleted as you carefully concentrate, listening to the recording progressing.

Occasionally, depending where you are, there might be an interfering background rumbling noise and shaking vibration such as from constant passing traffic. The ensuing "hum" has a very low frequency, but a loud noise. It's no good recording a historic novel with the sound of lorries or trains in the background. If that cannot be avoided, you can reduce or eliminate it by switching on a high pass filter (Audacity>Effects>High Pass filter).

Similarly, if there is a high frequency piercing loud noise, which hurts your ears, such as from a builders circular saw, drill or a hissing sound from somewhere else switch on a low pass filter instead (Audacity>Effects>Low Pass filter). Avoid using either of them if you can.

Actual recording is a very small component of the overall process, so it might be wiser to reorganise recording times to when the interference has gone or is predictable.

Once you have achieved three PASSES on each individual page of a chapter, each page identified with its own label box, and a Chapter label box running continuously through every abutting page, then shade highlight the whole joined up Chapter irrespective of how many pages there are.

It is essential that you conform to ACX's (Findaway's) common requirements on room tone at the beginning and the end of each Chapter. So, make sure you know what they are before you start recording. Failure to do so will result in rejection.

There are three technical requirements required by both ACX and Findaway if your recording is to be accepted by them. They are commercial concerns anxious about the consistent quality of the product which bears their name. They make no assessment of the narrator's voice. That is the author's choice and responsibility. They are predominantly concerned with avoiding background sounds and other distractions which make it difficult for listeners to focus on the story. For them it needs to sound as professional as they are.

Where the thin waveform between the narrator's words is "fuzzy" or thickened that is an indication of excessive or unwelcome noise adversely influencing the ACX-Check analysis and must be corrected.

An example of that is the deliberate creation of a space in the waveform into which in due course a character's speech will be copied and pasted. That imported "sound" replaces the vacant horizontal waveform and in the process may inadvertently have introduced "debris". So, if in due course that space is going to be replaced, there's no point in worrying about it.

In case your eyes have glazed over, all that means is that the submitted recorded sound, shown as a fluttering green band, on the main Audacity screen, must not go beyond the limits of the recording/playback meter. If it does it will go yellow/amber and red at the end. Don't worry as it will show up on ACX-Check when you decide to test it.

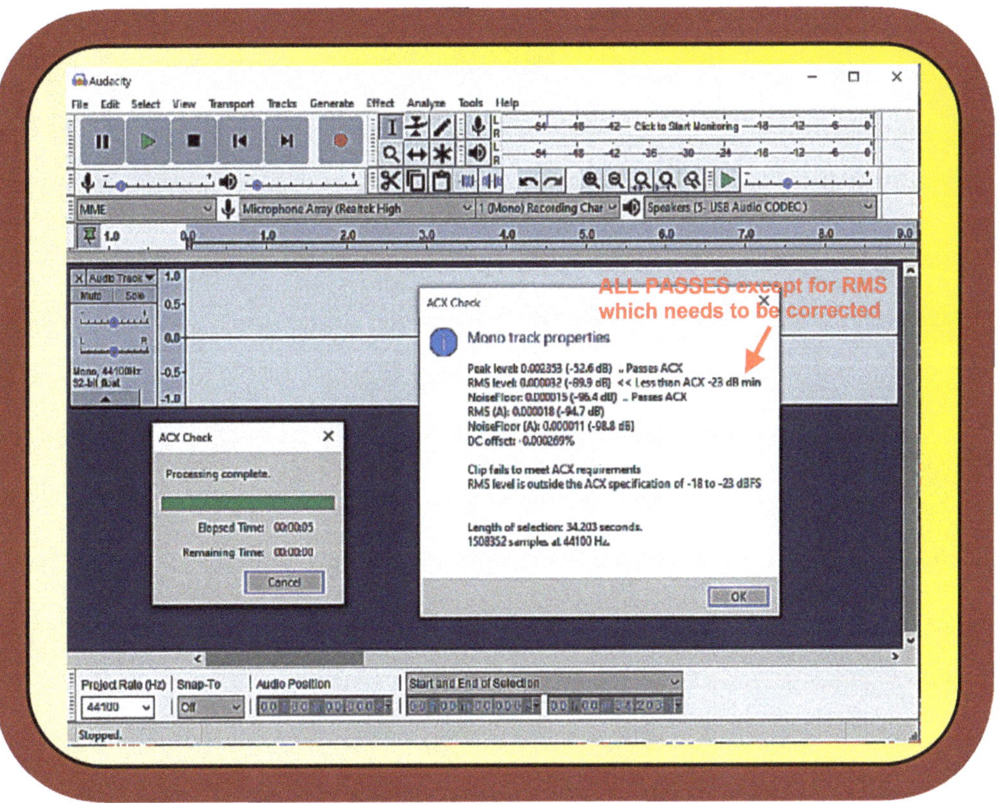

Peak Level: ACX-Check measures the maximum power output before sound distortion. You don't need to understand the technicalities. Just concentrate on the numbers. Must be no higher than −3dB, therefore, −3.1dB is alright because it is lower.

It is difficult to grasp that the higher number in each case is lower. That is because the measurement of decibels dB is based on a logarithmic (curved) scale, NOT a straight line linear scale.

RMS Level: This (Root Mean Square) average loudness is a measure of sound quality. Must be between −23dB and −18dB. So, −20.3dB is acceptable.

To appreciate this, sit or stand as quietly and still as you can, with no noticeable noise from elsewhere and click on the RED record button and record NOTHING for 17–20 seconds. Whilst you do, watch the recording/playback meter at the top of the screen. It should hardly move. The less it moves, the quieter it is. The recording will be represented by a very thin, horizontal blue line.

By applying an ACX-Check every 15–20 minutes worth of recording shown at the top of the screen, or on a Narrator's Script, on a page-by-page basis, you can best manage and correct any imperfections which can adversely affect the results, such as RMS Level. Best to deal with them as you go, otherwise it can be time consuming and disheartening if you've given yourself too much to do.

Noise Floor: The term Noise Floor is sound engineer speak. It has nothing to do with a floor in the normal sense of the word. All it is, is a measure of background noise or interference or consistency of Room Tone or perceived natural silence.

It measures all non-spoken sound. That is the gaps between and at the end of words. The submitted recording must be less than −60dB (decibels on a scale of noise measurement). For example, a measurement of −104.8dB is acceptable because it is lower.

Editing

Producing an audiobook as a merchantable product is a modern manufacturing process as it would be in most factories or businesses today. It requires the timely and orderly supply of quality-controlled components from a variety of sources. That is how they build motor cars and many other things.

In our case those components are Chapter recordings in accordance with the audiobook manufacturer's specification so that they can be efficiently assembled and checked without stopping their production line.

In this case, supplying ACX and Findaway, editing is just one in a series of inter-related processes, one after the other before it passes quality control tests before it can be incorporated into another set of disciplines.

So far, we have dealt with pages of raw recordings which have had their own regime of quality control in ACX-Check. That initial check ensures that basic technical requirements are met.

In this context, editing is largely concerned with adjusting and manipulating those recorded waveforms of varying spikes and spaces into a consistent MP3 form suitable for mass copying as shown in the earlier image at the beginning of this Part Eight (remember the playing cards?).

The first editing sequence consists of the EFFECTS of Normalization, Equalization and Compression, all accessed from the EFFECTS tab at the top of the Audacity screen. Shade highlight the whole selection or recorded page then apply them one at a time.

As the earlier screenshot mock-up shows the raw recording of the narrator's voice is interspersed with room-tone gaps. The raw recording is displayed as the thin blue horizontal Timeline with little bumpy bits before it becomes a waveform. Then with the application of EFFECT>NORMALIZE the Timeline changes into a noticeable waveform.

First Editing Sequence

Normalize

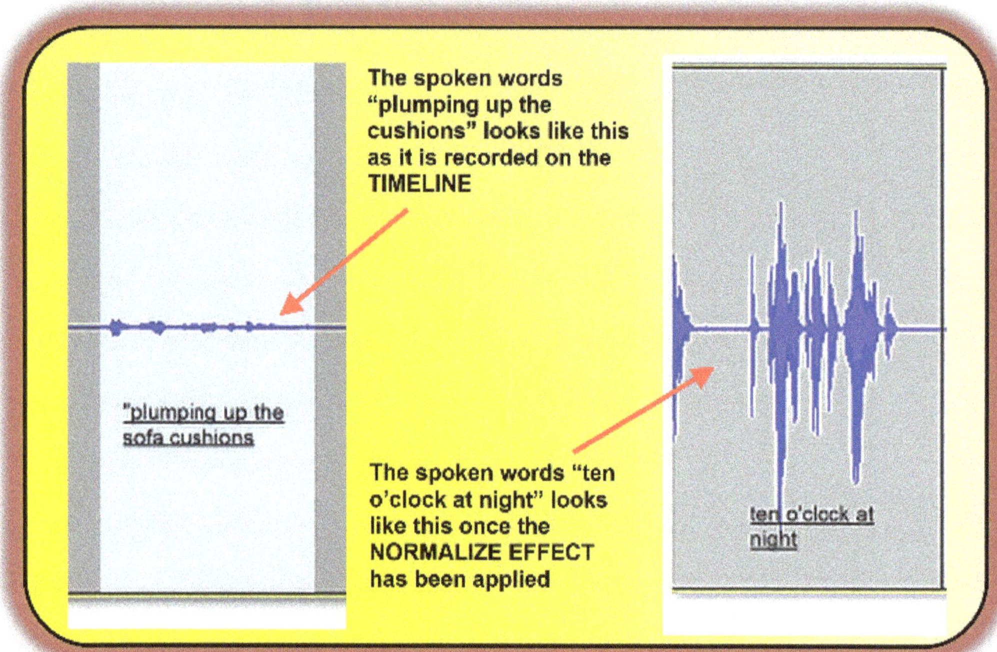

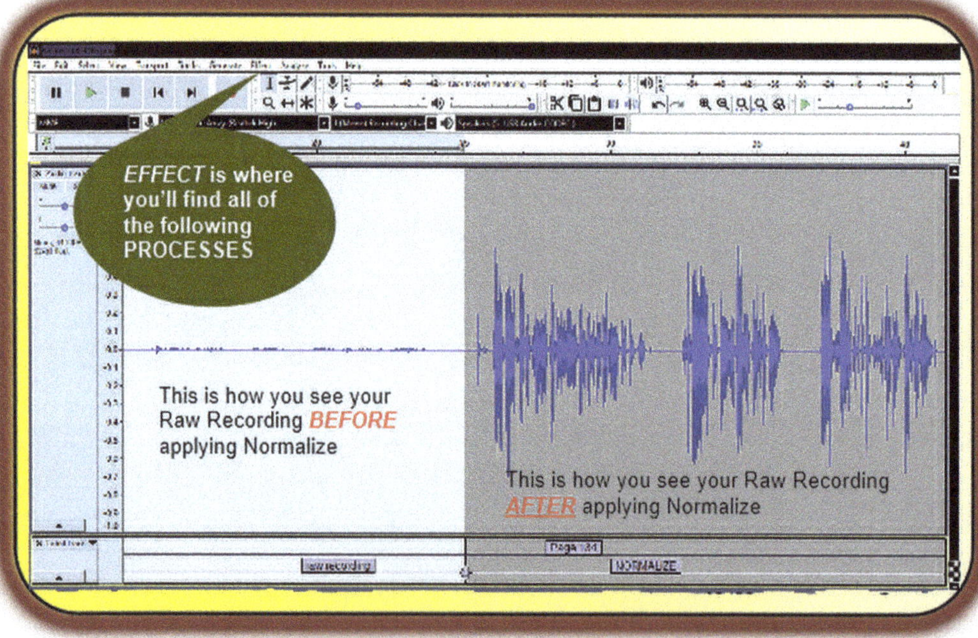

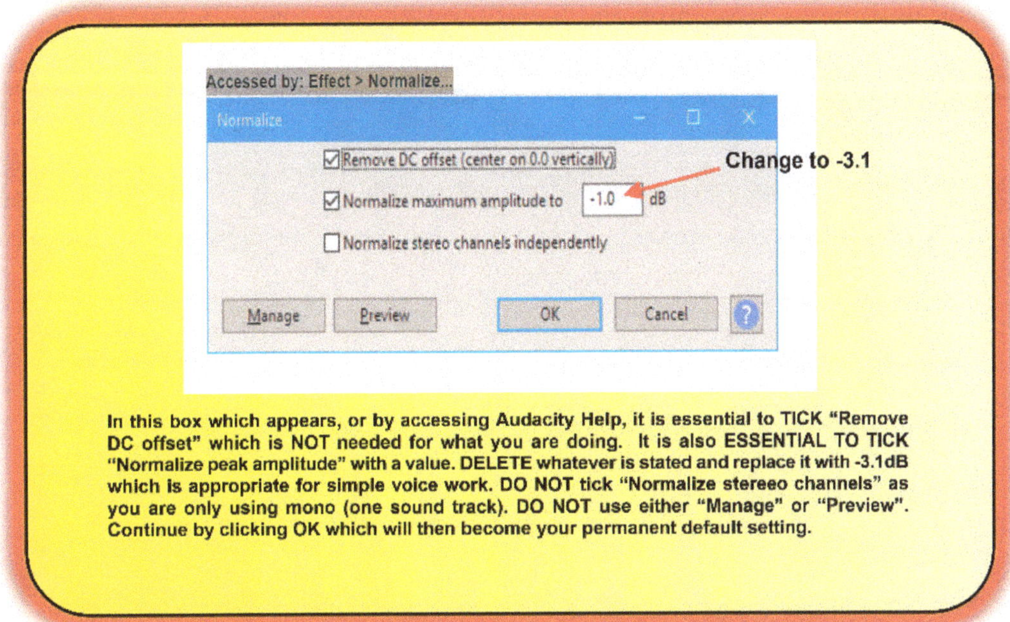

It is IMPORTANT to attend to the Normalize settings box which appears on your screen, or by accessing Audacity>Help. It requires adjustments to the factory supplied software and options to be addressed as per the image provided here.

As its name implies, the EFFECTS process of "normalization" adjusts the recorded volume to make YOUR sound "normal" as far as the technology is concerned. The human ear works naturally but perceives sound volumes and frequencies differently. That is to say, as far as the technology is concerned, a consistent sound modified to a suitable LEVEL of loudness, e.g. PEAK or LOUDEST volume, without changing the QUALITY of the sound itself.

You will apply NORMALIZE *again but not yet* after you've applied EFFECT> EQUALIZE and then EFFECT>COMPRESSOR. It is a progressive process of shuffling and consolidating spikey waveforms within the limits of the audiobook manufacturing process.

Equalize

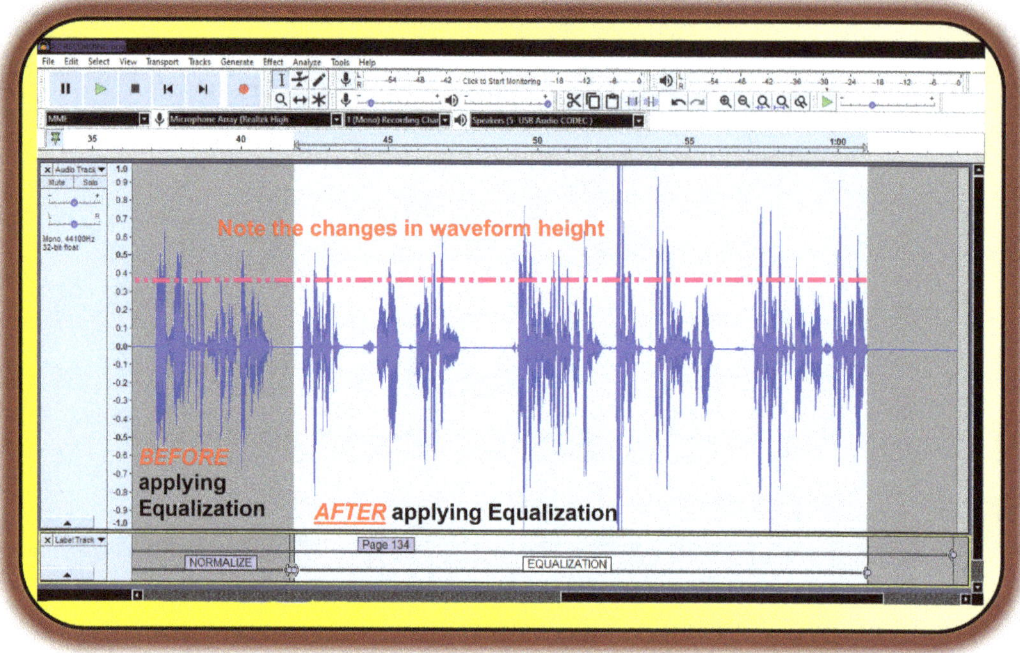

After normalization the first time, I shade and apply equalization. EFFECT>EQUALIZE involves the software increasing or decreasing the levels of different sound frequencies. That means automatically adjusting (equalising) the sound tone quality waveform which records the spoken word and the sometimes imperceptible background ROOM TONE between treble (high frequencies) and bass (low frequencies).

Although there are "things" YOU can adjust, DON'T! Once you get your sound right, leave it alone. RESIST the urge to twiddle knobs or fiddle with sliders. The process requires consistency across ALL chapters.

As you apply each EFFECT you should notice the sometimes very slight changes in the waveform. Some will be slightly more pronounced than others. It is important that you concentrate to reassure yourself that it has taken place. DO NOT be tempted to repeat any step (just to make sure) otherwise the sound will be inconsistent.

Compressor

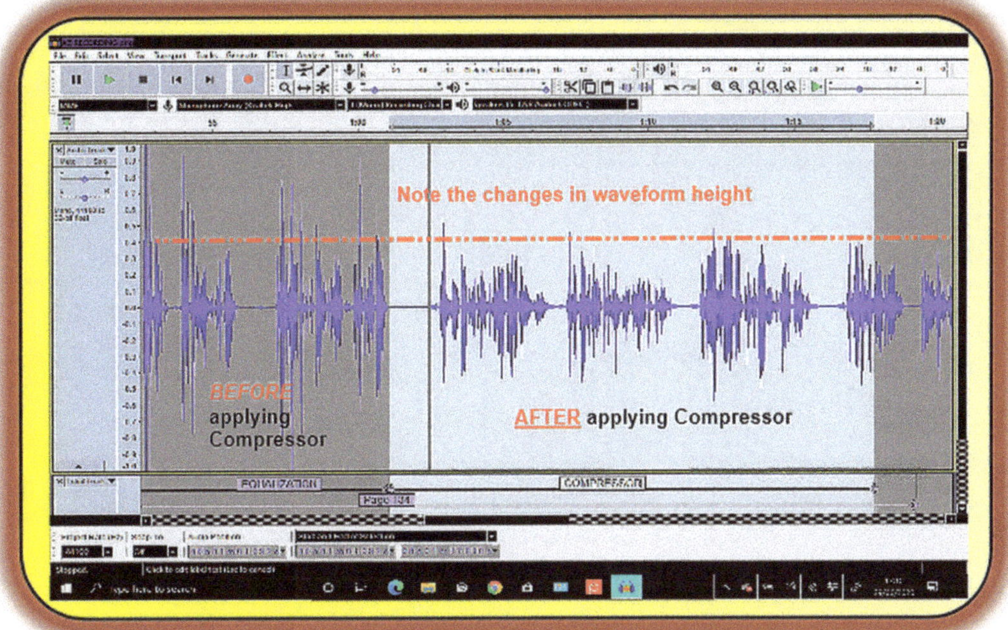

After equalization apply EFFECT>COMPRESSOR. That reduces the recorded sound's dynamic range to achieve "balance". Sound is measured in decibels (dB). In human terms meaning the difference between the quietest sounds (0dB) that we can hear and the loudest before it becomes painful (120dB).

It is worked out logarithmically (on a curve) where 120dB is many more million times that of 0dB. It does this automatically by turning down, or compressing, the louder sounds (or signals) to match more closely the quieter ones.

The otherwise diagonal line compressor has a "threshold" point, a bit like the knee on a leg, a dogleg on a golf course, a kink in an otherwise consistent slope, after which the sound is increasingly squeezed at a higher rate to manage or reduce excessive "loudness".

Normalize *Again*

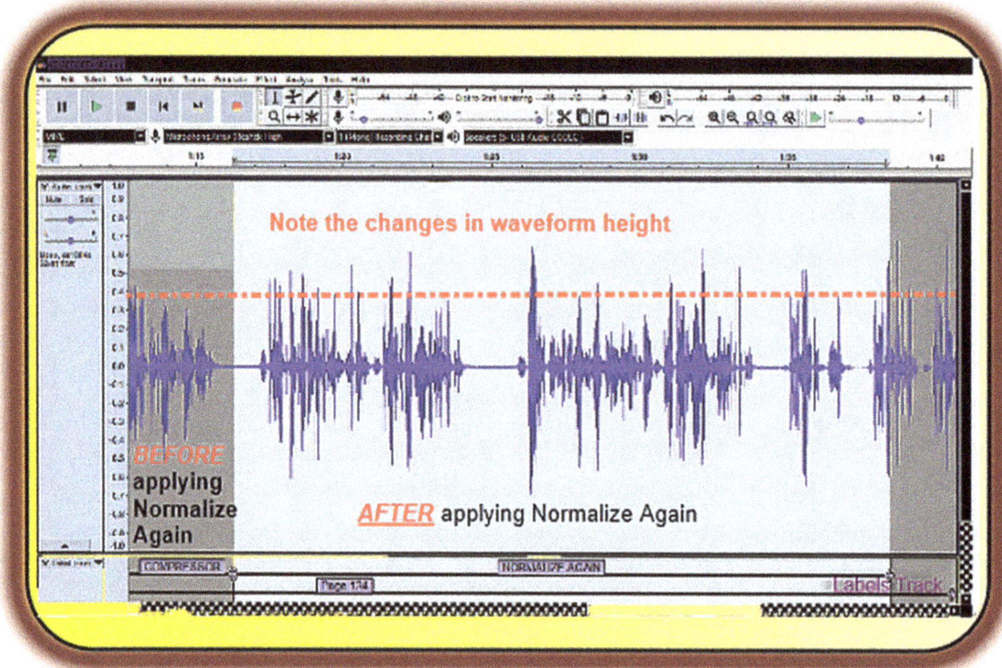

After that apply EFFECT>NORMALIZE AGAIN. The first editing sequence is complete once you have applied NORMALIZE for the second time. Whilst the waveform is still highlighted, apply ACX-Check.

Second Editing Sequence

To test to see if your recording passes ACX-Check, make sure that ALL of the text that you wish to check is shade highlighted. It may be one page or a whole chapter. Generally, the ACX-Check software has a limit of around 25 minutes or so. So, by looking at the elapsed time at the top of the screen you will know if you need to split your chapter into two. Then you have an A test and then a B test. If that appears problematical split them down further into C, D, E and so on to find out which section(s) carry a problem.

In each of those cases shade highlight ALL of that particular text again and repeat the EFFECTS as described – Normalize, Equalize, Compressor, Normalize again, then ANALYZE>ACX-Check

It does NOT tell you if your results will satisfy ACX Audiolab or the equivalent with Findaway Voices, but it would be surprising if that was not the case when you get round to trying to upload to them when they will be quality control checked again before manufacture.

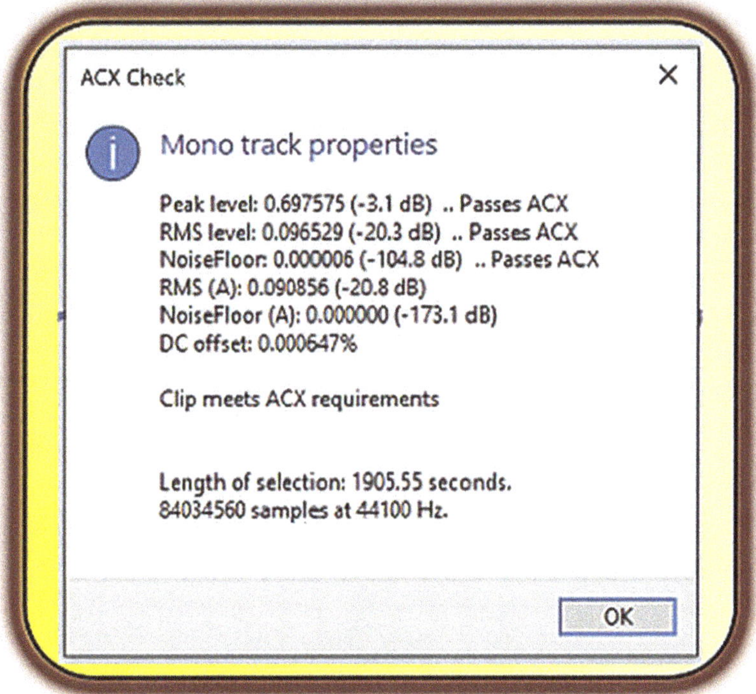

A small panel called **ACX-Check – Mono track properties** appears on your screen. Its moving green line shows that it is working. It shows the three important results, hopefully "Passes ACX" and brief helpful information.

Where it fails on any one of those measurements, ACX-Check will tell you by how much. If you have followed the advice given here earlier, you will see that the correction, if any, is usually marginal. Until you get used to this, it can be terrifying and demoralising – but DO NOT PANIC!

If ever you have need (hopefully you won't) to use High or Low Pass filters, one or both, although, really, you shouldn't need to, you may then commit yourself to having to use them on every page in the audiobook, otherwise it might sound odd and lead to ACX rejection through inconsistency, or put off your listener because you've broken his "suspension of disbelief".

If your ACX-Check has given you a PASS, you have a choice. You could take the view that "That's good enough", which may be acceptable on a long and involved novel. But if you don't get a PASS, what I do, to create a truly professional product, is to artificially "silence" (NOT shorten) just a few of those small gaps randomly which may have a noticeable benefit for the listener, but not be noticeable to any surveillance software in quality control.

You can decide by practice if you want to do that too and run the ACX-Check again and again until you do get a PASS. Shade highlight a few small gaps at a time then go to Audacity>GENERATE>Silence. Click to listen to make sure that your changes are not noticeable. Do not overdo it!

Just to recap. If you have done things my way, by now you will have recorded a PASS on your Noise Floor Level analysis. That is important, as it means you have achieved one third, the most difficult third, of your objective.

For now concentrate on the Peak Level. You can visually sense a problem by watching the Playback Meter Toolbar as you listen to what you've done. You need to watch for the colour going from a happy green to a neurotic orange/amber to a thundery red. You can study your waveform for erratic "peaks" which stick up higher and stand out more than the others do.

Limiter

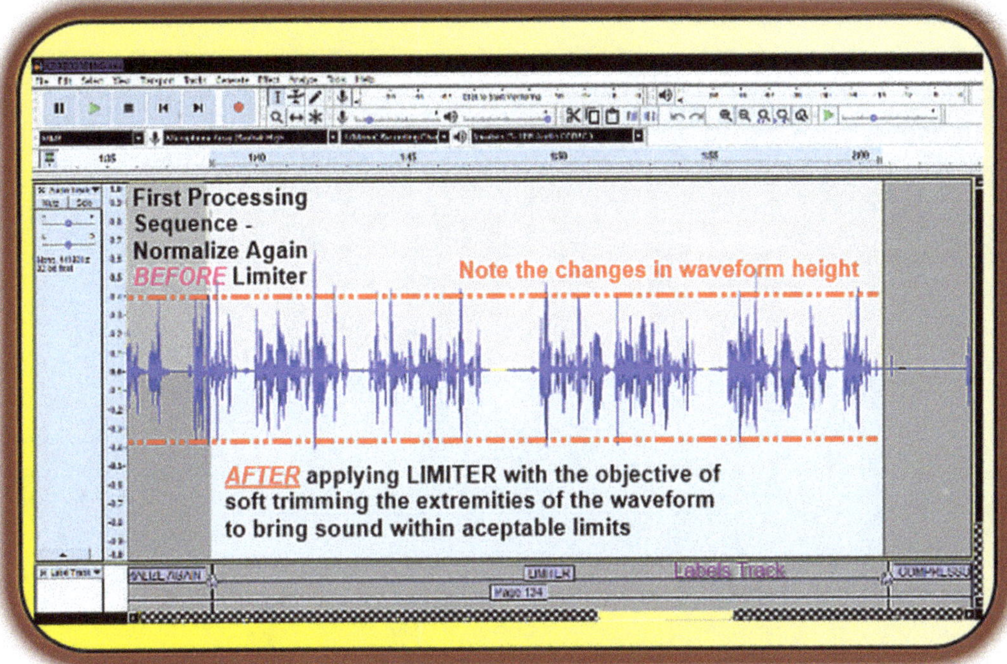

Your remedy is to go to EFFECTS>LIMITER. Using the analogy of shuffling and teasing playing cards back into the deck carton, the LIMITER encourages the waveform to be more orderly.

The Limiter is a form of Compressor. As the name implies, it stops stronger signals from exceeding the compressor's "threshold" point.

Hopefully the Limiter may well be the EFFECT which makes the difference between satisfying ACX requirements or not. It provides for Hard or Soft Clipping (further trimming the tops of waveforms like you would a hedge – topiary, if you like). Of those you should only use Soft Limiting. It progressively reduces the GAIN (input sound from the microphone) as it approaches the critical threshold.

Chances are, after applying LIMITER, that ACX-Check will give Peak Level a PASS.

Compressor *Again*

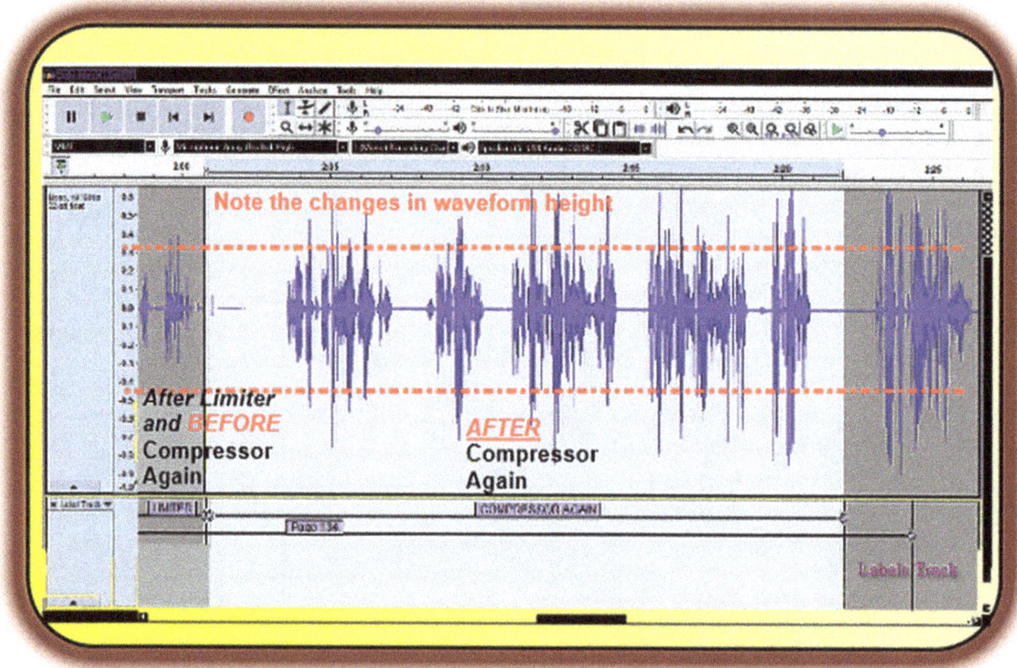

If it doesn't, then shade highlight and apply COMPRESSOR AGAIN. If that fails, try LIMITER AGAIN followed by COMPRESSOR AGAIN.

Listen to your recording carefully and critically again to ensure that there is no distortion or any difference to any other recordings in that project. If you fail again, you should consider re-recording that page again carefully following everything in this manual.

It is important to be honest with yourself. When your reputation and future commissions are at stake, "Just good enough" is not!

You cannot move on, until ALL of the pages in your current Chapter have three PASSES from ACX-Check.

If your only problem is your RMS Level try testing it on ACX Audiolab. It will tell you how to get over it.

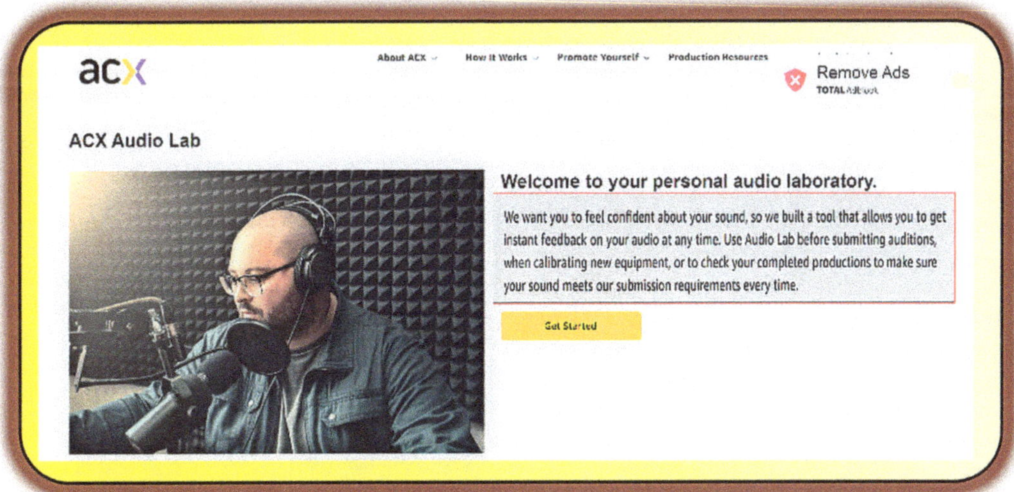

In getting this far as a narrator, I have had to redo numerous pages until I got them accepted and I was happy. I didn't have this manual to follow, which is why I wrote it, so that whatever frustration you get, just be aware that I've had far more.

You should by now have several pages each of which have gained three PASSES from ACX-Check.

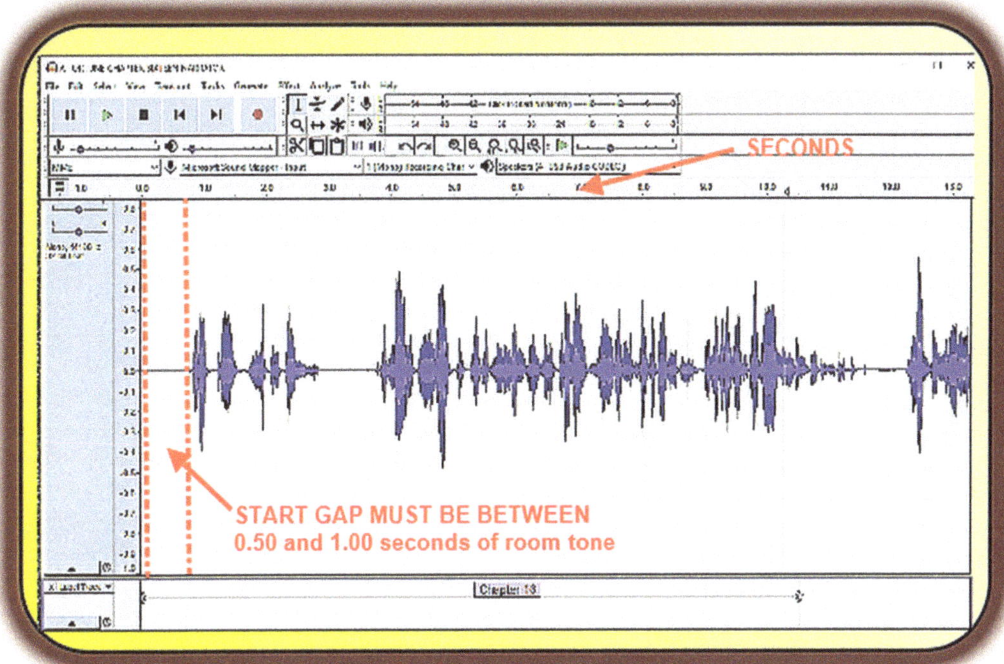

The first page of the chapter MUST HAVE a room tone gap of between 0.50 and 1.00 seconds. No more, no less! To ensure that you have this, before you begin to narrate, it is wise to SAY to yourself without recording "Start of Chapter whatever it is", and to have a LABEL saying the same.

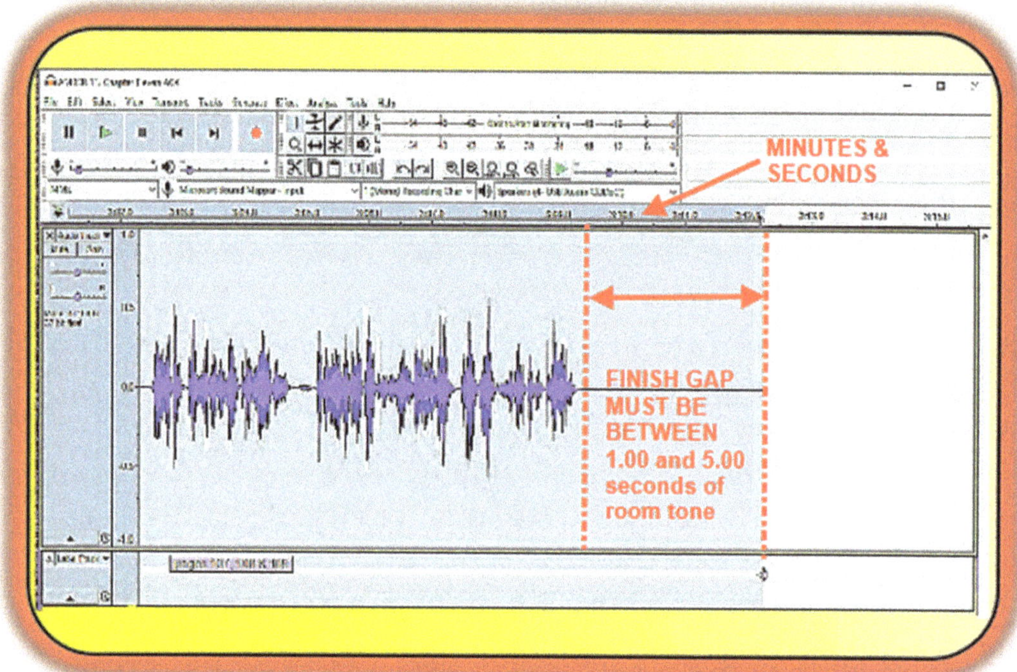

The last page of the chapter MUST HAVE a room tone gap of between 1.00 and 5.00 seconds. No more, no less!

To ensure you have this, when you finish narrating, it is wise to say to yourself "End of chapter whatever it is" and to have a LABEL saying the same.

Then one last check to make sure that you have three PASSES and correct Start and Finish gaps then you click SAVE which brings up the screen requiring you to ADD the metadata by which all computer systems manage the transfer of your audiobook's information.

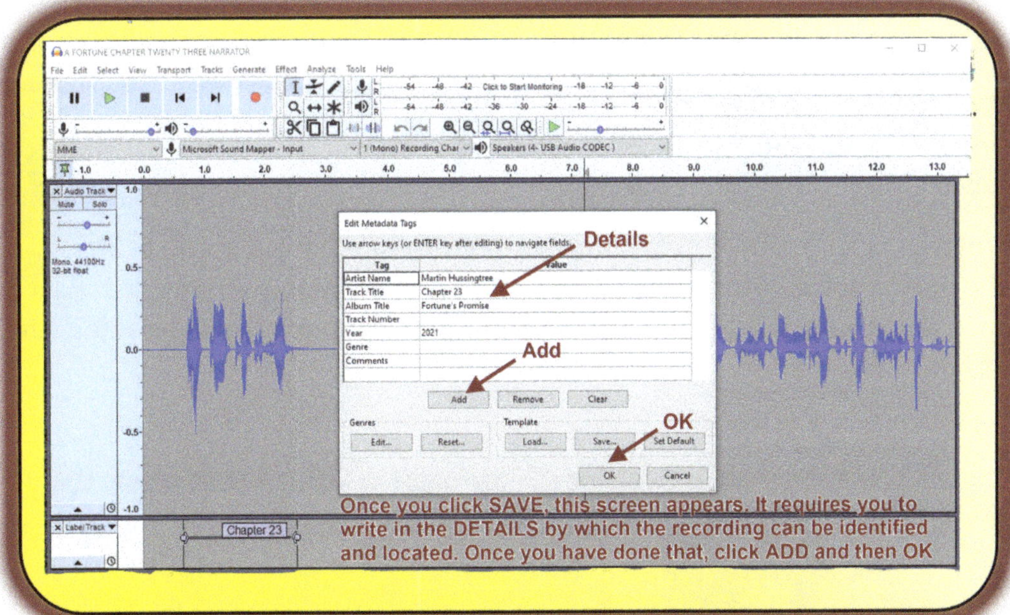

FILE>SAVE PROJECT AS … BOOK TITLE chapter ?? whatever it is ending in MP3. For example, BOOK TITLE Chapter 23 MP3 then

FILE>EXPORT>EXPORT AS MP3

ALWAYS use the suffix MP3 in the title to denote that it is finished and has been sent so that it is easily recognised in any list.

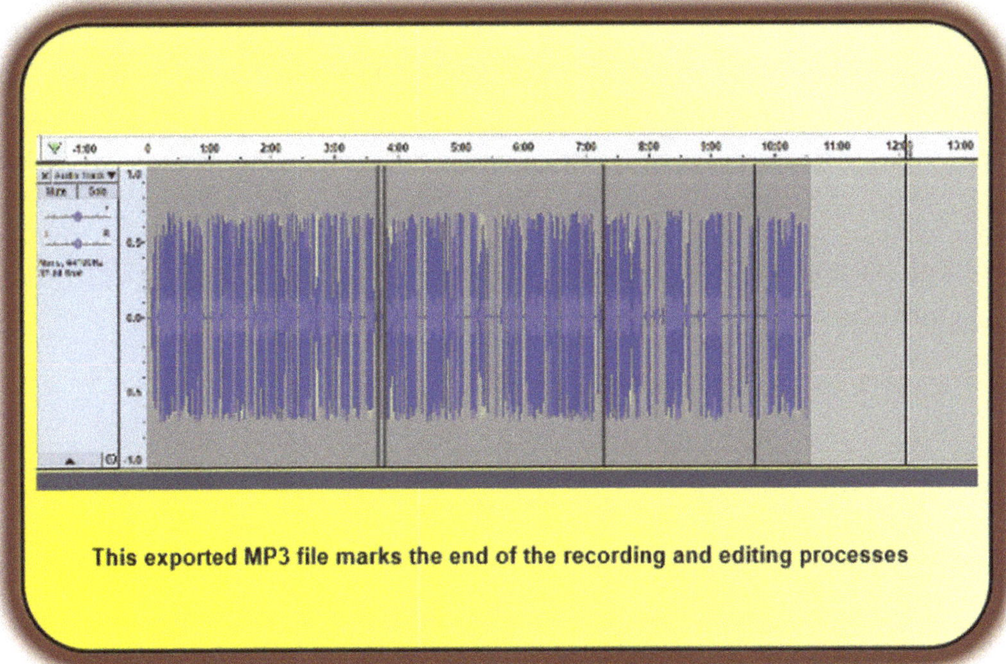

This exported MP3 file marks the end of the recording and editing processes

This is what each and every chapter MP3 tends to look like. Remember what I showed you at the beginning of this Part Eight?

It compresses your waveform into a smaller space for ease and economy of transmission and in a consistent form around which mass produced audiobook production is based.

When you click OK a green line briefly crosses the screen in a box then disappears to tell you that the Export has taken place. In reality, it hasn't gone anywhere, it has merely been transformed in readiness to being sent somewhere.

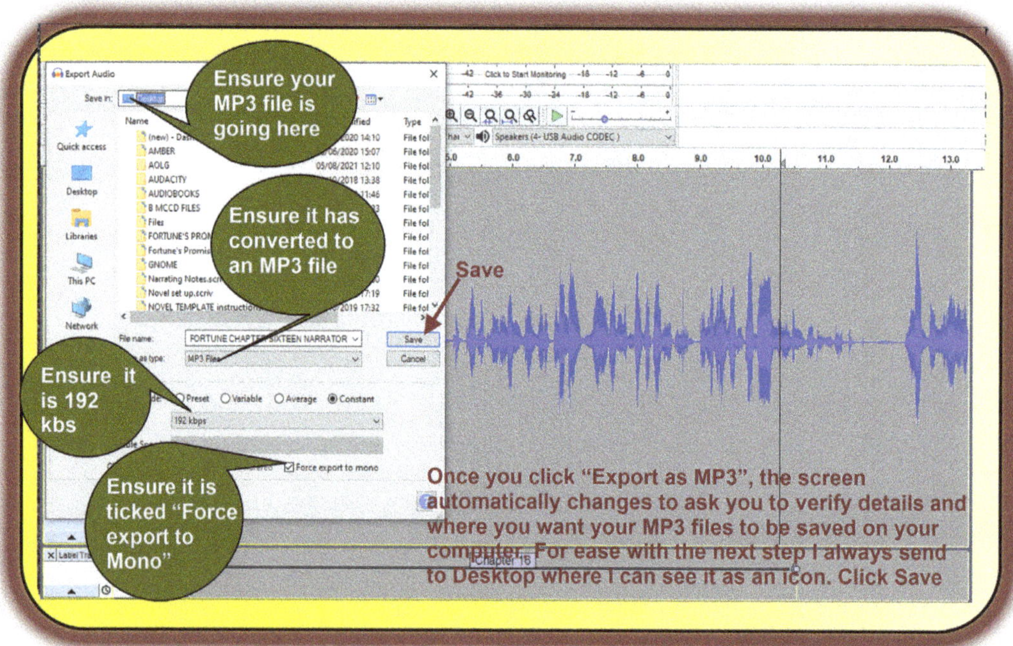

Then go to your Desktop, or wherever else you asked for it to be saved, and you should see this icon with a caption showing the name you gave it confirming what it is. All MP3 files look like this:

This is the sequence by which your browser takes you to ACX Audio Lab, which you'll find very helpful, if not indispensable.

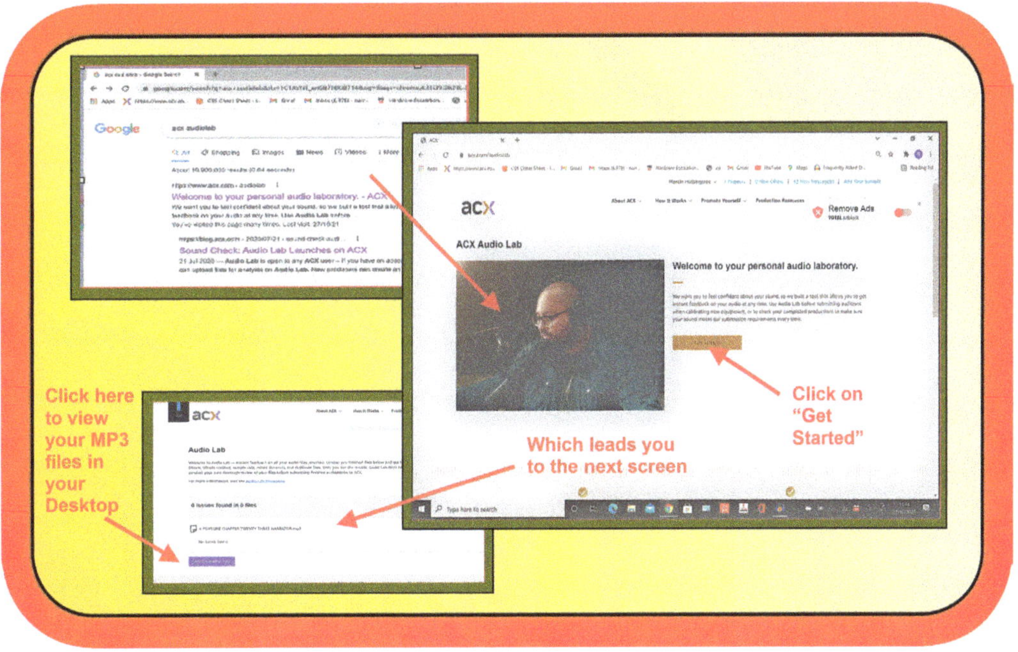

LABELS – your management system

Without the Labels Track, and its ability to tell you where you are, who is speaking, and when, and what you need to remember, or do, to correct and/or improve your recording, you would be unable to successfully or satisfactorily produce any audiobook recording, of any, but the simplest novel. One that is simply read, as opposed to one which is performed.

In order to make sense of the audible picture you have painted of potentially many speaking characters, it requires a management system to make sense of their many wriggly waveforms, which on the face of it, all look remarkably similar – too similar for easy identification and management.

Audacity provides such a system whereby speeches can have a tag or label attached to them so that they can be identified, stored, moved about and re-arranged to create an audiobook of speaking voices telling a story.

One wriggly waveform on a screen looks very much like another. It's a bit like looking at a flock of sheep on a hillside. A shepherd needs a way of controlling them. He has his dependable sheep dog. **LABELS** are your equivalent. They keep you sane! Without them you will go mad!

AFTER recording, go to Edit>Labels>Add at Selection (determined by where your mouse arrow is). The Label Track will appear below the recorded waveform. On the left-hand side, the Track Control Panel will appear.

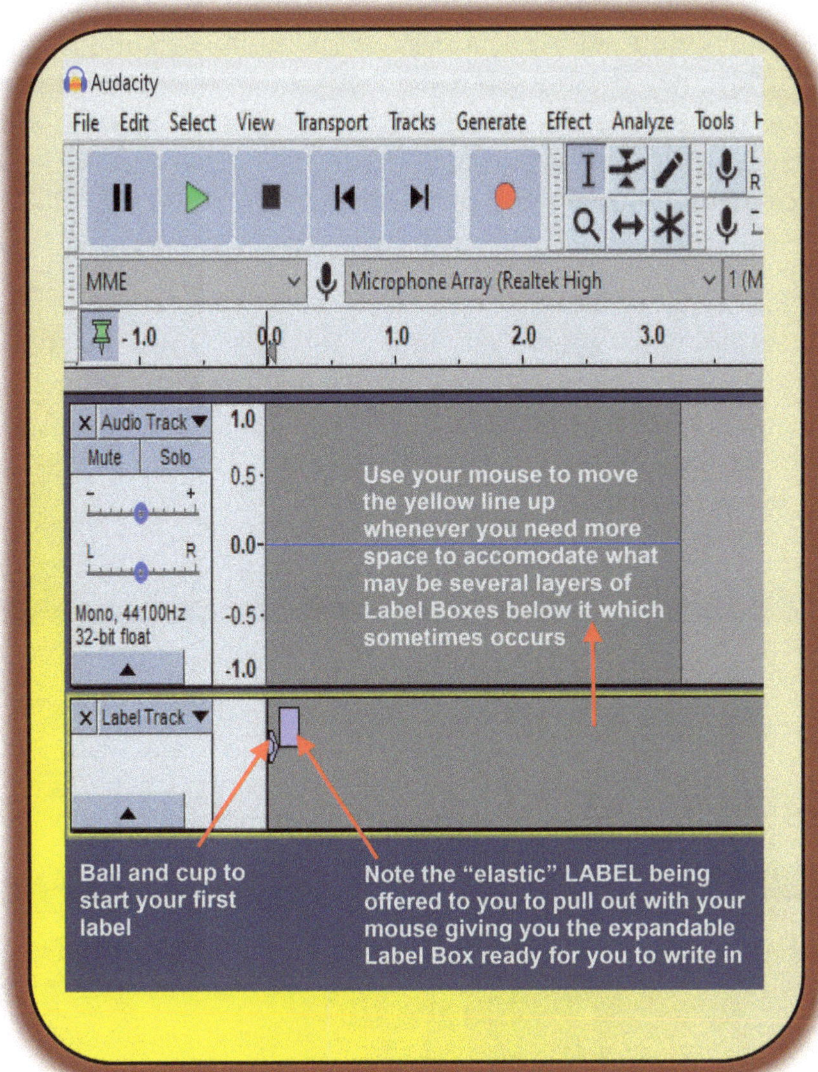

Labels are *YOUR* indispensable management tool. They can be called anything you type in the Label box provided, so long as it's meaningful, for example, it can be a page or chapter number, a character's name (and/ or four-part reference code as in Part Three) or anything else.

It can be an instruction to yourself, to remember to do something. It can be placed to identify where work needs **REDO**-ing and why, and any other editorial comment you wish to use to remind you or even to avoid. For example, whichever voice you have recorded, are they supposed to be shocked, excited, terrified, or to identify difficult locations where they are supposed to be, such as an echoing cave, where it's perishing cold, or pouring with rain – just like the Director of a movie or stage play might.

Labels are essential wherever dialogue is happening, generally allowing the narrator to avoid getting lost in his non-visual, seemingly otherwise "blind" world. They are the equivalent of the white stick that blind and partially sighted people use to know where they are. Failure to make the most of using labels will cause much frustration, error and delay. Making the most of them will make things easier, save time and improve the end result.

A label consists of a writable box on an elastic line which you can pull out between seemingly magnetic "cup and ball" ends. Unlike elastic, it stays stretched out where you put it. It's a bit like a knee or shoulder joint bone and socket. Click on the round ball and you can move it to where you want. Click on the cup bit and the ball stays still, but the elastic line goes to wherever you want it.

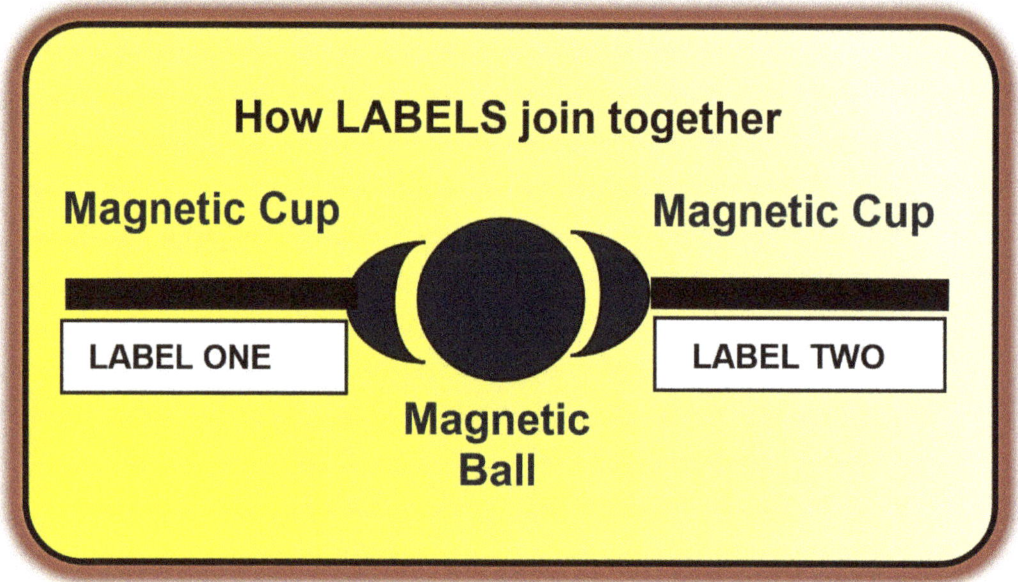

Being "elastic" labels can be lengthened or shortened and moved around to suit whatever you are doing. They can be SYNC-LOCKED to stay glued to any dialogue movement or change *in the same file*. Take care if you copy or cut and paste a speech and place it elsewhere to recreate that particular label as labels do not transfer with the dialogue.

Labels can be added in at any time. As your screen moves forwards containing the action, the identifying labels box will always move following your gaze as your screen changes, so if you have a label for each page and a label for each chapter you will always know whereabouts you are in relation to Narrator's Script pages. Using labels in this way allows you to always be able to relate the waveform to the script.

There is nothing preventing any number of overlapping labels, one above or below each other. They do not need to be erased. Like an artist's sketched outlines, in due course they will disappear. Automatically LABELS DO NOT appear in finished work.

Do not be afraid to move the horizontal yellow dividing line upwards. It has no effect on the squashed waveform whose sound qualities and volume stay the same.

Looking at waveforms all day inevitably becomes frustrating when you can't see the wood for the trees. If you don't intelligently use the Labels Track, you will always waste hours confusing yourself unless you have some way of marking and identifying them.

The old fairy tale of Hansel & Gretel is a case in point. They got lost in the woods, but on their way to being abandoned, sensibly dropped some white pebbles to mark their route so they could find their way home if they got lost.

The following images are typical examples of what Labels look like.

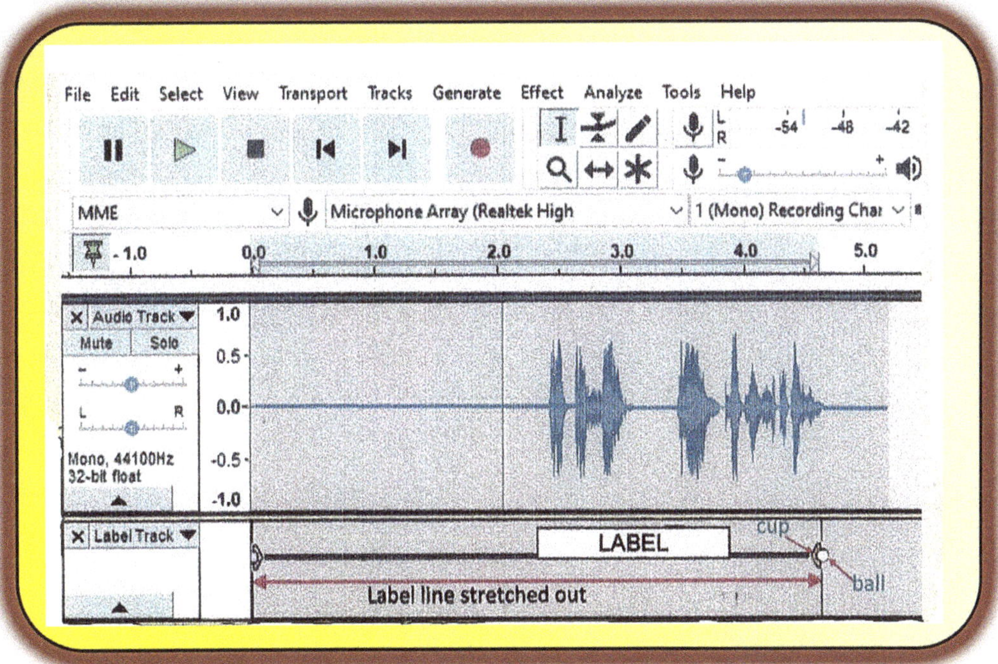

The first label will be half peeping out waiting for you to pull it out. The first thing you should do is to take it to the end of the page that you've just recorded where it will stay or you can pull it along with you as you go. Then within the writable labels box, you write "page one". At the end of that page there will be a cup & ball joint where the next page will begin. It will have its own labels box "page two" and so on. As you progress, you should have a labels box stating the Chapter number which you will continue to pull along with you across all of the pages in that Chapter. So, every recorded page of the Narrators Script will have at least two labels – page number and Chapter number before you have any characters saying anything.

DO NOT start the next Chapter with another page one. Use the Narrator's Script page numbers. Always write labels as text rather than numerals which can lead to confusion.

As you move along recording, the labels will always tell you more or less whereabouts you are. It is only when you have characters speeches, will you know precisely where you are.

Then on your first listen through, you stop at the first speech space you come to, and then you insert a coded label so you know exactly where you are in the text, and who is currently speaking. Then you go onto the next and so in until you come to the end of the page.

You might introduce other long running labels boxes saying REDO or something else you need to remember, so you can begin to appreciate that you might need to raise the yellow barrier above the Labels Track to accommodate all of those lines. You can adjust that divider as often as you like. It will affect all pages in that Chapter. It will not affect the recorded sound in the waveform. Squashing it will not affect it.

So far, I've covered page and speech labels, and barely touched on NOTE labels such as REDO or START HERE or REMEMBER TO or TIDY UP even. These are essential to producing a first-class product. None of those notes will ever appear, or be seen by anyone else, as the contents of the Labels Track does not migrate with the recorded sound.

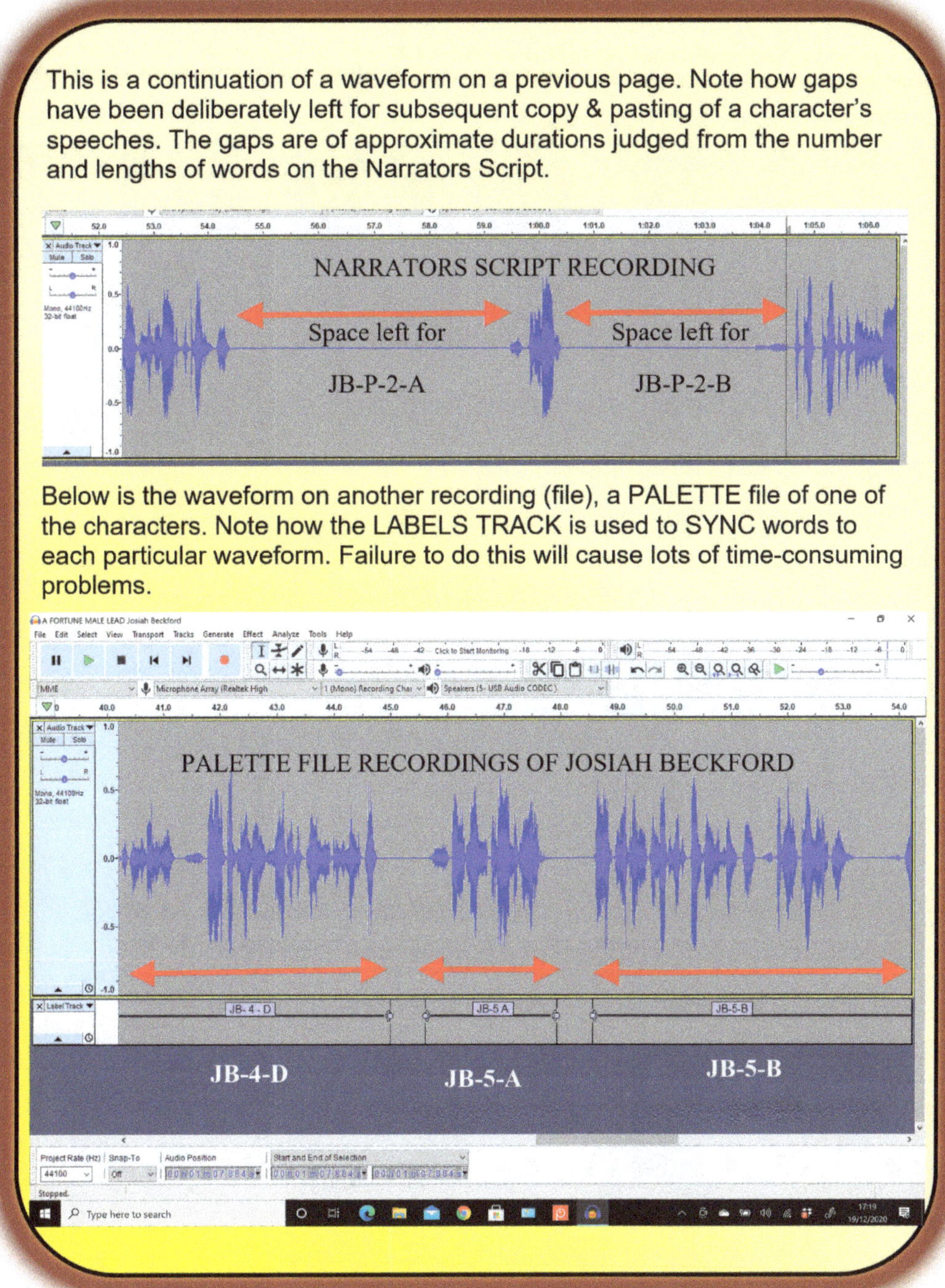

As you move along the waveform, the labels box moves along its line with you, so you always know whereabouts you are. The character's speech code as just described will tell you which CHAPTER you are on.

On the above, note how sloppy positioning of labels do not join at Page Transfers making it more difficult to follow, than, for example below, where with greater care, continuity is clearer and editing is easier taking advantage of the seemingly magnetic cup and ball interface

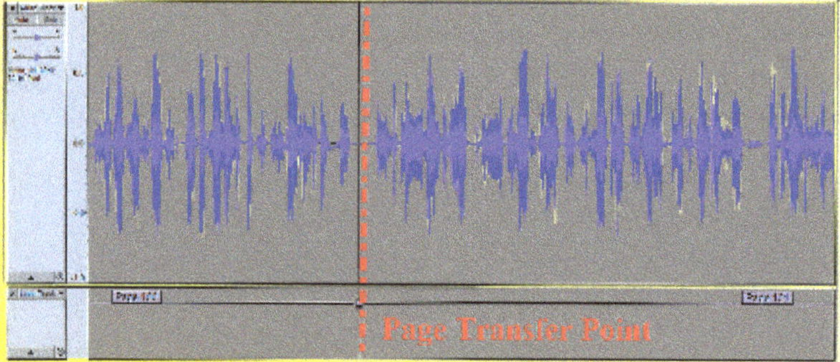

You can move the yellow divider up to create more space on the Labels Track if it starts to get congested during sorting or editing. It has no effect on the waveform whose sound qualities and volume remain the same.

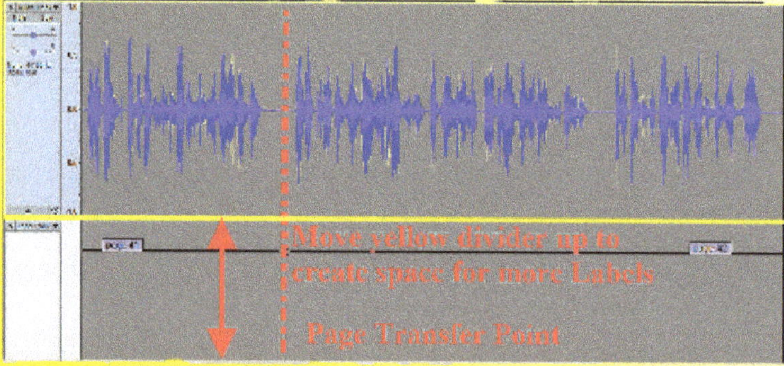

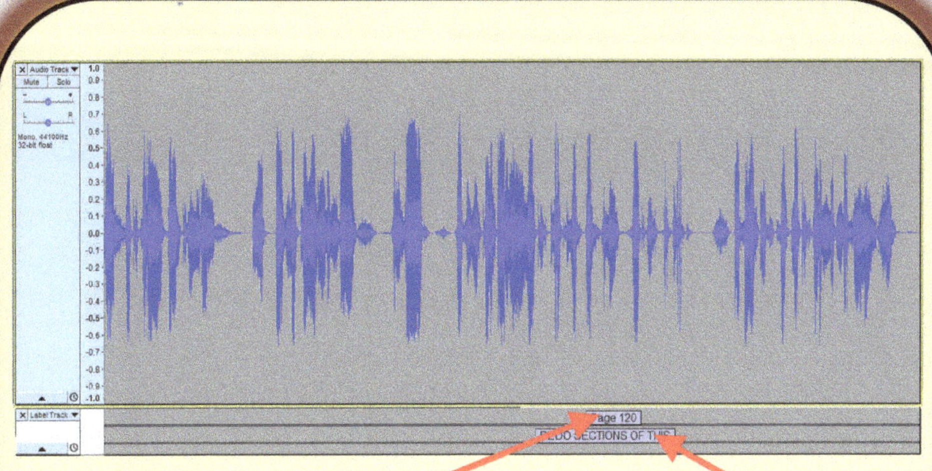

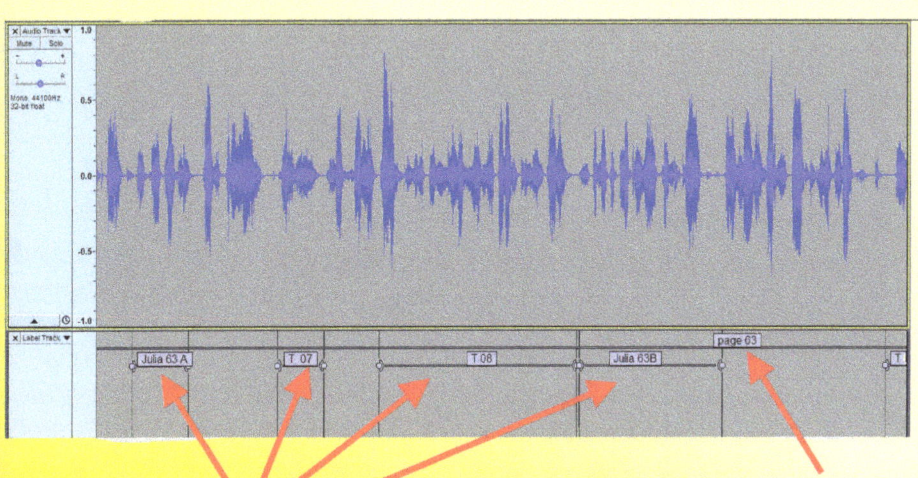

Without the Labels Track and its ability to tell you where you are, who is speaking and when and what you need to remember or do to correct and/or improve your recording you would be unable to successfully or satisfactorily produce any worthwhile audiobook recording to professional standards

Submitting

SUCCESS! ACX audiolab has confirmed the analysis of Audacity's ACX-Check. The MP3 file can now be confidently submitted to ACX or Findaway or both for their incorporation into the proposed audiobook.

By now all MP3 chapters, one by one, will have been sent to the Author for comment and/or approval which he will have given otherwise the narrator will not have arrived at this stage. As a matter of courtesy, the author should seek the narrator's agreement to submitting to his chosen publisher all of the chapters including the ancillaries.

Depending on whether the author chooses ACX or Findaway or anyone else, the process now involves a third party. For simplicity I will take you to ACX. Go to your browser and search for ACX audiolab as you saw earlier:

https://www.acx.com>audiolab

Their "welcome" page leads you to click on the button displaying the MP3 files on your Desktop.

Below is a real-life example of how I, as narrator, uploaded the Chapters of my audiobook of Sue Johnson's 70,000 word novel *Fortune's Promise – a Regency Romance*.

There are 38 chapters, plus Opening and Closing Credits, a Prologue and an Epilogue and a Retail Audio sample. Listening time is 7½ hours and covers the comings and goings of 83 different characters, male and female, whose voices had to be distinctly different.

The following screenshots show Opening Credits, the Prologue and Chapters 1–8. Followed by Chapters 37 and 38 together with the Epilogue and Closing Credits. Chapters 9–36 are largely repetitive and have been omitted for clarity.

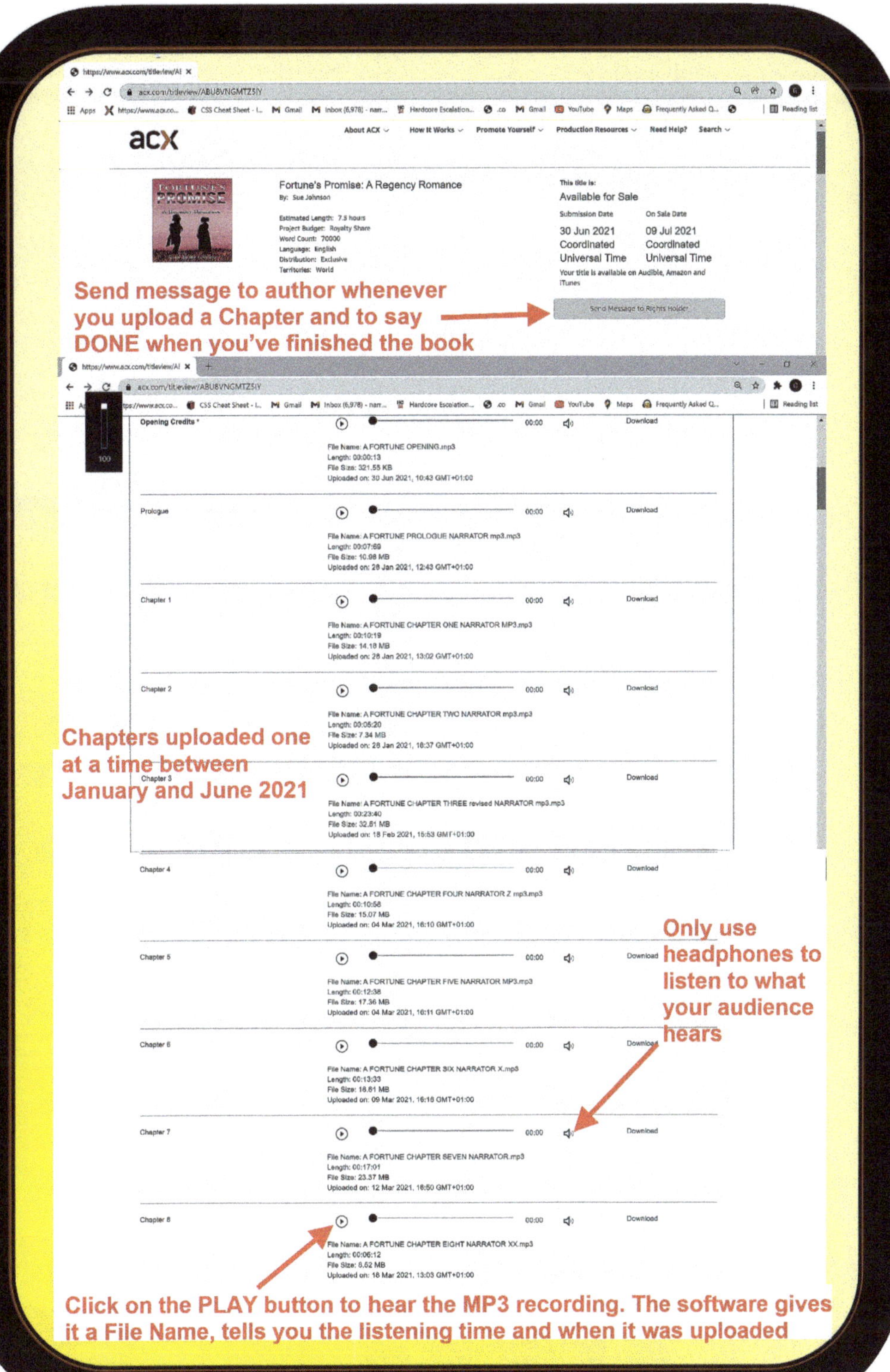
acx
About ACX   How It Works   Promote Yourself   Production Resources   Need Help?   Search
Fortune's Promise: A Regency Romance
By: Sue Johnson
Estimated Length: 7.3 hours
Project Budget: Royalty Share
Word Count: 70000
Language: English
Distribution: Exclusive
Territories: World
This title is:
Available for Sale
Submission Date
30 Jun 2021
Coordinated
Universal Time
On Sale Date
09 Jul 2021
Coordinated
Universal Time
Your title is available on Audible, Amazon and iTunes
Send Message to Rights Holder
Opening Credits *
File Name: A FORTUNE OPENING.mp3
Length: 00:00:13
File Size: 321.55 KB
Uploaded on: 30 Jun 2021, 10:43 GMT+01:00
Prologue
File Name: A FORTUNE PROLOGUE NARRATOR mp3.mp3
Length: 00:07:59
File Size: 10.98 MB
Uploaded on: 28 Jan 2021, 12:43 GMT+01:00
Chapter 1
File Name: A FORTUNE CHAPTER ONE NARRATOR MP3.mp3
Length: 00:10:19
File Size: 14.18 MB
Uploaded on: 28 Jan 2021, 13:02 GMT+01:00
Chapter 2
File Name: A FORTUNE CHAPTER TWO NARRATOR mp3.mp3
Length: 00:06:20
File Size: 7.34 MB
Uploaded on: 28 Jan 2021, 18:37 GMT+01:00
Chapter 3
File Name: A FORTUNE CHAPTER THREE revised NARRATOR mp3.mp3
Length: 00:23:40
File Size: 32.81 MB
Uploaded on: 18 Feb 2021, 15:53 GMT+01:00
Chapter 4
File Name: A FORTUNE CHAPTER FOUR NARRATOR Z mp3.mp3
Length: 00:10:58
File Size: 15.07 MB
Uploaded on: 04 Mar 2021, 16:10 GMT+01:00
Chapter 5
File Name: A FORTUNE CHAPTER FIVE NARRATOR MP3.mp3
Length: 00:12:38
File Size: 17.36 MB
Uploaded on: 04 Mar 2021, 16:11 GMT+01:00
Chapter 6
File Name: A FORTUNE CHAPTER SIX NARRATOR X.mp3
Length: 00:13:33
File Size: 18.61 MB
Uploaded on: 09 Mar 2021, 16:18 GMT+01:00
Chapter 7
File Name: A FORTUNE CHAPTER SEVEN NARRATOR.mp3
Length: 00:17:01
File Size: 23.37 MB
Uploaded on: 12 Mar 2021, 16:50 GMT+01:00
Chapter 8
File Name: A FORTUNE CHAPTER EIGHT NARRATOR XX.mp3
Length: 00:06:12
File Size: 8.52 MB
Uploaded on: 18 Mar 2021, 13:03 GMT+01:00
Send message to author whenever you upload a Chapter and to say DONE when you've finished the book
Chapters uploaded one at a time between January and June 2021
Only use headphones to listen to what your audience hears
Click on the PLAY button to hear the MP3 recording. The software gives it a File Name, tells you the listening time and when it was uploaded

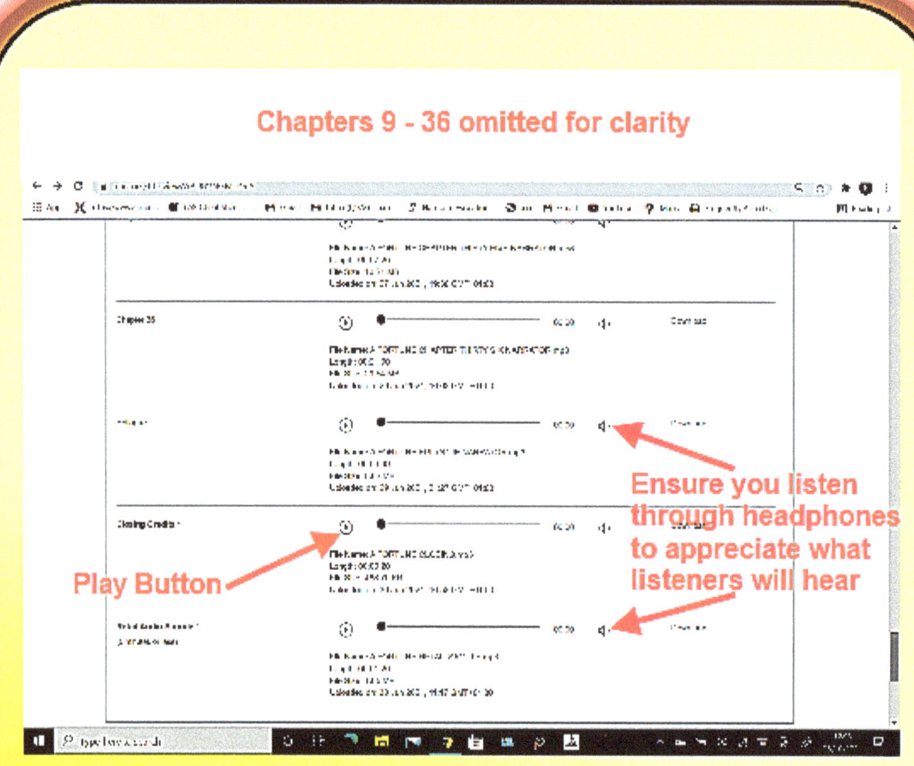

This is what the narrator sees on his computer screen. There are 36 Chapters, plus a Prologue and an Epilogue; Opening and Closing statements and a Retail Audio sample. A total of 41 recordings covering a PFH (narrators payment) of 7 ½ Finished Listening Hours).

The narrator's last act is to press his "I'm Done" button to advise the author.

Pressing the I'M DONE button on his Project page on their mutual management screen is the author's last act, having listened and approved all of the narrator's recordings above.

That submits everything to ACX, or the same for Findaway for further technical and quality checking. All being well, the audiobook will be on sale through their respective outlets in 2-3 weeks time thereafter, depending on their current situation.

Both author and narrator will then be advised of any changes necessary and/or likely publishing dates.

As you will see, the 43 separate MP3 files were uploaded one by one. In each case, I notified the author each time who could then hear them to satisfy and reassure herself that something was happening and that it sounded good from a listener's point of view.

It is crucially important that both author and narrator see this as a collaborative partnership, each having confidence and trust in the other.

When the whole book has been completed, I create a folder to contain all of the MP3 files sent to ACX. I then keep an ever-growing list of those audiobooks on my desktop which I can then use for reference.

Part Nine

Audiobook Marketing

Who and where are your audience?

Before you even consider who you might have an author/narrator relationship with and then how your mutual audiobook will be put on a particular market, you need to carefully consider your relationship with who is going to process and distribute your work to best effect. Each of the major audiobook distributors, ACX or Findaway Voices offer choices of where and how audiobooks will be sold, and who should sell them, or in some cases hire (lend/borrow) them from a library.

Both ACX and Findaway Voices rely on website catalogues as their virtual shop windows/shelves. Spotify who recently bought Findaway are a global audio streaming service for music, podcasts and audiobooks. To what degree that influences the market remains to be seen.

Only you know your situation and objectives so you need to carefully consider your strategy to maximise the return on your investment of time and money whether it be as an author or a narrator. You want to sell your audiobook to as many people as possible, or get as many library listeners as possible to hear it. Don't you?

Amazon's ACX dominate the huge, but highly competitive North American market, as well as the UK and Ireland whose combined total population of English speakers, as a first or a second language is roughly half of all global English speakers.

As for Findaway Voices they distribute (like a wholesaler does) to independent point-of-sale outlets and libraries across the globe including those also covered by ACX. So, there's an element of duplication. For example, Findaway claim to have a more advantageous relationship with Apple who some see historically as a direct competitor to ACX.

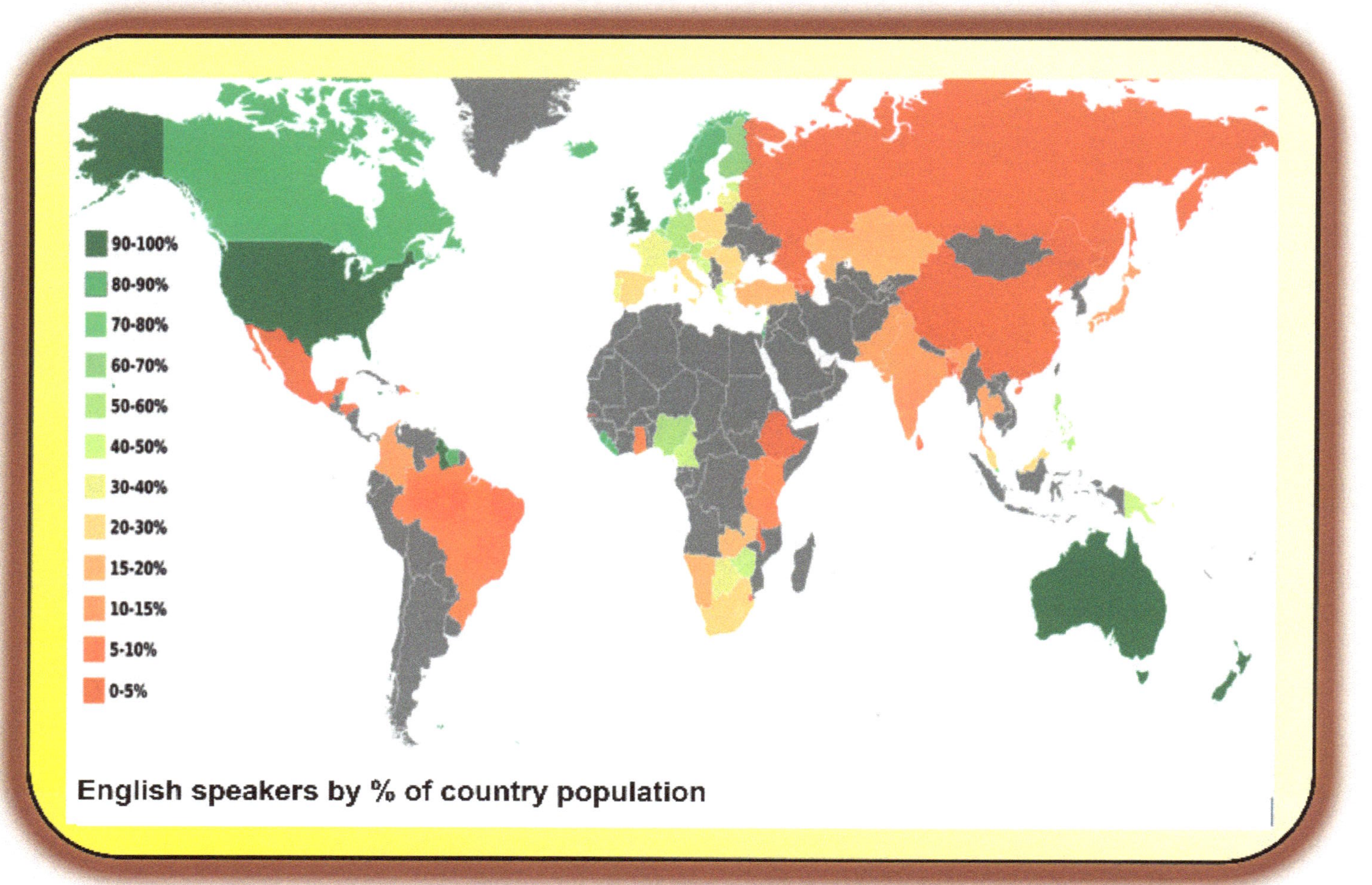

English first language speakers as a % of each country's population

Findaway's distributors to the "Rest of the World" have a widespread presence in lending libraries and also have audiobooks in other languages. They have audiences where second language English speakers may seriously outnumber first language English speakers consequently their main motive for listening to spoken English may be to improve their pronunciation and language familiarity as well as learn of different societies, or for some, just simply to feel "back home".

Findaway Voices (now part of Spotify) with a greater number of outlets in over 170 countries, most of whom are beyond the reach of ACX, also cover the North American market and increasingly the rest of the English speaking world, including all of the remaining Commonwealth countries in the southern hemisphere, comprising one third of the world's population, most of whom are adolescents, and others which once were part of the British Empire and others with commercial, educational and social connections to other English speaking markets.

It's easy to be blinded by the impressive numbers and coverage that either of the publisher/distributors claims. Somewhere within that coverage you will find YOUR AUDIENCE. They in turn will be looking for what interests them. What interests them will be covered by a specialist GENRE. It could be Romance, Crime or any other manner of groupings or sub-groupings. That's where they will look. They will be heavily influenced by the hidden metadata, the similarities with others, the title, cover design, promotional blurb and the narrator's voice of the free-to-listen-to brief audio excerpt. It is that intimate connection with the story teller's voice that they will spend several hours listening to. So, in making a sale the choice of narrator is crucial.

It is essential that you study your COMPETITION. Your audiobook needs to physically look, sound and feel "at home" amongst others. Supermarket shelves are deliberately stacked with similar products competing with one another as are libraries or bookstores. Buying or hiring an audiobook is a "comfort" buy. A familiarity. The comfort comes from what a buyer sees as making the right choice. It doesn't do for yours to sound or stand out like a sore thumb which might be considered as a risky purchase or criticisable by others.

Your audiobook is an entirely different dynamic commodity to a passive paperback/hardback book which is read silently, privately. An audiobook makes "sounds". It is a performance which is listened to. It also has to have its own character, title keywords and "cover look" which slots into how other similar audiobooks appear seeking the same buyer or listener, but it has to offer something more. In marketing speak it has to have a USP (Unique Selling Point) – a little something the others don't have, or a bit more of, an excitement, mystery, a *"je ne sais quoi"* – that unidentifiable quality, as the French say.

People read books and listen to audiobooks, not only for escapism and enjoyment, but also to learn and improve their spoken English. In the recent popular 2023 BBC TV show, *The Great British Sewing Bee*, Asmaa, the winner, was a full-time lady consultant breast reconstruction surgeon who came to the UK as a child refugee from Iraq, aged 14, not speaking a word of English. She said she taught herself the language by reading Mills & Boon romantic novels before going to university to study medicine.

Increasingly, speaking English is a "must-have" competence in many walks of international life. Even some Russian railway stations have their names in English on platforms. Increasingly in parts of south-east Asia, English (Authentic and American versions) are taught to children from an early age. Ever had a sales call, or one from a support desk in the Philippines or Nigeria?

You'll never know with any degree of certainty whereabouts *YOUR* audiobook listeners are in the world, now and in the future. You've no idea whether the smallest audience in terms of population might proportionately be your best or largest market.

You won't know if they are fluent and knowledgeable readers and listeners or whether they are just learning or improving their competence in the English language. You won't know if they are buyers or borrowers.

Aggregators, or middlemen, like Findaway Voices are best for getting a widespread exposure to a potential audience through their various distributors across the globe, which is why it is important to get to know in detail where each of them operates. It is not simple, and it is not obvious. Ask questions. Study the websites of Findaway distributors and others.

Unlike Findaway, ACX are NOT an aggregator. Nor do they supply anyone like libraries. They only promote your audiobook online through Amazon subsidiary www.audible.com in the huge competitive market of North America, UK and Ireland.

The following gives you a list of Findaway's global distributors as they are at the time of my writing. That may change. It is up to you to decide which of them is most suitable for your needs. They all operate differently.

Findaway Global Distributors 2023

These are the people who reach YOUR AUDIENCE

You must work out which suits you best

This list is in alphabetical order:

3 Leaf Group; 24 Symbols;

Amazon; Anyplay; Apple; Audible; Audiobooks.com; AudiobooksNow; Authors Direct; Axiell Media.

Baja Libros; Baker & Taylor; Barnes& Noble audiobooks; Bibliotheca; Bidi; Binge Books; Bokus Play; Bookmate; Books-A-Million;

Chirp; Cliq;

Downpour;

EBSCO; eStories;

Follett; Fuuze;

GooglePlay;

Hoopla; Hummingbird;

Instaread;

Leamos; Libro.fm

Milkbox; MLOL; My Audiobook Library;

Nextory;

Odilo; OverDrive;

Perma-Bound; Pool;

Radish; Rakuten Kobo;

Scribd; Storytel;

Ubook; Ulverscroft;

Walmart; Wheelers.

Recently in 2022, Spotify the world's largest and most popular audio streaming subscription service with 456m users, including 195m subscribers, across 180 markets paid $119m in cash to acquire audiobook distributor Findaway "representing (Spotify's) entry into the category dominated by Amazon's Audible".

Spotify CEO Daniel Ek went on to say *"we will expand the market and create value for users and creators alike. Spotify expects the market to grow from $3.3 billion today to $15 billion by 2027".* Nir Zicherman, Spotify global head of audiobooks said (June 2022) *"We believe this presents a unique opportunity to introduce music and podcast listeners around the world to audiobooks and drastically expand that market."*

To get things into perspective, it's best to look at some numbers provided by the Internet. The information provided are estimates for 2022. The figures given here are largely taken from the internet, rounded up to a whole number and approximated for indicative purposes only.

They are there for authors/narrators to begin to grasp where and how large their potential audience might be and if their chosen distributor, or a combination of them, is active in that region. Those who deal with lending libraries are particularly important for those who might be craving for enjoyment, knowledge and intellectual improvement but may not be able to easily acquire or afford it.

Population figures alone, or any imagined proportion thereof, don't indicate if, or how often, folk view the internet, let alone follow any particular website. Nor do they cast any light on their interest in reading any sort of books or listening to audiobooks. It could be argued that in the small numbers of people in any population a proportionately large number of them are avid readers or potential audiobook listeners.

The total population numbers are huge and difficult to visualize in any meaningful way. Somewhere within those big numbers will be many small numbers of people who speak English as their Mother Tongue first language, and many more whose second language is English to varying degrees of proficiency. Many of them will wish to better themselves by being more proficient, more capable so they can be better understood, not just in general conversation, over the telephone or in conference calls or webinars over the internet, but in learning new skills and specialist knowledge and a greater freedom to travel, learn and live in another country.

In the same way that learning foreign languages can now be achieved through listening to grammar and stock phrases through commercial audio tapes, the quasi-conversational way of hearing imaginable stories from a real English or an American English speaker, regional accents and all, can only be bettered by actually living with a few of them.

Fiction is frequently written about happenings in other countries, real and imaginary, often far away. Nowadays, folk who live there, or somewhere near, or know it well, might be a critical audience, particularly if the narrator is North American, unfamiliar with the character's dialect in a distant land.

It may be worth considering the relevance of a story's target audience to the characters, setting and traditions which it portrays. Careful thought needs to be given to how convincing local and regional accents and dialects are, getting that wrong can be disastrous.

According to United Nations estimates the current global population is 7.9 billion people. One third of those (2.6 billion – 60% of whom are under 30 years old) are in the Commonwealth, formerly the British Empire. Nowadays it is a collection of 54 independent friendly countries where English is an official language taught in schools.

Whilst most will revert to their local dialects, the increasingly ambitious minority see learning and language as a stepping stone to advancement and/or emigration in whatever field they aspire to join.

Globally, there are about 840 million English speakers, of whom about 40% have it as a first language and the other 60% speak it as a second language.

English is one of the world's international languages and is widely taught in schools in countries with their own language and no previous historical British connection, as in continental Europe for example.

Between 2002–19, between 25–41 million overseas visitors from all over the world travelled to the UK by air and by ferry and back home again. That's a lot of long round trips crying out for audiobooks to listen to on an aeroplane.

In the major market of North America, UK and Ireland, (total populations 442 million) serviced mainly, but not exclusively, by ACX there are about 325 million first language speakers and maybe 50 million have it as a second language, mostly of first- and second-generation immigrants, not counting the residents of Quebec in Canada where French is an Official language. However, audiobook creation and publishing is a very vigorous competitive market requiring a great degree of professionalism and marketing effort to do well.

The historic influence of UK culture and the more recent influence of that of the more modern USA through television and films has pervaded the evolution of many societies across the world. With the continuing increase in global communication satellites that is bound to grow.

In this context population figures alone might be misleading as they may well be heavily influenced by those who are socially immature, unskilled or still at school. Here are some examples.

In the numerous Caribbean island countries with heavy US and UK influences there are around 8 million people of different tongues whose common language is English or American English on account of the increasing influence of widely available American TV.

In Australia, New Zealand, Malaysia, in particular, and the more populous Singapore, Hong Kong and Philippines, together with the many Pacific and other island States the combined population is about 89 million.

In south and east African states, South Africa, Zimbabwe and others, with historic UK links amongst others, the combined population is believed to be 293 million, although proportionately relatively few will ever speak English.

The story is the same in west Africa. Nigeria and Ghana in particular, English is widely spoken, as it is the official language with a high degree of proficiency. Over all states the population is about 140 million.

In India, Pakistan, Sri Lanka and Bangladesh their diverse societies and many languages are heavily influenced by many years of being in the British Empire. English is the first or second language of many. Indeed, many families have relatives who have emigrated and settled in the UK and elsewhere. The total population is 409 million.

In the European Union of many states with languages of their own, the everyday second language of many is English, even though the UK is no longer a member, but English is still taught as a second language in most schools. Many will speak 2 or 3 languages. The total population is about 450 million with a high degree of language proficiency.

In some way or other, the English language has touched over 75% of the world's population. The other 25% including Russia. China, Japan, Ethiopia and Egypt and the whole of South America, where there is no English tradition as such, but intellectuals and businessmen with global connections are obliged to learn and speak it, many going to any number of overseas universities where it is commonplace amongst their peers.

Should you choose Exclusive or NON-Exclusive?

A fundamental choice to be made by the author alone, if he is the sole Rights holder for receiving maximum royalties, or jointly with his chosen narrator in receiving split royalties, is whether or not to be tied in for a long fixed period with one or the other publisher/distributor, or whether to go with both of them for less royalties but with greater exposure to potentially a much wider global audience and more sales numerically.

If authors and/or narrators wish to get maximum global exposure throughout the English-speaking world, there's a compelling argument for using separate NON-EXCLUSIVE arrangements with both ACX and Findaway, as their technical recording requirements are the same for both.

An EXCLUSIVE arrangement is where the publisher/distributor controls where and how the audiobook is sold and may, but not necessarily, control the selling price. The Agreement offered may tie the audiobook in for a number of years. That exclusivity usually gives the distributor a greater share of the revenue, and maximum royalties for the author and narrator, but if the competition is overwhelming and the marketing is poor and neglected, it may be a millstone around the author's and narrator's necks.

Established audiobooks already in an EXCLUSIVE arrangement with ACX, after a period of time, can be moved into a NON-EXCLUSIVE arrangement with Findaway Voices for example. That might be because the author/Rights Holder feels that the commercial performance of their audiobook would be improved by exposure to a wider global audience and the competition less fierce.

With the freedom of choice that that offers, and the formality of changing its status with ACX and registering the audiobook with Findaway Voices with its wider global distribution base, care must be taken to avoid the duplication where both ACX and Findaway are both serving the same distribution channel. Findaway supply Amazon, Google Play, Apple, etc., as do ACX, so choices have to be made. Findaway, for example, have a more financially advantageous tie up with Apple than ACX do.

Findaway Voices is by far the world's largest audiobook distributor. Unlike Amazon they don't deal in printed books or ebooks. They only compile and distribute audiobooks to vendors and a large number of library partners ranging from global brands (including Amazon subsidiaries and Apple) to fresh new start-ups across many countries.

The ubiquitous Sony Walkman portable CD music player type technology had been around for over 20 years before Findaway began with their Playaway device in 2006, and which is still in use in 40,000 libraries, schools and US military instillations worldwide.

In 2013 Findaway launched Audio Engine, the industry's largest B2B (business-to-business) audiobook delivery platform to service their ever-increasing numbers of distributors and others. It is that core technology and customer base which enables Findaway to have the widest reach in the English-speaking world and beyond, and no doubt is what attracted global streaming service Spotify to acquire them in 2022.

Findaway Voices with its wider global spread through its 40+ diverse distributors say it has 320,000 titles – more than twice as many as ACX. So even allowing for duplication, between them that is getting on for half a million audiobooks potentially sold to individuals and loaned out by libraries throughout the world.

Audible, with their own audio player, whom Amazon bought in 1997, now own and manage ACX, an online Rights marketplace and production platform launched in 2011. It became the largest audiobook publisher/retailer by far within the huge USA, Canada, UK and Ireland markets. At present ACX says it has about 150,000 titles.

Currently, at the time of writing, only Amazon and Audible.com sell audiobooks directly to customers via the internet.

It is possible for ACX, for reasons best known to themselves, to reject an audiobook causing the author to place it elsewhere if he can. As a narrator on a split royalty basis that has happened to me twice with an unexpected loss of income. Once bitten, twice shy!

If the author switches from ACX, it may be difficult for Findaway, without a satisfactory explanation, to verify that the contents of such a pre-published audiobook are fit and proper (and not legally actionable), that they're being asked to take on. They have a reputation to protect.

It will be prudent for the author/Rights holder to reassure Findaway that what will by then be a NON-EXCLUSIVE audiobook with ACX is exactly the same as it will be as a NON-EXCLUSIVE audiobook with Findaway and that no alterations have taken place in making the transfer.

NON-EXCLUSIVE arrangements enable the audiobook authors/narrator's relative freedom in distributorship, for example it could combine ACX with Findaway Voices to achieve a much wider global spread of points of sale and lending libraries. However, some distributors may pay lesser percentages on each sale, but if that creates greater exposure, more sales overall it could well prove the more profitable.

Who is going to promote your audiobook?

An audiobook is unlike any commodity you see for sale in any super-market, bookstore or library. You probably can't pick it up and inspect it. It only appears visually as a mock book cover on a web page in a distributor or promoter's website or virtual catalogue. It may or may not have the facility to listen to the brief retail sample.

So, when all said and done, the commercial fate of an audiobook is largely down to the visual packaging and where it applies, to the recognisable name of the celebrity narrator compared to an unknown, or to an audiobook with an anonymous narrator.

Purchasers in general like to know "what's in it for them?" What is it, if it's something new or novel? Who made it, how did they make it, where did they make it and how will it benefit them by eating or drinking it, being entertained by it, or using it to solve a problem or many problems? Will they enjoy it or will anyone close to them enjoy it? A gift maybe? Is it a risk? A waste of money? Likely to be disappointing? Purchasers need a reason to buy anything. Is it worth it? An audiobook will not be successful if it fails to address that.

In many respects the conundrum replicates the brand wars between rival cereal or chocolate bar producers and how they promote their products and aggressively fight for shelf position in supermarkets. It is deliberately beyond the scope of this manual to go into greater detail at this time as it is a subject in its own right. Worthy of a book on its own. Maybe I'll write one, let me know.

Over many years, traditional book sellers in shops, librarians, head office procurers of large book seller chain stores and anyone else with shelves to fill (if it were a printed book) or more likely, the virtual catalogue and website compilers of the organisations discussed at length here, study the global reference ISBN coded number to know where it fits in.

Where your audiobook is displayed depends on the critically important detailed metadata, a sort of virtual invisible specification input by the author/Rights holder before publication. It is worth checking. For a narrator, even more so because he has no say in it.

In that way your audiobook should be displayed, available for purchase, in the same category as its similar competitors in that genre so that buyers can see what they are looking for and can make a decision.

Books go on shelves built to contain and display books of standard sizes. That is why this manual is how it is. Shops and libraries like titles written on spines so they can maximise their display and for ease of browsing.

The problem with audiobooks is that they are of a different size and thickness to "proper books". Physically, they don't fit in. Unlike books which have been bought for hundreds of years, audiobooks are something of a novelty and in shop-fitting terms somewhat awkward. They have different display characteristics. Unlike music records or CDs, you can't play an audiobook in a jukebox.

On the face of it, a buyer's decision will depend on the cover design, the title, "blurb", the author and or narrator's name and a brief sample of the narrators voice. It will be influenced by what others have said, either in reviews, chats, articles, recommendations or by what they have read themselves in magazines, on websites or heard on podcasts, or seen on YouTube or direct mail shots.

If your audiobook were a printed hardback or paperback book with a commercial publisher behind it, most, if not all, of that would be done for you. In the case of a home-produced audiobook, you're on your own! You are largely reliant on being seen in a website or catalogue or by word of mouth. Many authors, fingers crossed, will leave it at that and move on to their next project wondering what happened to it and grumbling if sales are low.

Other, more enterprising folk, will have a website and/or a YouTube channel and/or a Facebook page or any other social media facility to draw attention to their audiobook and how to buy it. Some may indulge in mass email marketing to previous acquaintances. All of which is a huge subject interest which I will not cover here. Maybe another time.

What is important is whether your venture is author alone or author/ narrator jointly, in the case of split royalties. The position of narrator in this is uncomfortable, a bit like a pillion passenger clinging on a speeding motorbike. His contribution in this phase of things is largely superfluous. So, if a narrator has been persuaded to fulfil his role of bringing the story to life only to be rewarded by royalty payments alone, once he has thought about it, he might conclude that in financial terms it is or was not worth doing. Having said that, for a narrator, you have to start somewhere. At least that's what I did.

Who is going to buy your audiobook?

Last but not least, a VERY, VERY important question. The answer is neither easy nor straightforward. Unless you have an active time-consuming social media following and an even more involved ever-growing email list you will struggle if no one knows you. If they haven't got the means of listening to your audiobook, they won't buy it. If your subject matter doesn't excite them, they won't buy it. If they can't see it or touch it they won't buy it on impulse. Unlike a paperback book in a traditional bookstore or a record store, audiobooks tend not to be physically displayed unless the retailer is convinced that there is a commercial demand for them. They are not pop music. The only ones that stand a chance are commercial CDs usually recorded by a celebrity name, actively promoted by a major publishing house.

Libraries tend to have a limited number, if they have any at all, in popular categories which they know from experience will have a steady demand. ACX do not service the library market, whilst Findaway Voices thrive in it. Their audiobooks come integrally with an audio player which is ideal for library lending. That is how their business developed.

The vast majority of audiobooks are bought, downloaded, over the internet from Amazon, in the same way that about 70% of all paperback books are bought that way. Typically, each ACX audiobook offers a few minutes free sample for buyers to consider before purchase or not.

The competition, particularly in popular genres such as Romance is intense. The success or otherwise often comes down to the design of the "cover" and the title and whatever limited marketing "blurb" goes with it, the only visible means of enticing a buyer.

The easiest thing for an author to control is the choice of the narrator's voice. It must be appropriate to the subject. It MUST BE a "nice" voice, the sort of voice that you would happily listen to for hours, whether it's a happy or sad story or an exciting, scary or challenging one. The choice of text for the Retail Sample is crucial. It must excite, arouse, scare, intrigue or merely relax the listener.

As the statistics show, more and more people are turning to audiobooks, particularly now that Spotify have entered the market. It could be revolutionary. We'll have to wait and see. If you follow the advice in *THE Home Studio AUDIOBOOK HANDBOOK* there's every likelihood you'll enjoy some level of success and gain a lot more besides.

Finally and AI

It is now the end of October 2023, three years after I started bringing thoughts and intentions together. Tomorrow I'm sending all of my work off to the very helpful Fakenham Prepress Solutions for them to arrange it in a form acceptable to IngramSpark who will print and distribute it to all who might be interested across the world.

Over the last month or so, folk have become anxious about AI (Artificial Intelligence) making human beings redundant. In our case they worry about robots reading stories, instead of the likes of me. Evolution is always on the move, but to my mind it is difficult to imagine an artificial voice interpreting the subtleties, the feelings, of an author's words like a sensitive narrator can.

Having said that, as you will have read about the imperfections that currently exist, it might be better, if those who can, direct their attentions to what needs correcting now (I think I've made that clear) and leave the future to take care of itself.

The audiobook world is evolving. The recent emergence of streaming content through Spotify could turn out to be revolutionary. I can't wait to start writing the next Edition.

Finally, I must thank you for following me to the end. I hope you found it enjoyable, interesting and informative if not thought provoking. If you have, I'd appreciate you dropping me a line at narratorsuk@gmail.com. You might have a constructive suggestion or two for when I bring out the next version. You can also contact me at www.martinhussingtree.com and www.audiobookhandbook.com.

Appendices

Appendix Part Two – Authors

Checklist for an Author/Rights Holder to consider when appointing a Narrator

Recognise that it is a collaboration, a partnership, hopefully a long-lasting friendship in which you need to be confident in the narrator that you choose. This brief list is given in Appendix Part 2 A for you to copy.

✓ What's in it for him? It is important you know that.

✓ Is it just for money? For recognition? For experience? The challenge? Has he done it before? Does he intend doing more?

✓ Can you sense that he will enjoy creating your audiobook? If you can't persuade yourself on that, best find someone who will.

✓ Has he got other interests which may take precedence over your work?

✓ Does he have a steady income from another activity or source, or a pension or social benefit? Because if not he might be obliged to abandon your project to earn some money elsewhere.

✓ Has he other commitments or deadlines which will get in the way of finishing your audiobook?

✓ Is he in good health or expecting to go into hospital? Has he any problems with ailing dependents?

✓ Has he got a track record of similar work? Are there any reviews or any relationships with any other authors?

✓ Is his offer too good to be true? Is he over optimistic? Are you running a risk that he might give up part way through, or take a prolonged sabbatical?

All or any of those considerations, or other factors unknown can have an impact on an author's plans or aspirations.

Suggested Pro Forma to be given to a potential Narrator at audition

Title of book

Author

General location(s) of action

Total number of speaking characters

Male

Female

Number of textual chapters

Approx. number of words

Any language other than English

Any deadlines for completion

Distribution by

Cover design by

Marketing by

Narrators name on cover

Any contentious or potentially offensive wording

For each main and principle supporting character (max. 10)

Name

Gender

Age

Role in story

Locational history

Employment

Social background

Accent

Characteristics of voice

Idiosyncrasies, peculiarities and mannerisms, distinguishing features

Other things to remember

Appendix Part Five – AUDIOBOOK HANDBOOK AGREEMENT
(free to copy and amend)

AUDIOBOOK HANDBOOK AGREEMENT
between
Author/Rights Holder & Narrator

Title of proposed audiobook:

....

This AGREEMENT is between the Author and/or Rights holder of a published book, the basis of the proposed audiobook:

....

And the appointed Narrator:

....

1. This Agreement is between these two parties alone and has no connection real or implied with any other Agreement connected to the creation of this proposed audiobook, its subsequent sale or distribution to others.

2. This Agreement does not prejudice or override in any way any other Agreement associated with this audiobook.

3. Both parties recognise and accept that the methods, principles and procedures laid out in detail in the latest edition of the manual *THE Home Studio AUDIOBOOK HANDBOOK* are the basis for their collaboration in producing the above titled audiobook.

4. In the event of any dispute arising which cannot be amicably resolved otherwise or by referring to *THE Home Studio AUDIOBOOK HANDBOOK* itself, the author Martin Hussingtree or his successors offer to mediate for a nominal sum based on written submissions appertaining to this manual by email or online to www.audiobookhandbook.com.

5. Both parties accept the conclusion of such mediation, which will be given in writing, will settle the matter and that the unsuccessful party will bear the total cost. There will be no appeal.

6. The contents, text and format of this **AUDIOBOOK HANDBOOK AGREEMENT** is FREE for readers to use and adapt as a template. There is no cost. Its purpose is simply to facilitate a harmonious, mutually agreeable method of producing a recording, suitable for sale and distribution as an audiobook by ACX, Findaway Voices or by anyone else. It is provided here as Appendix Five for photocopying purposes.

7. **The Author/Rights Holder accepts that they are totally responsible for:**

a) The decision to choose and appoint the Narrator. The conduct of any auditioning process involving one or more potential Narrators which will include selecting those available and willing, and providing Narrators with a detailed synopsis of the story, number of chapters, including the front and back statements and retail sample, total word count and a listed number of characters and their detailed biography, accents, characteristics and idiosyncrasies of ALL main and numbers of supporting characters (ages and sexes) whose voices the Narrator will be expected to consistently replicate throughout the recording. That will enable a Narrator to estimate how long it will take him and bid for the PFH (price per finished hour) of workflow measured listening time that he should be paid for doing his work. That is *NOT* the same as the recording and editing time including all research and production time which will be much longer).

NOTE: Failure to do this thoroughly may entitle the Narrator to ask for an increase in PFH!

b) A carefully thought out, representative audition script sent by email, typed text, to each potential Narrator, double-spaced with wide margins for the Narrator to annotate and work from and also comprehensive biographies of those characters who appear in the audition script and any other relevant information which the Author/Rights Holder might require to enable him/her to make a judgement of the most suitable Narrator for bringing their words to life.

NOTE: Failure to do this thoroughly is a recipe for disaster!

c) The review and approval of any initial sample of the Narrator's recording.

d) Keeping the Narrator informed of any indisposition, holiday or absence which might delay the Narrator's work.

e) The Author/Rights Holder will advise the unsuccessful Narrators as soon as possible after reaching their decision.

f) Once the Narrator has been appointed, the timely (within a week), formal approval or otherwise of EACH AND EVERY submitted recording on a Chapter-by-Chapter basis. The Author/Rights Holder CANNOT change their mind or quibble over minor details on matters which they have already supplied and/or approved or sought to incorporate as an afterthought. The Narrator cannot continue without that formal approval, and has grounds for complaint if the author's approval is unreasonably slow or repeatedly so.

g) The Author/Rights Holder and Narrator may negotiate a private reimbursement regime beyond the scope of any other Agreement. Upon approval of each recorded and uploaded chapter or finished piece, the Author will pay into the Narrator's bank account money by electronic transfer calculated on that chapter or piece's PFH x the workflow stated time as requested by the Narrator. The Author/Rights Holder will message the Narrator confirming that that has been done.

h) The Author/Rights Holder CANNOT re-write or revise any chapter's text which the Narrator has already begun recording or has been recorded unless to correct an error or oversight not previously identified, in which case the Narrator may claim an additional payment.

i) The Author/Rights holder will properly manage their own tax affairs. All payments from ACX or Findaway or any other paid directly to him/her should be declared in whichever tax regime they abide. No-one else will be responsible for that.

Failure to comply with these responsibilities will discharge the Narrator from their responsibilities and entitle them to seek recompense as they think fit in a civil Court.

8. **The chosen Narrator accepts that they are totally responsible for:**

a) Providing the Author/Rights holder with evidence of their previous similar work and any references from third parties, as well as information about their availability and ability to undertake the proposed project.

b) Diligently and purposefully applying their knowledge, experience, ability and technical competence to the audition script provided to him. To use his best endeavours throughout all chapters to faithfully and consistently reproduce their audition performance and apply it to all and every situation not covered by the audition.

c) If successful at audition, based on the comprehensive information as described and provided by the Author, the narrator is to give his best and realistic time ESTIMATE in calendar weeks (including statutory holidays) of approximately how long the Narrator might take to totally complete the whole recording excluding time taken by the Author/Rights holder to give approvals. This is indicative only. It is NOT a guarantee! However, the Narrator's monetary quotation of total cost per finished hour (PFH), as measured and shown by the workflow IS GUARANTEED and cannot be varied.

d) Providing recordings of the Author's text on a chapter-by-chapter basis to the technical standard specified by ACX and/or Findaway or both or any other and a request for payment of that item calculated on that chapter or piece's PFH x the workflow stated time. It is for the Narrator to advise the Author each time by way of an invoice message on the workflow and for the Author to check and provide payment under a private arrangement.

e) Alerting the Author by email, as well as through the workflow, that the latter's attention is required to listen and approve recordings on a chapter-by-chapter basis as well as any re-submitted chapters and any proof-reading oversights and inconsistencies identified by the Narrator which might require correction.

f) Advising the Author by workflow message and email if, for whatever reason, he is experiencing difficulty in maintaining progress against his original time ESTIMATE together with his proposals for recovering his schedule or extending it.

g) As appropriate, where the audiobook is sold on a split royalty basis, the designated and acknowledged (on the front cover) Narrator shall use his best endeavours, in consultation with the Author/ Rights holder, to contribute to any on-going marketing effort.

– 4 of 6 –

h) The Narrator will properly manage his own tax affairs. All payments made for their services should be paid directly and be declared in whichever tax regime they abide. No-one else shall be responsible for that, nor will anyone else be responsible for any obligations they may have to any associated trade union or trade body.

i) If during the course of recording, which potentially might take several weeks or even months, the Narrator chooses to abort his contribution for whatever reason, repaying the Author all monies paid to them. That will be the limit of their liability as it was up to the Author in the first place to evaluate the risk of them doing so. Failure of the Narrator to do so may permit the Author to recover that money with costs through a civil Court action.

j) Keeping the Author/Rights Holder informed of any indisposition, holiday or absence which might delay the Narrator's work.

9. Split royalty payments:

a) Where such situations occur, both ACX and Findaway have provisions for remitting royalty payments direct to both Author and Narrator usually on a monthly basis providing numbers of sales warrant it. That is governed by a separate Agreement with whichever publisher/distributor is involved.

b) In the unlikely event that the publisher/distributor, ACX, Findaway or another, terminates their Agreement with the Author so that the audiobook is withdrawn from their list, meaning that split royalties cease and that the Author cannot get it re-listed with another of equal standing, if any, then the Narrator may have grounds for suing the Author in a civil Court for loss of expected income unless an amicable agreement for compensation can be agreed between them.

c) In the unlikely event that the Author, at any time in this Agreement, chooses to divorce the Narrator, and providing the chapter-by-chapter stage payments are up to date at that time, the Narrator is entitled to keep what he has been paid then the Narrator may also have grounds for suing the author in a civil Court for loss of expected income unless an amicable agreement for compensation can be agreed between them.

10. Cover art:

   a) Where the Author is the sole Rights holder, or the Rights holder alone, and the Narrator has no commercial interest in ensuing royalties from sales, the Narrator has no automatic right to have their name on the promotional front cover. THAT is not good practice. However, the Narrator MUST be given the OPTION, at no cost, to have their name on the front cover prominently and proportionately displayed.

   b) Whether or not the Narrator has a commercial interest in the sales of the audiobook, they will have an on-going reputational interest, which at the outset may influence their decision whether or not to provide their services.

   c) The design of the proposed front cover matters as it is influential in the audiobook's commercial success. It is the prerogative of the Author and MUST be established and openly displayed before the Narrator is appointed at which point the Narrator has the discretion to withdraw.

   d) The design shall be produced both in a portrait and in a square formats suitable for use in either an ACX format or a Findaway format in accordance with their requirements.

   e) Where the Narrator is to have a commercial interest due to the Author/Rights holder electing to employ split royalties, which will impact the on-going royalty payments and reputational interests of both, the Narrator will have the power of veto on the cover design offered by the Author/Rights holder. If a satisfactory compromise cannot be reached, the Narrator must withdraw.

11. Territories:

   a) With differences between ACX and Findaway, the Author/Rights holder and the Narrator must discuss and agree on where sales are best targeted.

   Signed this day:..

   Author/Rights Holder:..

   Narrator:..

END OF AUDIOBOOK HANDBOOK AGREEMENT

Appendix Part Six – AUDIOBOOK HANDBOOK acoustic alcove

How to make an AUDIOBOOK HANDBOOK acoustic alcove

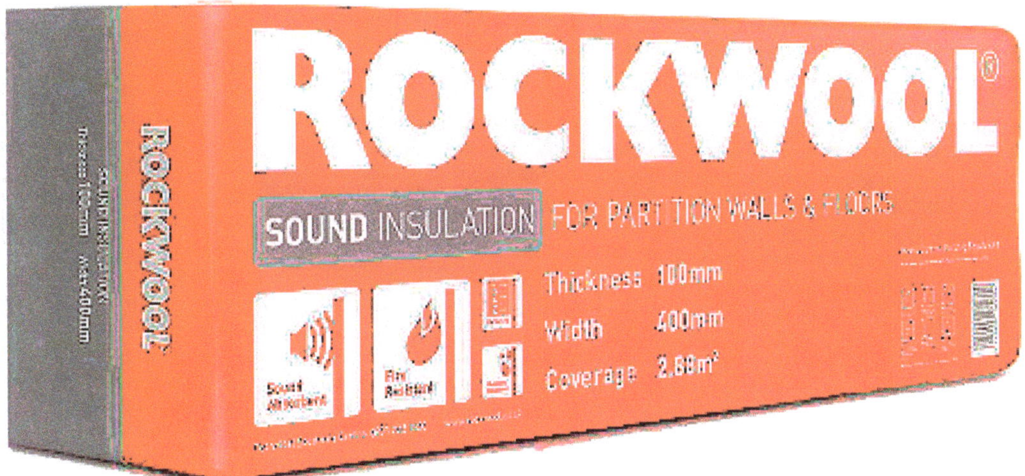

Making an acoustic alcove like mine is straightforward. It requires little skill, but it does require care. The first thing you need is pack of 6 no. thick semi-rigid ACOUSTIC slabs from a DIY store or builders' merchant as in this image. They are used normally to insulate buildings where the passage of sound is a problem, such as partition walls. Nowadays, they are commonplace.

They are NOT the same as floppy THERMAL insulation which typically comes in roles for preventing heat loss through roofs and which is NOT fit for this purpose.

This acoustic alcove was designed to be dismantled and portable so none of the components are permanently fixed together..

A, B, D, E, are all 120 x 40 x 10
C, F are both 100 x 40 x10

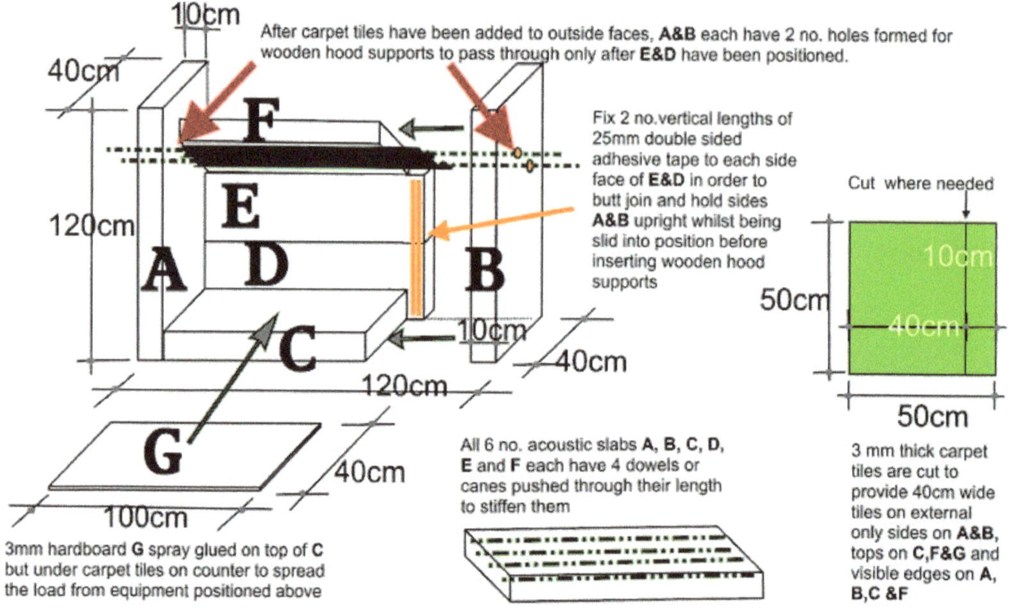

3mm hardboard **G** spray glued on top of **C** but under carpet tiles on counter to spread the load from equipment positioned above

All 6 no. acoustic slabs **A, B, C, D, E** and **F** each have 4 dowels or canes pushed through their length to stiffen them

3 mm thick carpet tiles are cut to provide 40cm wide tiles on external only sides on **A&B**, tops on **C,F&G** and visible edges on **A, B,C &F**

To make an acoustic alcove like mine which when assembled will measure 1.200 mm wide x 500mm front to back x 1.200mm high, you need:

- 1 no. pack (containing 6 no. acoustic slabs each measuring 1.200mm x 400mm x100mm) of ROCKWOOL stone wool insulation used as sound insulation for internal walls and floors.

ROCKWOOL has outstanding acoustic properties. It absorbs sound waves and dampens vibrations. It is best in class for fire resistance and withstands temperatures of over 1000°C. Highly stable and durable – works for the lifetime of a building. It is environmentally friendly, made from abundant, naturally occurring volcanic rock which is 97% recyclable. Obtainable from local DIY stores and builders' merchants. Current UK 2023 price is approx £58.00.

- 24 1.200mm lengths of approx. 8–10mm dia. round wooden dowel or 4ft (1200mm) long, heavy duty, sturdy, professional gardeners' bamboo canes. These are essential to reinforce and stiffen the otherwise semi-rigid or floppy acoustic slabs by pushing them through the middle of the fibres from one end to the other. Precision is not required. Effectiveness is.
- 2 or 3 old bed sheets, preferably cotton and coloured plain, to cut up as they will be necessary to neatly wrap around each sheet to contain the mineral wool fibres.
- 1 roll of 50mm wide heavy duty Gaffer tape to securely fasten the old bed sheet shaped to each acoustic slab.
- A strong pair of scissors and a Stanley knife.
- 9 cheap carpet tiles (50cm x 50xm) neutral colour preferable.
- 1 large can of instant spray glue.
- 1 roll of double-sided adhesive tape (see diagram).

Lots of old newspaper whilst you spray the backs of carpet tiles and a face mask preferably.

- 1 no. piece of 3 mm thick hardboard or ply 1000mm x 400mm (to support equipment, e.g. laptop; microphone – "G" on diagram).
- 2 lengths of 20mm x 10mm PAR (planed all round) softwood 1200mm long to support the slanting roof.
- 1 no. 1500mm length of stiff wire.

PLEASE NOTE:

ROCKWOOL is NOT a nice material to handle and work with. It is itchy and loses fibres into the atmosphere, so for comfort you should always use kitchen rubber gloves, a face mask, and wear an old shirt or overall and work on it in a well aired place such as a large garage or shed with open doors. It is NOT asbestos and won't harm you.

01. Take two of the slabs and reduce their length to 1000mm in each case by carefully sawing off 200mm. They will be the horizontal counter "C" and the sloping hood "F". Put them to one side, so that they don't get confused with the other members of a different size.

02. Prepare 24 round 10mm dia. wooden dowels by sharpening or diagonally slicing one end in each case as if they were an arrow or trimming the ends of 4ft long (1200mm) heavy duty gardeners' bamboo canes from a garden centre. There will be four to each acoustic slab. The fibrous slabs are easy to push through.

03. Remember that two acoustic slabs are shorter, therefore, those dowel rods or bamboo canes will need to be shorter too.

04. Once the reinforcing dowels or bamboo canes have all been pushed through their acoustic slabs, they should be notably firm and able to stand up on their own. If not, add an extra rod/cane until they do. Then measure the surface area of each slab and cover it with cut-out old bed sheet allowing for generous overlaps, all on one side which will be subsequently covered, (by carpet tiles in most cases) hiding any folds and the unsightly Gaffer tape.

Do not pull the bed sheet tight because it will cause the soft acoustic slab edges to "round" which is not what you want. The attached carpet tiles will need to present a clear sharp as possible edge. You just want one side on each slab which is "presentable".

In the case of sloping hood "F", leave a dangling "apron" from the selvedge of the old bed sheet, as you will see from the photograph, where it will hang over "E" covering the hinge gap.

05. Spray glue 3mm hardboard "G" on top of counter slab "C" ensuring that there are no bumps underneath to stop it being completely and consistently horizontal.

06. Spray glue two top and bottom 400mm x 500mm and one middle 400mm x 200mm make-up carpet tiles to outside hidden back sides of wing slabs "A" and "B" covering any Gaffer tape and folds in the covering sheet. One will be on the left-hand side and the other will be the right-hand side, opposite handed.

07. Spray glue 100mm wide carpet tiles on one long (front) and one short (top) visible edge with joints matching those carpet tiles on the outside face. Where the carpet tiles meet, the corner edge should be presentable, like a furnishing would.

08. Spray glue two 400mm x 500mm carpet tiles on to the already glued hardboard counter top "G" above counter slab "C".

09. Spray glue two 100mm carpet tiles on to the front edge of "C" matching the joint of the carpet tiles on "G" above. The leading edge should be presentable, like a furnishing would.

10. Slabs "D" and "E" have no carpet tiles added to them. They are joined together by carefully glueing two long edges together so they line up vertically. Failure to do that will mean that there will be gaps against "A" and "B". An option is to spray glue a disused cardboard box opened out on the back, (or four extra carpet tiles making 13 in total) joining them together where it won't be seen.

11. Spray glue two 400mm x 500mm carpet tiles to the top(back) face of hood slab "F" and two 100mm carpet tiles to the front edge as before. This hood slab will rest in position supported on a slope created by two lengths of 20mm x 10mm PAR softwood 1200mm long.

12. This next bit requires much care and concentration. Lay "A" and "B" on a solid bench together matching like a sandwich with the carpet tile of "B" uppermost and the carpet tile face of "A" furthest away at the bottom of the sandwich.

Work out where the lower of the two wooden hood supports will need to go to carry sloping hood "F". Drill a pilot hole through the carpet tile on "B", through the fibres behind it and pierce a small hole in the inner facing bed sheet covering beyond.

Using something like a long-handled screwdriver pushed through those holes through "B", to mark the inner facing bed sheet covering "A" so that you can then make a hole through the fibres of "A" and through the carpet tile on the far side.

13. Using the double-sided tape, as in the diagram, loosely assemble all of the components together. Then using a long length of stiff wire about 1500mm long, thread it through "B" and across the space then through "A". Then rest the hood slab "F" on the top of "E" and the wire. If you're happy that it looks like it should be in the diagram and the photograph, then make the holes through "A" and "B" wider so that one of the 20mm x 10mm PAR softwood 1200mm long wooden supports can replace the wire.

14. Repeat that process with the second support, higher up, as you'll see on the diagram and the photograph so that you can press all of the components together.

The construction creates sufficient soft gaps for wires and cables to be threaded through to electricity points. It was designed to be dismantled and be portable so that it can be transported elsewhere or if the room or space is required for other purposes.

Ideally, decorators collapsible portable wallpaper pasting tables, which are cheap and easily obtainable from DIY stores and builders' merchants give the greatest flexibility in mounting your lightweight acoustic alcove above.

As you will see from the photograph of my prototype, the side walls are bowed. That is because of their self weight, albeit that they are lightweight, and the addition of heavier carpet tiles requires stiffening. To combat that, four wooden dowels/canes rather than the three that I used will provide a better solution for cosmetic purposes. But my original still does the job well.